A LOUIS SEARING AND MARGARET MCMILLAN MYSTERY

THE MARINA Murders

Richard L. Baldwin

Buttonwood Press
Haslett, Michigan

OTHER BOOKS BY
RICHARD L. BALDWIN

Fiction
Mysteries
A Lesson Plan for Murder (1998)
ISBN: 0-9660685-0-5
Buttonwood Press

The Principal Cause of Death (1999)
ISBN: 0-9660685-2-1
Buttonwood Press

Administration Can Be Murder (2000)
ISBN: 0-9660685-4-8
Buttonwood Press

Buried Secrets of Bois Blanc: Murder in the Straits of Mackinac (2001)
ISBN: 0-9660685-5-6
Buttonwood Press

The Searing Mysteries: Three in One (2001)
ISBN: 0-9660685-6-4
Buttonwood Press

Spiritual
Unity and the Children (2000)
ISBN: 0-9660685-3-X
Buttonwood Press

Non-Fiction
The Piano Recital (1999)
ISBN: 0-9660685-1-3
Buttonwood Press

A Story to Tell: Special Education in Michigan's Upper Peninsula 1902-1975 (1994)
ISBN: 932212-77-8
Lake Superior Press

DEDICATIONS

This book is dedicated to my grandchildren: Benjamin Baldwin, Hannah Hoffmeister, Nicholas Baldwin, Thomas Hoffmeister, and Jackson Baldwin.

✥

My passion is to tell stories by writing books and publishing them. While I may not live long enough to enjoy watching each of you fulfill your dreams and follow your passions, I know that if you do, you will experience immense joy. Please know that I love each of you and will be eternally proud of you in whatever you do with your lives.

This book is also dedicated to the memory of my friend, mentor, and inspiration, William X. Kienzle. Bill believed in me, encouraged me, and advised me. He read every one of my books, answered every one of my letters, and was always there giving me a supportive pat on the back. I will miss his friendship, his marvelous stories, and his compassion for people.

This novel is a product of the imagination of the author. In many instances the actual names of people are used, but only with their permission. If permission wasn't sought or given, a fictitious name is used. None of the events described in this story occurred. Though settings, buildings, businesses exist, liberties may have been taken as to their actual location and description. This story has no purpose other than to entertain the reader.

Published by Buttonwood Press
PO Box 716
Haslett, Michigan 48840
www.buttonwoodpress.com

Publisher's Cataloging-in-Publication Data
Baldwin, Richard L.
    The marina murders / by Richard L. Baldwin. – 1st ed.
    p. cm – (Louis Searing and Margaret McMillan mystery; 5)
    ISBN: 0-9660685-7-2

    1.   Murder--Michigan--Fiction.
    2.   Detective and mystery stories. I. Title.

PS3552.A451525M37 2002   813'.54
                QBI33-451

Printed in the United States of America

Contribution Policy: Buttonwood Press will donate fifty cents of each copy of *The Marina Murders* sold to the Eugene Pattison Talented Writers Award Fund. This fund is named after Dr. Eugene Pattison will provide scholarships to talented writers in the English Department of Alma College in Alma, Michigan. Richard L. Baldwin attended Alma College from 1959-1962, was a member of the Tau Kappa Epsilon Fraternity and was a member of the Alma College Golf Team. Alma College has a special place in the hearts of the Baldwin and McMillan families. Richard's parents, Louis S. Baldwin and Margaret McMillan graduated from Alma College in 1932. Richard's maternal grandmother, Maybelle Howard McMillan graduated from Alma College in 1902 and taught music at the College for a short time.

Acknowledgments

One of the nicest compliments ever given to me was that I surrounded myself with quality people who share their talents to present an entertaining story. Such has been the case with the writing and the publication of this novel.

My editor Gail Garber has once again done a masterful job editing this story. I appreciate the excellent advice given to be by Karen O'Connor who patiently waded through the manuscript pointing out a variety of suggestions to improve the tale. My friend Ben Hall offered many positive suggestions in the text as well. Last, but certainly not least, I thank my wife Patty for her thorough review of the story, her numerous suggestions for consistency and clarification and her countless words of advice. Most importantly, however, is Patty's constant love and support for my passion of storytelling. It is most comforting to have a loving partner, spouse, and best friend beside me providing unconditional love.

Sincere thanks are given to Joyce Wagner, my friend who has proofread most of my work since 1998. Joyce's red pencils are consistently worn down due to my endless production of minor inconsistencies with the rules of grammar and punctuation. I also must thank my typesetter and masterful cover designer Marilyn "Sam" Nesbitt. Once again, she has put together a book that is easy to read and attractive to the eye.

There is always a significant set of advisors in a major effort such as writing a technically accurate book. First, on my long list of people who proved helpful, is Chief of Police and Harbormaster for Manistee, Michigan, David Bachman. Chief Bachman answered tens of questions and was always available to assist me. Thanks, too, to

ACKNOWLEDGMENTS

Kathy Kubanik of the Manistee Police Department for her help with this story. Additional law enforcement advice was willingly offered by Lieutenant Toby Archambault, Michigan State Police/MCD and Chief of Police for Big Rapids, Kevin Courtney. Thank you to Captain Greg Hammond, EMS coordinator for Meridian Township for thoroughly explaining EMS procedures.

Sailors were needed for this story. I thank Greg LaMore of Holland, Dennis Nemeth of Sturgis, and David Wiksail, Harbormaster, City of Muskegon, for their technical advice, as well as Tom DenHerder of Yacht Basin Marina in Holland for allowing me to use his marina in my story. Scuba diving questions were answered by Don Tomas. Fishing in Lake Michigan expertise was shared by Charles and Elinor Mange of Arcadia.

Several people served as advisors and these are Jan and Wayne Birkmeier, Jenny Geno, Grace Kammeraad, Stephanie Ammel, Joseph and Amanda Hoffmeister, Lynwood Beekman, Marc Rottinghaus, and Gayle Brink. Medical advice was offered by Dr. Karen Blackman. Information about drug interaction was provided by Duane Warren, PharmD, BCPS. Psychological profile information was willingly given by Elaine Stanfield. Procedures used by Mackinac Bridge employees were provided by Hank Lotoszinski, Administrator of the Mackinac Bridge.

Jan Kenny, a well-known artist in Manistee provided a drawing for this book. It is found on the following page.

The beautiful golden retriever shown with me on the back cover of this book is Snooker, the proud show dog of Jim and Barb Kallman of Haslett, Michigan. Thanks to Snooker, Barb and Jim, and photographer John Zink for allowing me to add Samm's alter ego to the Buttonwood Press family.

To each of these people and others who offered support, I am truly thankful. The joy is in the writing and the creation of the book, but great joy comes from those who always seem to be present when needed to perform some service, be it listening, advising, or simply nodding a head. The story has been born, and in thankfulness for all who played a part in its development, I offer my deepest gratitude.

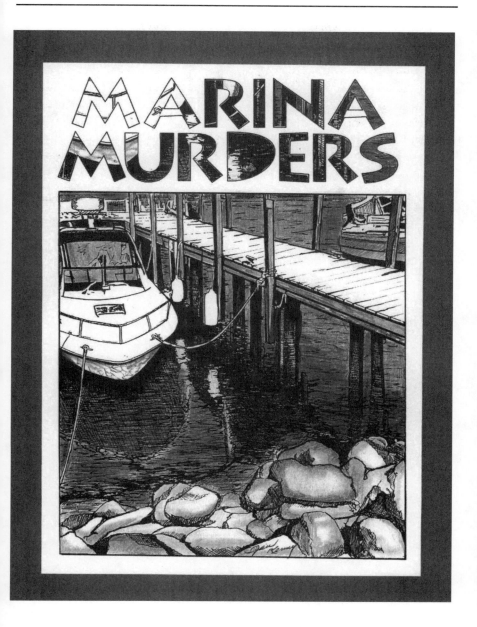

CHAPTER ONE

May 23, Saturday
Traverse City, Michigan

J ake Prescott looked at his watch and saw an illuminated 1:50 a.m. He took his cell phone and called the answering service for Dr. Glenda Knoble. He pretended to be Dr. Iaani, chief of surgery, calling from the Munson Medical Center in Traverse City. He said that he was aware that Dr. Knoble was on her yacht in a Traverse City marina and could she go to the hospital to assist with surgery.

Glenda and her physician husband Tom slept aboard their yacht, *Rx: Smooth Sailing*, which was moored in the Duncan L. Clinch Marina. Stars were shining and a half moon peeked in and out of slowly moving clouds coming off Lake Michigan. It was against this backdrop that a murder would turn the peace and quiet of the area on its head.

One minute later, Glenda, awakened and in a stupor, put her cell phone to her ear and listened. "Doctor Knoble, I'm sorry to bother you at this late hour, but you've been asked to go to the Munson Medical Center in Traverse City. There are surgeries taking place and Dr. Iaani has asked for your assistance. There has been a multiple vehicle accident."

"OK, thanks. Anything else?"

"Nothing needing your attention. Your other calls are being handled by the doctor on call or patients are going to an emergency room. Mrs. Duncan wanted you to know that her son's fever has broken. She is relieved."

"That's good. Thanks. I'm going to the hospital now."

Glenda sat on the edge of her bunk, rubbed her eyes and sought the energy to get up and help out. *No sense waking Tom*, she thought. She'd go to the hospital, assist in any way she could and return to the marina. Tom wouldn't even realize she'd been gone.

Dr. Knoble went topside, stepped onto the dock, walked to her car and drove to the hospital at 6th and Elmwood. The trip took about five minutes. The Munson Medical Center was not her hospital so she looked for the Emergency Room entrance and followed the signs. When she got out of her car, she saw a man in scrubs coming toward her.

"Dr. Knoble?" Jake asked, walking under mercury lights in the almost empty parking lot reserved for doctors and administrative staff of the hospital.

"Yes. I understand I'm needed in surgery," Glenda replied, moving from a walk to an easy jog. She thought it strange that an intern would come outside to greet her. That had never happened before, but perhaps every second did count and Dr. Ianni wanted her to have an escort.

"Definitely. Follow me, please. Short night, huh?" Jake asked.

"Typical, comes with being a doctor."

"We're going into that door over there," Jake said, pointing straight ahead.

"OK," Glenda replied.

Jake stepped aside to let the doctor lead the way and then pressed a small pistol into her back.

"Turn around and walk to the red pickup. Say nothing, do nothing. Understand?"

Once in the pickup with the all-door lock in place, Glenda Knoble was a trapped woman. She was in the presence of a very strong man about 24 years of age who was on edge and intent on striking terror into her soul.

Glenda, age 46, blonde, petite with tanned skin, had no idea why this was happening to her. She was tired, confused, and following a few seconds of denial thought the moment wasn't real. But it was. She did what she was told.

Jake was nervous and excited. He had killed before, mostly animals, plotted other deaths and even came close to killing a high school teacher once, but tonight, murder was for real. His heart was beating faster than normal. He was about to carry out a murder that had been on his mind for the past three years. Actually the seed of revenge had been planted seven years ago when his mother Sara told him why his father had committed suicide seventeen years earlier.

Glenda went from confused to scared. "What about the surgery I am supposed to perform? I'm needed in that hospital."

"There is no surgery for you to perform."

"But, my calling service told me ab..."

"Your calling service received false information."

The pickup left the hospital parking lot. There was no traffic in Traverse City at 2:10 a.m. Most traffic lights were flashing caution on the main roads. The pickup went south on U.S.31 with Glenda still not comprehending what was about to happen to her.

A mile further down the road, Dr. Knoble decided to try her bedside manner to get out of this.

"Want to talk about something? Do you need money or some help?" she asked.

"Nothing to talk about unless you want to apologize for killing my dad."

"Killing your dad?" Glenda said confused. "I don't understand."

"Dr. Brad Prescott. Does that name ring a bell?" Jake asked.

Glenda knew the deceased Brad Prescott but chose to deny it.

"I'm afraid I don't know anyone by that name."

"Seventeen years ago you and the members of your investment club killed him."

"I think you're mistaken. I didn't kill your father."

"That's not my understanding," Jake replied.

As Jake drove on to the county park where Glenda would die, he had a—

FLASHBACK: It was the afternoon of September 12, 1985. I was seven years old. I came home from school. I put my books and homework on a kitchen chair and went to the garage to get my bat and glove so I could join my friends at the neighborhood ball field. I opened the door and looking up, saw my father's limp body hanging beside the family car. I stood there in total disbelief of what I was seeing. I called to my mom. When she saw Dad, she became hysterical, screamed, and cried. She pulled me into the house, closed the door and held me close. "I love you, Jakee. I love you, honey." she said, while both of us were sobbing and holding each other.

"What happened to Dad?" I asked.

"I've got to call the ambulance. Daddy needs help, now."

As the pickup continued south on U.S.31, Glenda pleaded, "Listen. I'm very sorry. I really am, but please understand, I did not kill your father."

"Mom didn't feel we should know all the details until seven years ago when we were seventeen. I guess she thought we could handle it. We couldn't. Still can't. It ruined us, my brother and me. It ruined us emotionally and psychologically. It affected all of us. When you killed my dad, you also killed me, sort of, or at least that's how I see it."

"If you're referring to the marina investment, yes, I was a part of that, but killing your dad is not what I did."

"You took his money, his share, a million dollars, most of it from his home equity account and you dumped on him. He couldn't handle the double-cross."

"There was no double-cross! As I remember it, the county wouldn't approve the marina being built because of an environmental impact analysis. The project had to be scrapped."

"Right, and he lost all of his savings, went into debt, became guilt-ridden and depressed. He apparently thought hanging himself was his only way out."

"I'm really sorry about that. We all took a hit and had to adjust."

"Taking the hit is not the issue, the double-cross is."

"Double-cross? I'm not getting it," Glenda replied.

"You knew the land was toxic and the marina could not be built. To bail yourselves out, you invited my dad and others to put in several million dollars with the understanding that the marina was a windfall. You took his money into your investment club, cut your losses and left him out of money and looking at a useless piece of land."

"That's not what happened. As I recall, we ..."

"It doesn't matter what you recall," Jake replied angrily. "What matters is what my mother recalls."

"Again, I'm sorry," Glenda said, holding her face in her hands.

Jake drove on to a county park, empty in the dark of the night. He parked in a spot hidden from anyone driving by. He left the truck running in case he needed to make a quick escape. Jake retrieved a syringe from under his seat. His brother had gotten several syringes and a supply of midazolam in doses of ten milligrams. "Here's a syringe. Inject this into your body. It will relax you, that's all. You'll be OK, just inject it."

"What is this?" Glenda asked, looking at the vial for some indication of the drug composition.

"It will make you feel real good, you know what it is, you've prescribed it often, takes you to lah-lah land."

"I'm not going to..."

Jake swung at her and the back of his hand hit her on the bridge of her nose and her forehead. The force of the blow snapped her head back. "Do it now!" Jake said forcefully.

For a second Glenda didn't know what hit her, literally. She quickly concluded that she really didn't have any choice. If she didn't inject the drug, her kidnapper would, so she did. In a matter of a few seconds she was out cold.

Jake took Glenda and placed her in the bed of his pickup. He snapped on the cover and then inserted a tube from the exhaust pipe into the bed of the truck. He listened to the radio as the carbon monoxide fumes went into Dr. Knoble's lungs. At that point, her body, poisoned by gas, shut down. He turned off the radio and had a—

> FLASHBACK: I can still see the look of disbelief and horror when Mom saw Dad hanging lifeless in the garage. Crying and trying to comfort me, she called the police. I heard the sirens in the distance as Mom called Mrs. Murphy who immediately came over to take me to her home. As I was taken from our house, the police car and an ambulance came up. I saw the flashing lights, police officers and firemen running toward the garage. I saw neighbors coming out of their homes. For months I couldn't open the garage door, I wouldn't go into the garage. Each time I put my hand on the door knob I'd see my Dad's body and I just couldn't open the door.

Jake turned off the ignition, left the cab of the truck, and opened the cover to allow fresh air into the bed of the pickup. He also needed to be assured that his victim was dead. She was. He removed the tube from the exhaust pipe and threw it in the back of the truck. He snapped the cover back on and drove north on M-31 to the parking lot of Smith-Barney, a bit west of the Duncan L. Clinch Marina on Grandview Parkway which separated downtown Traverse City from the West Arm of the Grand Traverse Bay.

The dead of night was perfect for slipping into the bay undetected. He put a noose around Glenda's neck, symbolic of his father's death, put a buoyancy compensator and a weight vest on her to keep her body under water but not too far under the surface. He put on his scuba outfit and made sure his illuminated compass was working. Jake entered the water and with Dr. Knoble's body in tow, swam underwater toward the marina and the piling beside the Knoble's yacht, *Rx: Smooth Sailing*.

Once there, Jake tied Glenda's body to the piling. He then slit her wrist adding one more symbolic gesture of death by suicide. He quietly swam underwater, away from the marina and surfaced near the investment firm. As he was coming out of the water he noticed a police car with siren and lights flashing moving at a high rate of speed along the Grandview Parkway. His heart dropped into his stomach because he was certain someone had seen something and called to report it. But, the police vehicle went right on by. Its siren could be heard getting fainter and fainter the further east it went.

Jake put his scuba equipment, the buoyancy compensator, and weight vest that Glenda had worn in the back of his pickup. He drove away certain that his mission had been successful. He took his cell phone from the front seat. He dialed a number and in a few seconds said, "She's dead and floating." He pushed the "End" button before setting the phone on the seat beside him. He started his pickup and headed for Room 118 in the Quality Inn by the Bay, four and a half miles east on North U.S.31. On his way to the motel, he saw why the police vehicle was in such a hurry. A bad traffic accident had occurred at the intersection of Garfield Road and Front Street.

When Jake arrived in Traverse City the day before, he had asked for an extended check-out time the next day. When he got to his room, he undressed, pulled the covers back, and got into bed. He was tired and felt no remorse about what he had done. Maybe his father felt better about it. Jake did, and he felt his mom and brother would be proud. It had taken a long time, a lot of research, and a lot of training, but all of the work had paid off. The perfect crime had just been committed, and Jake had a—

> FLASHBACK: The neighbor's cat had died in the same way as Dr. Knoble. I said "Here kitty, kitty, kitty," and she came to me. Even purred. I picked it up and then for some reason it seemed to be afraid as if it knew what was going to happen to it. I took it behind the garage where nobody could see me and I injected her with a drug. I put her soon-to-be lifeless body in

a box, taped the lid and ran a hose from the exhaust pipe of my mom's car to a hole in the box. I started the car and waited till I thought the cat was dead. I opened the box. The cat just lay there, peaceful looking. It was easy. It was exciting. I dug a hole, dropped it in, covered it with dirt, and then helped the neighbor look for her cat. I even made "Lost Kitten" signs and put them on light poles in the neighborhood.

Chapter Two

May 23, Saturday
Grand Haven , Traverse City,
and Gaylord, Michigan

Lou Searing and his wife Carol, along with their golden retriever Samm began the holiday morning by taking a long walk along the shore of Lake Michigan. Their home, south of Grand Haven, was set in a sand dune looking down at the golden beach. Their front yard was the clear and cool waters of Lake Michigan. Lou and Carol, both retired from careers in education, enjoyed sharing time on the beach: walking, soaking up warm summer sun, and feeling the gritty sand underfoot. The couple walked hand in hand as intermittent, cool waves washed to shore and bathed their feet.

Samm begged for something to be retrieved, and Lou would comply by tossing a small piece of driftwood down the beach. The weekend seemed to be the perfect beginning of summer. Lou and his crime fighting partner, Maggie McMillan, were not investigating a murder at the moment. Lou was writing his next novel and Maggie was relaxing from a lot of consulting work. Carol was relieved that Lou wasn't off seeking danger. He was home and enjoying the Lake Michigan shoreline. He was right where Carol wanted him, home.

While Lou and Carol were returning from a long walk, a collie was yapping at the end of the "A" dock at the Clinch Marina, near the Zoo, in downtown Traverse City. Like Lassie, the dog tried to get someone's attention. An older man, taking a walk and looking at all the beautiful boats, must have sensed some problem. He walked out to the end of the "A" dock.

"What's got you all upset, boy?" the man said to the collie. "See something, do ya?"

The dog looked at him and then looked back into the water. The man looked down and caught sight of a woman with a noose around her neck and tied to the piling beside the yacht *Rx: Smooth Sailing*. She was undoubtedly dead.

The old man gasped a bit, took a deep breath and quickly walked along the dock and up to the marina office where he reported what he had seen.

Within minutes EMS, police, and county sheriff vehicles were screaming to get to the marina which was immediately cordoned off. The medical examiner eventually certified death. Dr. Knoble's husband Tom went into shock and was taken to the hospital where he was treated and then questioned thoroughly. The Knoble yacht was impounded by the authorities.

Jake saw the whole thing, joining a crowd of curious people near the marina. It gave him a rush to know that what he had done could cause so many people to be interested, involved, and to spend a part of their holiday talking about and gawking at his work.

Jake returned to his pickup once the body had been taken from the water, placed in an ambulance and removed from the marina. Jake could see the police continuing to talk to people and to look for some evidence of the crime. There would be no clues found. Jake was proud of the well-executed murder, but he knew that he had sinned, he had violated a commandment, "Thou shall not kill." But, in doing so he felt that he had honored another commandment, "Honor thy father and mother."

Jake picked up his cell phone and placed a call.

"St. Joseph rectory. How may I help you?" the housekeeper said.

"I'd like to speak to Father Thomas Murphy. This is an emergency."

"One moment please." While Jake waited for Father Murphy, he had a—

FLASHBACK: I had a good friend when I was growing up. His name was Thomas Murphy. We went to St. Ann's together and were altar boys at many of the masses. Tom was always going to be a priest just as I was always going to be a doctor. He accomplished his goal a year ago. I was invited to the service where he was ordained. I was proud of him and praised him for having his life together. His mom and dad gave him everything he needed to successfully enter his chosen career. In fact, Mrs. Murphy was Mom's best friend, still is. His dad tried to be a substitute father for me. He was a kind man, taking me to ball games and fishing and doing what most fathers and sons do. I appreciated his kindness, but all I could think of was that I was not doing this with my dad, and then I would see Dad hanging, dead in the garage, and I couldn't get my mind off of it.

"This is Father Murphy. How can I help you?"

"Father, bless me for I have sinned," Jake said. "I have killed a woman, but it was because I want to honor my father and mother."

"Who's calling?" Father Murphy asked. He was certain it was Jake Prescott, but he prayed the voice was not his friend's.

"This is Jake, Tom."

Jake had divulged his deadly intentions in the confessional several months ago. Father Tom had prayed fervently that his friend wouldn't go through with his plan. He hoped that since Jake told him how much he hated the people who he believed had killed his father that would be release enough.

"I'm very sorry, Jake. Very, very sorry."

"Yeah, I know, but it had to happen."

"Murder is a mortal sin. You know that Jake. To receive the sacrament of reconciliation, you need to be in the presence of a priest. I cannot administer the sacrament over the phone."

"I wanted you to know. I thought you, being a good friend, would listen."

"Can I arrange for you to see a doctor, Jake? What help can I get you?"

"I don't need or want any help. I do want to be absolved of my sin, but I don't want any doctor or anything. I simply wanted you to listen and know that what I had set out to do, seek revenge for my father, my mother, my brother and me, has happened."

"I know you think it's justified, Jake. But murder can never be justified in the eyes of God."

"God says an eye for an eye, doesn't He?"

"Jake, I know a lot of doctors and others who can help you, but you need to want the help."

"That's right and I don't. Thanks for listening, Tom. I'll see you."

"Peace be with you, my friend."

"Thanks."

The two men hung up. Father Murphy called his mentor, Father O'Brien. Tom needed some help. He knew another would die. He couldn't simply let this happen, but he was bound by his vows not to reveal what he had heard in the confessional. He also knew that he could discuss what he had heard with another priest as long as the penitent was not identified.

⟡

Father O'Brien was at the same parish and lived in the rectory with Father Tom. Father O'Brien was a godsend to Tom as he was learning his way in a rather large parish in Gaylord. The two met in Father O'Brien's office. The office always reminded Tom of being in a leather store. If it weren't for Father O'Brien's obsession with Cuban cigars, the place would smell of fresh leather.

"What can I help you with today, Tom? This cigar bothers you doesn't it? Want me to snuff it?"

"That's OK," Tom replied. "Thanks for asking, though."

Father O'Brien put the half-smoked cigar aside, turned on the fan to clear the air, and then gave his full attention to the novice priest. "What's on your mind, Thomas?"

"Once again I come to you needing your advice about a difficult situation."

"You'll find that they don't get any less difficult, Tom. I'll help if I can. What's on your mind?"

"Well, I wanted to talk to you about something that ..."

"Excuse me, want some coffee, Tom?"

"No, thanks."

"Sorry to interrupt. What's the situation?"

"I learned in the confessional six months ago that a penitent planned to kill. He confessed and explained that he sought absolution for his sin. I forgave him believing that he was truly sorry and that I had convinced him not to go ahead with his plan to murder."

"He did, I take it. Commit the murder, I mean."

"Yes. He'll be coming to me seeking absolution. If I recall correctly, I learned in the monastery that I can refuse absolution if I don't think the penitent is sincere in his asking for forgiveness or if I think the penitent plans to sin again."

"You recall our obligations and responsibilities exactly."

"But, how can I allow another life to be taken? I mean, I sit here knowing that another will die. I have an obligation to the penitent, yes, I understand that, but it seems I have a greater obligation to one about to die. Is there nothing I can do to protect this person?"

"Frustrating isn't it?" Father O'Brien said looking down and shaking his head from side to side. "I've been there too, Tom. It tears your heart out. I've never heard of a plan to murder, but I have heard of pending violence. What's worked for me and I think quite successfully, is counseling. If the penitent respects you and holds you in high regard, meaning that your words mean something to him or her, you can counsel. You can offer help, you can try to intervene by seeking help for the person."

"And, if that doesn't work?" Father Murphy asked.

"You can't control another, Tom. We all wish we could. I've been wanting to control the Bishop since I became a priest." The two enjoyed a laugh as the Bishop had made their lives difficult on more than a few occasions. "But, we can't control others. We can only be God's representatives on an earth that's full of human emotions; anger, jealousy, fear, revenge, and a host more. In sum, you can counsel."

"That's it? Counseling the penitent?" Father Tom asked, frustrated by his short list of ways to solve this problem.

"Well yes, you can also refuse to give absolution and help the penitent realize that in not obtaining absolution, he will go to hell. Maybe that will change the course of the events."

"Can't the penitent go to another priest? You know, shop around till he or she gets absolution?"

"Sure. It happens."

"Why couldn't I just have penitents seeking absolution for judging others or being selfish for example? Why do I get this one so soon after my vows? I don't have enough experience for this."

"You'll handle it well, Thomas. You are a compassionate soul with a good head on your shoulders. And, speaking of that, I think I could use your counsel on a difficult case I am facing."

"If you think I can, sure, I'd be glad to."

The conversation shifted to Father O'Brien's issue, but Father Murphy never let go of the frustration and dilemma that he was about to face. Thirty minutes later the two parted respectful of the thoughts and opinions of the other. Thomas Murphy paused to give thanks for the fellowship and guidance of Father O'Brien. Tom silently wondered what young priests do in rural areas where a mentor doesn't exist. Thankfully, this wasn't his reality. He'd pray about what to do when Jake came into his confessional.

☙

It was a very hot afternoon in June, June 8th to be exact. Confession was at 4 p.m. The door opened beside the name "Fr. Murphy" and in stepped Jake. He said what most Catholics say when they enter the confessional, be it behind a screen or face to face, "Bless me Father, for I have sinned."

Father Murphy nodded and awaited the confession.

"I've committed a murder and I seek to be forgiven."

"Murder is a very serious sin. It is a mortal sin as you know."

"Yes, I know. I think my killing was justified, but I do realize that in God's eyes it is a sin and because of that I wish absolution."

"Can I get you any help, Jake? As soon as he said that Father Murphy had a—

FLASHBACK: I was in high school with Jake. He hated our physics teacher, Mr. Snyder. Old Man Snyder, as we disrespectfully called him, was going to give Jake a "B" which would take him out of the running for valedictorian. Jake was angry and temporarily out of control after school. I feared for him and for Mr. Snyder that night. Jake confided in me the next morning that Mr. Snyder would become very sick in class and maybe even die. Jake said to minimally expect a flurry of cops and paramedics to descend upon the school. He told me he was going to drop something he had concocted into Mr. Snyder's coffee at the beginning of class. I saw Jake go up to Mr. Snyder, distract him and reach toward his coffee cup. Jake returned to his seat and I did what I thought best.

I got out of my seat, went up to Mr. Snyder and then pointed toward the window and said loudly, "Hey, look out there!" On cue, Mr. Snyder and everyone in class looked out the window; I then knocked his cup of coffee into the lab sink. The cup broke. The drugged coffee went down the drain and so did the pending crisis. I picked the pieces out of the sink and turned on the water to wash the evidence away.

Mr. Snyder was upset. I was directed to go to the office to be punished by the assistant principal. But Mr. Snyder lived and I was able to calm Jake down after class by telling him as his friend that I would have turned him in if Mr. Snyder had become ill. Jake knew I would have too.

"I don't want help. I came for absolution."

"Jake, taking the life of another is a serious matter. As your friend, I beg of you to stop this. I cannot disclose this to the police, but I feel as responsible to a potential victim as I do to you."

"You lived with me all those years. You saw what they did to Dad. You saw how it affected us. You saw how there was no justice in this, Tom. You saw my mom suffer. You saw John and me suffer. In a sense THEY killed four people."

"But, Jesus taught us to forgive seven times seventy. He taught us to follow the commandments. He taught us to love. It is not for you to avenge what happened, Tom. The Bible says, 'Vengeance is mine, says the Lord.'"

"Well, I'm helping the Lord, OK? They've got it coming and it will come, one at a time, death will come."

"Jake, I can understand your not wanting to accept my offer to help you. I hope you will accept my decision not to absolve you of your sin."

"What? You have to! You've got no choice."

"That's not true, Jake. Under two conditions I can withhold absolution. If I do not believe you are truly sorry or if I think you will deliberately continue to sin. I believe you know right from wrong and that you realize that you broke a commandment and that you are sorry for having sinned, but I also believe you will continue to sin. You've told me so, six months ago and today. Because of this I cannot and will not absolve you of your sin."

"That means I'm going to hell, doesn't it."

"That's what we believe, yes."

"These people can kill my family and become millionaires with big yachts and not have to pay in any way for killing the four of us?

Is that what God wants to have happen? Must be, because that IS what is happening and I don't see anyone planning to hold these people accountable. I will make them accountable, Tom. I will for my dad, my mom, my brother, and myself. If I go to hell, four of us will feel that justice occurred and to hell with heaven if need be." With that, Jake became angrier and eventually stormed from the confessional, startling two elderly ladies who had been waiting patiently to confess their sins.

While Father Tom listened to the ladies' minor transgressions, he was also thinking of Jake and wondering how he could have handled the session better and if he might become a victim of Jake's mental instability. Now Jake would have two reasons to hurt Father Tom; ruining the attempted plan to kill Mr. Snyder, and now, the decision not to absolve him of a mortal sin.

⟿

Lou was sitting in front of his computer. The Searing cats, Luba and Millie, were by his feet, curled up into fluff balls and catching a nap. Carol was working on a quilt piece. Her quilting group would be meeting soon and she wanted to have something to share with them.

Lou, Carol, the cats and Samm, were comfortably in Lou's writing studio on the second floor of their home south of Grand Haven. Every once in awhile, Lou would leave his computer and stand in front of the bay windows overlooking Lake Michigan. The beautiful and ever-changing scenery seemed to help his creativity. Many of his characters came to mind while standing in front of the bay windows. He had watched summer storms coming ashore, snow squalls in winter, warm breezes in spring and huge cumulus clouds warning of the coming cool days of fall.

The quietness was broken when the phone rang. Lou answered, "Hello."

"Lou?"

"Yes."

"This is Charlie Mange up in Arcadia."

"Well, my goodness. Good to hear from you. What's on your mind?"

"I've been wanting to take you fishing for sometime and I just figured that if I didn't pick a date and invite you, we'd never get around to it."

"You're probably right. What do you have in mind?"

"How about July 5th and 6th?"

"Sounds good to me."

"Carol is invited too. She and Elinor can quilt to their hearts content."

"Thanks, I'm sure she'd enjoy that, but she is planning a Nana and grandchildren trip to Chicago that weekend. Every 4th of July she and our grandchildren take a train to Chicago to see the Windy City and to enjoy the fireworks. It has become a tradition. They stay in a hotel, go to a museum, and just have fun creating memories that will last a lifetime."

"You don't go?"

"Oh, no, I'm not allowed, Charlie. This is a Nana and grandchildren trip, no Grandpas allowed."

"So, you could come up for some fishing?"

"Sure. I'll arrive in the early afternoon of the 5th. Would that be okay with you?"

"That would be great. You don't need to bring anything. We've got all you need."

"OK, thanks, Chuck. See you and Elinor in about a month."

"It's in ink on the calendar. I'm glad this is going to work out."

⌇⌇

June 19 was a critical day for Jake and the future victims of his murderous plan. Jake thought seriously about his not being forgiven for the murder of Glenda Knoble. Jake was raised a good Catholic. He had been an altar boy, educated in the Catholic schools, and was quite serious about all the doctrines. He was greatly troubled by Father Thomas's refusal to absolve him of his sin. He truly believed that he would go to hell if he should die before being forgiven.

The decision of whether to end the killing and be forgiven versus continuing to carry out his plan to murder more people was a difficult one. After all, years had been spent tracking the victims, learning their habits, personalities, life styles, and hobbies. He had spent a lot of time in weight rooms, in underwater aquatic classes, and in studying how to commit the perfect murder. Would he simply throw all of this away to gain eternal life in Heaven?

Maybe he was doing God's will in killing the people who he felt to be responsible for destroying his dad, and thereby his whole family. He did believe that life has a way of balancing and for every wrong, some price would eventually be paid. It could be that he was being used as the vehicle for paying the price. The more he thought about it, he knew that murdering someone was not God's will, but his own.

But it was more than his conscience or his thinking about his dilemma that would be of significance. It was a trip to the mall. Jake was seated on a bench watching people go by when he glanced over and saw a 6 -or 7-year-old boy with a man, presumably his father. Immediately as is often the case, the clock turned back 17 years when he saw his dad hanging in the garage. But, he also had a vision of the little boy growing up without a father, just as he had been forced to do. Jake thought, *If this boy's father died, he would have a life of adjustment and loneliness, just like I had to endure.*

Then it hit him. In killing another, he would take a parent away from children. He would be responsible for several young lives growing up without a father or mother, and not only that but a few grandchildren as well. So, yes, he would have revenge for his dad, mom, brother and himself, but was it too much to deny a parent or grandparent to all of these youngsters? The realization hit Jake hard. It was the first time in all of his years of planning that he seriously came face to face with the effects of his murders.

Jake stood up and walked away. Now, he wasn't sure what to do. Should he stay the course or return to Father Tom, seek absolution for his sin of murder and promise to sin no more and have a chance at going to heaven? The choice was his and remained in his mind for several days.

CHAPTER THREE

Sunday, July 5
Manistee, Michigan

It was almost six weeks after he murdered Dr. Knoble that Jake pulled into Manistee, Michigan. In addition to being very strong and muscular, Jake had a full head of sandy-colored hair on top of a six-foot frame. He was a soap opera star look-alike. He always drew stares from admiring females of all ages.

While most young men want to do something with their lives other than what their parents wish for them, Jake wanted to do exactly what his father, and especially his mother, wanted him to do, become a physician.

Jake came from a long line of physicians and many of them distinguished in a variety of specialties. His father Brad had been a plastic surgeon prior to his committing suicide. Jake's grandfathers were general practitioners and the physician line goes even further into the roots of the family tree. However, his mother Sara who was very bright, worked to put her husband through medical school and did not have a college degree. After Brad's death, it was necessary for her to work to support her sons.

〜

Manistee, the Victorian City, is one of many port cities on the eastern shore of Lake Michigan. Citizens take pride in the Victorian style homes throughout the community, many built in the lumbering era of years past. Stores in the downtown area adopted the Victorian theme and visitors feel they have taken a step back in time when they visit this friendly and unique home to thousands of tourists every summer. The Chamber of Commerce always looks forward to summer because of the tourists, the gamblers going to the Little River Casino located north of town, boaters and fishermen, and the tens of thousands of people who come to enjoy a variety of festivals in the area.

Jake was not in town as a tourist, a gambler, a boater, a fisherman, or a festival goer. He was in town to commit his second murder. The deep-seated desire for revenge was strong enough for him to allow this emotion to rise above the feelings of compassion for those who would be left behind.

Dr. James Rothchild was cleaning his boat, docked in Slip 2 of the Manistee City Marina, home to a line of expensive pleasure craft along the Manistee River that separated Lake Michigan from Lake Manistee. He had taken his 43-foot Tiara Sport Fisherman out into Lake Michigan earlier in the day to try his luck at some salmon fishing. This afternoon, he would clean up the boat and take a nap. After all, he was on a well-deserved vacation.

Jake turned onto River Street. He went along the one-way street past shops, and restaurants, and followed the signs out to Douglas Park. He was constantly checking out everything. When he got to the parking area near the beach he parked his Ford Ranger pickup. Pleasure boats were in the river and people were busy enjoying the warmth and the water.

Jake stepped from his 1999 pickup and stretched. He appeared to be heading to a baseball game as he was wearing his favorite Detroit Tigers baseball cap with the Old English D on the front. Jake wasn't married, didn't even have a steady girl. He played the field, so to speak. He figured now was the time to do so because once medical school started, there wouldn't be much time for anything other than studies and a lot of late-night reading.

He had applied to the traditional in-state medical schools, University of Michigan and Michigan State University, but was not accepted at either school. He couldn't understand this because of his almost perfect grade point average, a significant pile of letters of endorsement, and the rich tradition of his family. The rejections devastated him and were second only to seeing his father's lifeless body as upsetting events in his young life. He had subsequently applied to Ohio State and the University of Minnesota and while he hadn't heard from them, he was certain he would in the near future.

Jake walked around to the passenger side of his truck, opened the door, opened his valise and took out one of his detailed reports. He wanted to read it one more time. The report contained directions for the murder of Dr. James Rothchild. This was not the first time Jake had read his briefing. He had been memorizing it for a couple of days. Jake got back in his pickup and after reading the report one last time, he began to tear it up into little pieces, put them all in a plain white envelope, crushed the envelope into a little ball, and put it under his seat. He would throw it away later.

⤳

Jake drove his truck back to the downtown area. He parked and walked up and down River Street. He carried a camera to give the impression that he was a tourist. He stopped in the City Drug Store to buy a newspaper. He then walked to the bridge where he could take a set of steps down to the walkway. He followed the foot walk down to the city marina and as expected, Dr. Rothchild was docked and was alone.

Jake looked across the channel and saw the Chalet West Apartments. He saw the short incline that he'd back into in several hours. He returned to his red pickup and took a few minutes to check out his scuba equipment, oxygen tank, weights, buoyancy compensator, knife, and wet suit. Everything was in place and ready.

The night before at 3 a.m. he swam underwater across the channel to the city marina. The practice trip was uneventful, perfect for a dress rehearsal and his luminated wrist compass worked perfectly allowing him to swim directly to the marina under the cover of darkness. Tonight it would be for real. The perfect crime was hours away and had been planned to perfection, its execution was predictably assured.

⌇

At exactly 4:30 in the afternoon Jake approached his victim, "Excuse me, are you Dr. Rothchild?"

"Yes, I am."

"I'm an orderly at Memorial Hospital in Ludington," Jake explained while wearing a scrub outfit. "You are needed in an emergency, sir. Dr. Christian Svetnicka has asked for your help and sent me here to give you a ride to the hospital."

Dr. Rothchild immediately wondered why this message was brought to him in person. It would be more logical for him to get a call from his office, but then he wouldn't have a car to drive to Ludington as his was parked in the Petoskey marina parking lot. What difference does it make, he thought. He was needed in an emergency and to this call he would gladly respond.

Soon after leaving the city limits of Manistee, Jake hinted that the doctor's eventual death would be revenge for his father's misfortune at the hands of the group of investors.

"Does the name Brad Prescott mean anything to you, Dr. Rothchild?" Jake asked.

"Yes. He was a physician who took his life about 15 or so years ago. I don't remember the details."

"He was my dad."

"Well, I assure you he was a fine man, an excellent doctor, and ..."

"And now dead because of you guys, stealing his money and wrecking my life and the lives of my mom and brother," Jake said with an angry voice.

"Now wait a minute. If you think I had anything to do with your father's death, you need to know that I ..."

24

"Too late. Double crossing a fellow physician is about as low as one can go."

"Double cross? Listen, young man ..."

"No, YOU listen. I found my dad hanging from a rafter and I will never forget seeing his face. Can you imagine? I was seven years old."

"I'm very sorry, but ..."

"You scam artists thought he was a sucker, someone who would risk all of his savings for a phony land deal."

"It was not phony!"

"You killed my dad. You and the others literally stole our money and left Dad embarrassed, devastated, confused, hurt and in a vulnerable position. He felt cornered with no way out. He was in debt and couldn't imagine ever recovering."

"Listen, we all were in the same boat."

"No, you threw my dad out of the boat and watched him die. It was what you did to him that caused him to kill himself, to leave me without a father or any means to support ourselves."

"Again, I'm sorry, but ..."

"Does the name Jake Prescott mean anything to you, Dr. Rothchild?"

"No, should it?"

"You signed the rejection letter I received from the U of M Medical School."

"I probably did. We send hundreds of those out every year. That's life, a lot of competition, you know that."

Jake listened and experienced another—

FLASHBACK: My mom said there was a letter for me from the U of M. I opened it, fully expecting to be accepted. I couldn't miss, my grades were perfect except for one "B" in quantitative statistics and nobody gets an "A" from Dr. Wilson. My letters of recommendation were excellent, Dad went to the U of M and graduated high in his class. My acceptance was assured. I opened the letter and read, "We regret to inform you that your application to the medical school at the University of Michigan has been denied. We suggest you consider other schools as your credentials are extraordinary, or perhaps you could reapply next year." The letter was signed by Dr. James Rothchild.

I was stunned. My mom cried. I stood there and the anger welled up inside of me. I remember thinking that this happened to me because of my dad. Not only was I denied a father, but now I was denied the opportunity to fulfill a life-long dream, to become a doctor like my dad, to continue the work he began. I read the letter again and then I went out and got drunk.

⌇

Late in the afternoon as carbon monoxide poured into the covered bed of Jake's pickup, Manistee's Chief of Police Mickey McFadden was sitting in the Four Forty West Restaurant with an old friend from his days on the police force in Jackson, Michigan. His friend was Eamonn Kelly. The two Irishmen had been friends since they shared a desk at the police academy. Eamonn was now chief of police in Big Rapids.

Mickey and Eamonn were strapping, middle-aged men with military-type crew cuts. Both were happily married to understanding and attractive wives and were fathers to happy and active children. The two chiefs of police were tall, strong, well tanned; each gave the impression of being in control and was a symbol of law in their towns.

Each summer they met once or twice for dinner. For one evening they would put aside their stresses and strains and enjoy a meal and some light conversation. After drinks were served and orders taken, their conversation began.

"Quiet summer, Mickey?" Eamonn asked.

"Yeah, I'd say so. We've had the usual summer problems that come with a lot of people in town, at the beach, and around water, but nothing major. How about you?"

"Well, with most of the students home from Ferris State, and Big Rapids not being a summer tourist attraction, things have been rather quiet. Young kids restless with no homework always lead to some minor destruction of property, noise, and well, you understand all of that, but like you, nothing major. It's been quiet."

"You had your annual motorcycle rally come into town?" Mickey asked.

"Yeah, that happened a week or two ago. I look forward to it. In fact, once I hear they're coming, I get on my Fat Boy and lead them into town."

"Bet they welcome having a police chief brother with them."

"Yeah, it cools the tension right away. I momentarily slip out of my police chief role and put on my Harley-Davidson vest, and become one of them. We usually have a few arrests for drinking, but it is usually the groupies and not the riders. You know, if ever there was a misunderstood group of people, it would probably be Harley riders."

Little did Mickey know that his dinner with a good friend would be prologue to a murder in his quiet Victorian town. In twelve hours he would be leading a murder investigation, handling the media, holding press conferences, and trying to assure a summer community that they could move about safely.

⌦

As Dr. Rothchild lay dead beside scuba equipment in the bed of Jake's pickup, Lou Searing was in Arcadia fulfilling his promise to do some fishing with an old friend from his special education days. Chuck Mange was one of the pioneers of mandatory special education in Michigan. He along with Marv Beekman, generally known as the Father of Special Education in Michigan, and Marv's son, Lynwood Beekman, had crafted the language for mandatory special education in the late 60s and early 1970s. Chuck had been a professor at

Michigan State University, a guru in special education finance, and an all around quality man committed to programs for children with disabilities. He worked tirelessly for decades and established himself as one of the premier professionals in all of the United States.

Chuck and Lou spent the late afternoon talking about old friends and getting caught up with their interests in the past five or so years. Lou learned that Bob and Nancy Marshall lived down the road from Chuck and his lovely wife Elinor. Lou knew Nancy from her work at Project MATR, a special education initiative downstate. Small world. Following a delicious salmon fillet dinner and lively conversation, the day came to a close.

CHAPTER FOUR

Monday, July 6
Manistee and Arcadia, Michigan

Sunday became Monday as the moon was full over Manistee. The air was cool. Jake would stay up until about 2:45 a.m. and then drive to the Chalet West Apartments parking lot. If all was quiet, he'd place a knotted noose around the doctor's neck, attach the buoyancy compensator and weight vest onto him in order to assist him in pulling the body underwater. Then in a wet suit and with scuba equipment attached, Jake'd swim underwater with Dr. Rothchild in tow to the western edge of the City Marina. He'd surface, tie the victim to the piling at the end of a vacant slip, slit the doctor's right wrist and then swim underwater back to his pickup. This time the slit wrist would symbolize Dr. Rothchild signing the letter that denied Jake entrance into medical school.

~

Eighty-five-year-old Rose Crandall lived in Apartment 6 on the 3rd floor of the Chalet West Apartments. She was a light sleeper and because of a couple daytime naps, she was often up at all hours of the night. Her routine under these circumstances was to part the curtains and look out onto the dimly lit marina, and the night lights of a sleeping Manistee. The moon reflected on the almost ghostly still Manistee River.

This middle of the night view was different. She thought she saw a fish jump by a piling over at the marina. Then she thought she saw a light or a reflection of a light in the same spot. A fish jumping was the only explanation for the disturbed water and the reflected light.

Rose always had a pair of binoculars by the window. During the day when people were walking along the boardwalk, she would be entertained for hours watching people and boats in and across the channel.

Rose took her binoculars, looked toward where she saw the fish jump and saw an outline of something, but couldn't make it out. A few seconds later she saw an object break the surface of the water, but before she could train the binoculars in on it, it was submerged once again. *Could the Lock Ness Monster be here in Manistee*, she thought.

Rose Crandall would have quite a tale to tell at breakfast. She'd seen a giant fish in the channel and there was surely some monster out there that appears in the middle of the night. She saw nothing else and soon placed the binoculars on her dresser, drew the drapes shut, and went back to bed.

~

It was 5 a.m. when Chuck awakened Lou from a deep sleep. Chuck had been up for awhile. He put fishing tackle, bait and some food in his boat assuring that he and Lou would pull away from his dock at exactly 5:30 a.m. Lou quickly got dressed, splashed some water on his face, made sure he had his cell phone, hearing aids, and wallet. Chuck had a hot cup of coffee on the kitchen table for Lou. Elinor was up to see them off. She offered breakfast, but Lou declined except for some juice to wash down a few vitamins and to give him a shot of sugar.

Chuck and Lou walked down his path and steps to reach his twenty-four foot welded aluminum craft with a 170 horsepower motor. Lou glanced at his pocket watch and saw 5:25 so he knew

Chuck would be happy getting an early and on-time start to a day of fishing on Lake Michigan.

The sun was coming up as a thin layer of fog rested on the Lake. The slow moving boat cut through the mist as if seeking its way to light. Chuck and Lou rode out of the channel and made their way into Lake Michigan. Chuck steered the boat due west for about a mile. At this point, the Lake drops to a depth of about one hundred feet.

Chuck told Lou he likes to fish at the "Steeple Hole" which is about a mile west of Arcadia. If you look to land, you can see the steeple in town. The temperature of the water is around 53-54 degrees which, in 70-80 feet of water, should be where the salmon and trout are waiting for a pro-king spoon to appear hanging from a downrigger with an 8-10 pound weight.

The two men were all set for action. Lou knew to keep his mouth shut. Chuck didn't like to talk when he went fishing. Talking was something to do over a cup of coffee or a dish of ice cream. Lou figured this out last night when Chuck relayed the story about a neighbor who often wore a T-shirt that read, "Shut up and fish!" So, Lou let Chuck initiate any conversation and even then tried to keep his reply short.

Chuck's handle on his ship-to-shore radio was "Charlie Tuna" and Elinor's handle was "Mama Tuna." People in the area tuned into channel 10 and always knew when Chuck and Elinor were on the radio. Their names are as common in the area as butter and jam are to a piece of toast.

Chuck and Lou had only been fishing for about a half hour when Chuck brought in a couple of Chinook Salmon. Each fish weighed at least 20 pounds and was placed in the ice box. Lou caught a 6-pound brown trout and had hooked a salmon, but it broke free and lived to swim another day.

⌘

While Chuck and Lou were landing huge fish, ten-year-old Billy Lorimer set his minnow pail on the Manistee City Marina dock. The sun had been up for about an hour, the air was warm, and a gentle breeze was ushering in a bright and hot day in Manistee, a popular summer destination for boaters, campers and tourists looking to vacation in a nice, small town on the shore of Lake Michigan.

Billy looked a bit like Tom Sawyer, shoeless, wearing a short-sleeve shirt, rolled up blue jeans and a broad-billed fishing hat. He also wore a bright orange life preserver, which was the condition upon which he was allowed to go fishing at the marina. He knew how to swim, but his mother insisted he wear a life jacket.

Billy's mom told him if he caught several bluegills and cleaned them, he could have them for his birthday dinner. He was not supposed to be in the marina as only registered boat owners and their guests were allowed on the premises, but Billy was quiet and polite and nobody ever questioned his being around. Actually, he was sort of the resident fisherman giving others reports of the fish biting and making small talk of what he had caught.

While baiting his hook and casting it out into the channel, Billy knew he'd catch a lot of fish because this was his best spot for fishing. Getting a good dinner was predictable.

When Billy slowly reeled in his line, he noticed that the water was discolored. He didn't think much of it. A few casts later he noticed some bubbles coming to the surface or floating out from under the dock. This usually meant a turtle or maybe some fish were underwater. Once again, he didn't give it much thought.

It wasn't until Billy pulled in his first perch that he realized something wasn't right. He took the fish off the hook, put it in his pail. Some liquid that looked like blood seemed to slide off the fish. Billy was enough of a fisherman to know that the blood wasn't from his fish. He decided to look under the dock to see what could be there. While he got down on his knees he was thinking, it might be a dead seagull, a stringer of dead fish, or maybe a dead cat or dog. He wasn't expecting to see what he saw; a dead body, wearing a T-shirt and shorts, floating face up, eyes open but fixating on nothing, floating and swaying a bit with the water's movement. A rope was around the man's neck and tied to a piling.

Billy felt like he might throw up. He took a deep breath and got control of himself. He left his pole and minnow bucket on the dock and ran to the marina office. He didn't scream, didn't try to arouse anyone on a yacht, nor did he tell two older men sitting on a bench near the marina office what he had just seen. Billy ran to the phone, picked up the receiver and with his finger shaking and his chest heaving from an exhausting run, he punched 911.

"What is your emergency?"

"A guy's dead at the marina. He's under the dock."

"Slow down, young man. Where are you?" The dispatcher asked this rhetorical question as his 911 enhanced system immediately told him the call was coming from the City Marina.

"I'm at the marina."

"OK, we'll send someone. A police car is on the way. Tell the officer where the body is. OK?"

"OK."

"You all right, young man?"

"Yeah, but I'm scared."

"What's your name?"

"Billy Lorimer."

"Is your mom or dad there?"

"No."

"Are you with an adult you can put on the line?"

"No, just me fishin' off the dock."

"Do you recognize the person under the dock, Billy?"

"No."

"OK, Billy. Help is on the way. You stay on the phone till the officer arrives. OK?"

"OK."

"Can you hear the police car coming toward the marina?"

"Yeah, I hear it."

"Good. You can hang up and talk to the officer. Wave at him so he sees you. He'll be looking for you."

Billy hung up the phone and waited for the officer to pull up. The police car came up to the marina office and an officer quickly exited.

"You OK, fella?" the officer asked when he got to Billy.

"Yeah, a guy's dead, under the dock, down there by my minnow bucket," Billy gasped pointing to the end of the 3rd slip dock.

"OK, you stay here with Sergeant Simons. She'll take down what you know. We'll also call your mom and dad and have someone come down and get you or we'll take you home."

Billy got in the police car and began talking to Sergeant Simons while the officer ran toward the end of the dock. In the background could be heard more sirens and then an ambulance came into the marina. By now, curious people were gathered around.

The officer looked down in the water and saw a layer of blood, mixed with some gasoline or oil and some seaweed. It looked like someone had emptied a bottle of dark red wine into the water.

One would not suspect it was human blood from glancing down at the water. It was only when you looked under the dock and saw the corpse, the lifeless mass of matter, that you knew that murder had occurred in the marina.

The right wrist was slit. While inspecting the body and awaiting the medical examiner, the paramedics believed that the person had been strangled. With dark red marks around the throat, purple lips and an ashen color to his face, it was obvious that the victim was dead.

Within minutes police officers descended on the scene, and under Chief McFadden's direction, were taking down the registration numbers of every boat in the marina, rounding up the boat owners and directing them not to leave. Other officers were up the hill on River Street writing down the license plate numbers of every vehicle parked along the street. Their trained eyes combed the area looking for anyone watching from a distance or from any window in stores along the street.

Another officer went into Four Forty West and told the owner that no one was to leave. There were only a few early patrons for breakfast and they left their names and addresses and told the officer that they didn't see anything out of the ordinary.

Lou's cell phone went off while he and Charlie were awaiting the next strike of a salmon or trout. They knew from looking at their fish finder that they were teasing the fish about 80 feet down into Lake Michigan.

"What did ya bring that thing out here for, Lou?" Chuck asked shaking his head in disbelief. "When I bring you out here to fish, you're supposed to leave that thing at home."

Lou smiled and removed the phone from his belt. "Hello."

"Lou, you got a call from Mickey McFadden, Chief of Police in Manistee," Carol said with a serious tone in her voice. "He wants your help with a murder at the city marina."

"OK, got a number?" Lou asked as he reached in his pocket for a pen and small notepad.

"Yes. It's 231-555-7564."

"I'll call him. I take it you had a safe trip home from Chicago?"

"Yes, we got home rather late last night. The kids had a rough night in the strange hotel. They slept most of the way home on the train. I didn't, but they did and we all got home safely."

"Thanks for the message from Mickey. I'll be in touch with you after I find out what's going on in Manistee. Love you."

"You be careful, Lou. You hear?"

"I hear," Lou said. "Rest today. I'll look forward to hearing all about your Chicago trip."

"I'm off to Mass. I'll miss you beside me."

"Likewise."

"Love you, Lou. Bye."

Lou dialed the number for Chief McFadden while telling Chuck that there had been a murder in Manistee and he'd probably be needing to get back to shore.

"We'll just pull up our lines and head down to Manistee. I can have you there in about a half hour," Chuck said. "That would actually be faster than going to our home and driving there."

"Thanks, Chuck. Sorry about this," Lou replied.

"No problem. You make that call and I'll pull in the lines."

Lou got Chief McFadden on the line. He gave Lou sketchy details and asked if he could get there ASAP to assist in the investigation.

Lou said he was fishing with a friend and would be coming into the Manistee harbor in about 30 minutes.

Once the lines were up and Chuck was free to take his boat to Manistee he called Elinor to report his plans. Elinor was busy quilting a piece for her oldest granddaughter who was to graduate from high school in a couple of years.

"This is Charlie Tuna calling Mama Tuna."

A few seconds later he heard, "Mama Tuna here. How they biting?"

"We got some nice ones, but Lou just got called to Manistee to help with a murder investigation."

"A murder?"

"Yeah, at the marina, I guess. I'll be awhile. Wanted you to know where I was and that I'll be getting home later than usual."

"OK, your friend called and wanted you to bless the fishing rods of his charter group."

"Tell him the Reverend Tuna Fish has other things on his mind, but if he brings his folks to Steeple Hole and goes down about 80 feet, they'll find all the fish they can handle."

"OK, I'll pass the blessing, or rather, the advice on to him."

"Check in later, Mama Tuna."

"Thanks for the call, Charlie Tuna."

While Chuck was taking his boat south toward Manistee, Lou asked Chuck about this blessing business. "Oh, it's something that started a long time ago. I took on the role of a fishing saint and began to bless the rods of fishermen. By luck, chance, or divine intervention, people started catching fish after my blessing. It caught on and the local folks think a blessing from me will bring them some fish. It's all in good humor. I have no spiritual powers. At least none that I know of."

"Ever have any excitement out here besides catching the big salmon? As if that wouldn't be enough."

"Oh, once in a while something happens. A guy drowned out here once."

"You saw it?" Lou asked.

"No, someone in a cottage across the road from our home spotted a boat trawling around in a circle. The witness came to our house and got me up from a nap. The two of us went out into the Lake. I boarded the boat, cut the engine, and found everything in place, just no fisherman."

"Was he ever found?"

"Yeah, his body washed up a few miles from here."

"Tough way to die."

"Yeah. Then there was the CIA training exercise along the shore."

"CIA? Here in Arcadia?"

"Yeah, I never did get all the details, but my friend and I spotted some men who seemed to be hiding in the dunes."

"We contacted the authorities because we thought it certainly out of the ordinary. We didn't hear anything for weeks until we learned that some military types were involved in a training exercise. You know, get dropped in some remote area and try to get to some common point without being detected."

"High drama for these parts."

"Yeah, but the most excitement is hooking a steelhead or a chinook and bringing it in to say nothing of eating 'em the way Mama Tuna cooks 'em. Dying and going to Heaven, Lou. I'm here to tell you, she makes one fine meal."

Continuing on to Manistee, Chuck asked Lou how he got involved in investigating murders. Lou told him the story he'd told so many times, but each time the memories came flooding back into his consciousness. One would think it would be good therapy to talk it all out, but all it did was bring back vivid memories of a night in hell. But, asking why Lou investigates murders is a logical question that deserves a logical answer, so Lou answered him as best he could.

"About 6 years ago, I would have been about 54, I was on a motorcycle camping trip with a Harley-riding friend of mine. We were camping in the Appalachian Mountains in Eastern Kentucky and sometime in the middle of the night I was awakened and attacked. My friend was stabbed to death, but I had on a thick leather coat and the knife jabs couldn't penetrate it enough to kill me. I got help on a cell phone but it was too little too late and my friend died on the way to the hospital."

"Man, terrible experience!" Chuck replied in disbelief.

"Yeah, it was. Carol came down as did my friend's wife and family. The police said they couldn't do anything. I took time off to find my friend's killer and eventually did. I couldn't save his life, but I could get some justice."

"Who killed him?"

"Bunch of punks on drugs, getting money to keep their habit going. To think my friend lost his life for such meaningless activity still disturbs me. Anyway, I found I had a skill for investigating murders so once that word got around, I got called on to help investigate one or two."

"The cops don't mind your being involved?" Chuck asked.

"Oh, yeah, some of them do. I guess I'm a threat to their competence. Most feel they can handle it on their own and they can. They're trained and have up-to-date techniques and resources."

"The Manistee Chief called you, though?"

"Yeah, Mickey and I go way back. Mickey's dad and my brother Bob were good friends in Vietnam. Bob came back and went into the State Police Academy where he earned a good reputation as an investigator. Mickey's dad became a paramedic putting his Vietnam training and experience to good use. His son Mickey went into police work. He served on the Jackson force and then had a chance to be Chief of Police in Manistee. He's got good leadership skills, good communication skills and works well with government officials. He's a natural for an administrative position.

"Anyway, yeah, Bob and Mickey's dad maintained their friendship. Because of his interest in criminal justice, Mickey followed Bob's career as well as mine. We've talked on occasion about my cases. I guess Mickey wanted all the resources he could have at his disposal to solve this thing quickly."

"He's got a detective on his staff, doesn't he?"

"Oh, yeah, I'm sure he has. I'm not being called on to replace anyone, only to be one more head in trying to figure out who thought murder was a way to solve a problem."

"Since I've read your books, Lou, I know about Maggie. She's a big help to you," Chuck said.

"Oh, you got that right. Maggie is the brains in our duo. She gets around in her wheelchair better than most with healthy legs."

"Sounds like you two are a good team."

"I think so. We've solved four cases to date. I wouldn't be successful without her."

"There's the Manistee harbor up ahead," Chuck said, pointing south. 'See the pier out into the Lake?"

"Yeah. Won't be long till I'm into another case."

ঌ৵

While Chuck and Lou were approaching the Manistee pier, Chief McFadden had sent two officers to the Chalet Apartments to find out what they could learn. Mickey knew that on any given moment in time, at least 100 eyes were fixed on the channel and marina. He didn't know when this crime was committed, but chances were good that somebody saw something.

The manager of the apartments offered a general announcement to all the residents: "Could I have your attention please. As most of you can tell, there is an emergency across the channel at the City Marina. Chief of Police McFadden has sent a couple of officers over to see if any of our residents has any information to share about what might have happened at the marina last night. If you saw anything suspicious or have any information at all, please come to the lobby or call my office. Thank you."

The announcement came as many of the residents were eating breakfast and watching the drama unfold across the channel. Many were gathered around Rose Crandall who offered her "monster in the Manistee channel" theory. Most knew of Rose's outlandish tales and her vibrant imagination, but were enthralled by her storytelling and most hung on every word.

Tom Zopinski, a long time resident, interrupted, "Rose, you hear that? The police want to talk to you about what you saw."

Rose brightened up. She knew she'd soon have the officers mesmerized with her account of the channel monster. The manager had already warned the officers, "My guess is Rose Crandall will come to the lobby, but you need to know that Rose tells whopping big stories. Her imagination and her love for attention combine to provide all of us with the most outlandish stories you've ever heard. So, if she comes up, listen, but know that this is the same woman who was in the Oval Office when President Clinton and "that woman" were carrying on. She'll also tell you that she is John Glenn's cousin and went with him the first time he went into space. She isn't crazy, just loves to hold people's attention as she throws around a lot of, pardon me, Officer, BS, if you know what I mean." Both officers nodded.

Shortly after the announcement and plea for help was given, two men, Eric and Stan, appeared. "We were here in the lobby playing cribbage late last night," Stan said. "We saw some car lights come into the parking lot."

Eric added, "We looked at the clock and saw that it was about three o'clock in the morning. The cops come by on the even hours so it probably wasn't the cops."

"Sometimes kids come around to drink or talk or sometimes go swimming in the channel so that's probably what happened," Stan surmised. "About a half hour later, we saw a vehicle leave."

"Did you see the car?" an officer asked.

"Just the lights," Eric said, with Stan nodding in agreement. "It's dead around here in the middle of the night. Every sound or any light is very out of the ordinary."

"Did you hear anything?" an officer asked.

"Just that car or truck or whatever and that was faint. Neither of us hears very good," Stan said while pointing to his right ear where an in-the-ear hearing aid was placed.

The officers took down names and phone numbers and thanked them.

A moment later, Tom appeared. "You've got to talk to Rose Crandall. She's got a story for you. She saw something last night out in the water. There's a channel monster out there—comes out of the water, snatches people, strangles them, ties them to a dock, and goes off looking for more people to kill. Rose seen it. She's telling everybody around the breakfast table."

"Thanks, Tom," the manager said with a smile. Tom left and the manager said, "Well, I told you. The channel monster. Godzilla comes to Manistee. Oh, pahlease!!" The two officers looked at each other and smiled.

"We'll miss Rose when she dies, but till then we couldn't ask for cheaper entertainment. It's so sad, but so humorous. Our social worker says to just let her have her imagination and delusions. It's too late for therapy and no one is harmed by her stories. So, we just turn her on and off like a TV show, which is exactly what she is."

As predicted, around the corner came Rose, about five feet tall, shuffling along, pushing her walker, frail, with stringy grey hair combed into what looked to be a slept-on bun, glasses about to fall off the end of her nose, and hose trying to cling to spindly legs. She had a smile on her face as she slowly approached the officers.

"I know you officers are good at dealing with people, but try your best not to laugh too hard," the manager urged. "Just go along with the story. The more you chuckle the more she turns on the imagination and you could be here for at least an hour. If I were you, I'd stick to the words of Joe Friday, 'Just the facts, ma'am, just the facts.'"

"You must be Rose," the taller of the two officers said.

"Yup, Rose Crandall's my name, information's my game," she said with a smile. "You ready to hear about the monster that rises out of the channel? He especially likes boaters, strangles them and ties them to the marina dock."

"We want to hear whatever you've got to share, Mrs. Crandall. If you saw something last night we want to know about it."

"I couldn't sleep. I pulled back the curtains and pretty soon I saw, over by the marina, this big thing come up out of the water. First I thought it was a fish jumping, but then, it rose out of the water, up ten to twenty feet in the air, sort of like a dinosaur, long neck, big head, spiked tail. You guys ever hear of the Loch Ness monster over in Scotland?" Each nodded. "Well, this thing looked like that!"

The officers took notes and tried to remain serious and respectful. They knew their families would have a story at the dinner table that evening the likes of which they'd never heard in quiet, Victorian Manistee.

꒰ꔛ꒱

Chuck and Lou pulled into the harbor. Lou glanced to his left and saw a grandmother and a little girl standing on the end of the pier. He had a flashback to Dawn, a Harley-Davidson motorcycle-riding friend, telling him she used to walk with her grandmother to the end of the Manistee pier, and while there, enjoy some Sweet Tarts. This seemed to be a generation re-enactment of Dawn's childhood memory. Lou waved to the two and they returned the greeting. Lou wondered if that little girl would grow up to be like Dawn, feeling the wind flow through her golden hair as she sped down a country road on a Harley Sportster.

Lou could see the commotion up ahead as they got closer to the marina. There were a lot of swirling red, blue and white lights atop police cars and emergency vehicles by the marina area. Lou could see the yellow caution tape. Up on River Street a throng of people were gawking, talking, and hoping to see the victim of a brutal murder.

Chief McFadden saw Lou on Chuck's boat and directed them to pull into a slip in the marina. They tied up and got out of the boat and onto a dock. Lou introduced Chuck to Chief McFadden. The three shook hands.

"What do we have, Mickey?" Lou asked.

"It wasn't an accident. He's been murdered. It's brutal, Lou."

"Shot or stabbed?"

"I'm not sure how he was killed. The head is in a noose. Probably hanged. The body is still under the dock. We're waiting for the medical examiner. He's tied up with some case. I'm not sure where. Hopefully, he'll be here any minute."

"Who found the body?"

"Some 10 year-old kid, up early, fishing off the dock. He saw some bubbles, some blood, and then the body. He's pretty shook up.

His mother took him home. We thought it best to get him away from all of this commotion. It's the kid's birthday too. What he saw this morning will stay with him for a long time."

"Yeah. Hopefully, time will heal," Lou replied.

"Take a look under the dock, Lou. Look at the dark red marks around his neck, and also notice the slit on his right wrist. Almost looks like the killer tried to cut his hand off."

Lou knelt down, looked under the dock, and was sorry a youngster had to see what he saw. "I've seen a lot of corpses in my work, but most have been in a morgue, face up with a sheet covering a still, pale, and lifeless body. This is gruesome, chief." The movement of the water and the blood still leaking from the victim's wrist, from his mouth, as well as some air bubbles still exiting his nose gave the impression that maybe there was still some life in the victim. If Lou was into morbidity, he'd have looked longer, but all he needed to do was confirm Mickey's observations. Lou had a thought that maybe it wasn't a murder so he stood up and asked Mickey, "Could it have been suicide?"

"No, I quickly ruled that out."

"If he slit his wrist and then hung himself, he'd have no way to get under this dock and tie the rope to the piling," Lou reasoned.

"Right. My guess is someone wanted him dead and they sure made an ugly mess of it," Mickey said, before Lou could voice the same conclusion.

"Yeah, you know, I can't believe all of this activity could take place here in a marina full of boats and with so many people around in the middle of our tourist season."

"I thought the same thing," Chief McFadden replied. "The pathologist will give us a time of death, but it had to have been early this morning or perhaps late last night."

In order to get some identification, the detective on the scene removed the waterlogged wallet from the back pocket of the victim. The driver's license was in the first plastic insert. The wallet belonged to Dr. James Rothchild. His address was Cadillac, Michigan. Registration records in the marina office indicated that Dr. Rothchild owned the boat, *Relax the Sphincter*. He came into port Saturday morning from Muskegon. He paid for two days and was assigned to Slip 2.

҉

Walking toward the marina from downtown Manistee was Jake Prescott. He walked alone, joining tens of others in downtown Manistee who had heard about a possible drowning at the city marina.

While he was in the Sunrise Bakery he had gotten word of the commotion at the marina. It didn't faze him. Jake expected the body to be found. But, he was certain that there would be no way the murder could be attributed to him. Jake had been doing research for the perfect murders for the past year. While walking to join the curious he had a—

> FLASHBACK: I can still see Mom talking to my brother John and me. She sat us down at the kitchen table and said "You boys are old enough to know why your dad committed suicide. I decided to wait until you were older to tell you. I think you are ready and so I will tell you what happened." My brother and I were all ears. She said our dad had joined an investment club. When the original club members saw they were going to lose millions of dollars from a land development investment, they invited a few other doctors to join them, knowing they would take a hit, but thinking they could all cover some of their lost money with the investment the new doctors were willing to make. Our dad was one of the doctors asked to join them.
>
> Mom went on to say that the others who joined Dad in this potential windfall were fiscally able to take the hit. However, I'll never forget the moment I heard her say, "Your father told me that he and the

other three had been double-crossed." Mom said that for the original members, forgiveness and wise financial planning helped the losers get back on their feet, but Dad quickly became depressed, took on tremendous guilt for putting us and his own future at risk, and came to believe that his only recourse was to escape by death.

As we knew, she said he must have gone into the garage, fashioned a noose, tied it to a rafter, stood on the hood of his car and jumped. His neck snapped before his feet hit the cement floor of the garage and his death was instantaneous. He had not told Mom of his plans nor was there any note.

⌁

While Jake and hundreds of citizens and tourists gawked and talked, the medical examiner arrived, did his work in a timely fashion, certified death and then ordered the body removed from the scene. You would have thought a major movie production was underway. TV cameras were on hand, a radio personality was taping an interview, and a photographer from the *News Advocate*, Manistee's daily newspaper, was snapping shots for tomorrow's edition. Hundreds of necks were stretching from behind yellow tape all around the marina hoping for a glance at the removal of the lifeless body which looked more grotesque out of the water than in it.

Lou went right to work. First, he thoroughly inspected the dock area. Chief McFadden allowed him to board Dr. Rothchild's yacht and look around. Lou didn't see anything out of place, no sign of a struggle, nothing amiss. In fact, the yacht was immaculately clean and organized.

Mickey's officers were looking for evidence, taking photographs, and securing the yacht. It would soon be impounded and taken from the marina to an undisclosed location for further study. Chief McFadden said family members may not be happy about it as the boat is sometimes kept for months, but there could be crucial evidence somewhere on that boat and it had to be kept.

"How long you going to store it, Mickey?" Lou asked.

"Till the case is solved. Could be a long time."

After carefully looking around the yacht, Lou was satisfied that he wouldn't learn anything on board to help him with his investigation, so he stepped from the beautiful Tiara. Lou took some time to join Mickey's officers in talking to boat owners in the marina. He wanted to be assured that no one heard a struggle, strange sounds, or anything that would lead them to think that a murder was happening within a few feet of their floating palaces.

As the body was taken to the West Shore Medical Center on East Parkdale Avenue, the detective was trying to find relatives of the victim. He called Anita Rothchild who told him that James had decided to take his yacht from Manistee out into Lake Michigan for a day's ride and a little fishing. He had come to Manistee yesterday and her last contact with him was a phone call about 3 p.m.

Anita was close to a state of shock when she got the news. She was able to give Lou some helpful information. Lou learned that James Rothchild was a proctologist. He had no enemies that she knew of, and was well known in Michigan as a highly respected doctor in problems of the gastrointestinal track and especially cancer of the colon.

Before Lou left, he walked up to Chief McFadden to thank him for calling and inviting him to assist in solving the murder.

"I think we've got a serial killer here, Lou." Mickey said, matter of factly.

"Really. This has happened at other marinas?"

"I read a bulletin several weeks ago that came from Traverse City, I think. I'll have to dig it out, but I remember a marina being mentioned and the right wrist being slit."

"Yeah, check that out and let me know, will you?"

"Sure."

"Did you pick up any clues?" Lou asked. "I didn't find anything that would be helpful."

"We didn't either," Mickey replied, shaking his head.

Before leaving Manistee Lou decided to stop and see if he could talk to the young lad who first spotted the body. Lou asked an officer to drive him to Billy Lorimer's house on the corner of 2nd and Pine. When Lou arrived, he explained to Billy's mother why he was there and asked if he could talk with her son. She thought it would be okay. A school psychologist who happened to be a friend of the Lorimers was with him to help the lad adjust to this morning's disturbing discovery.

Billy came out and sat on the porch. "My name's Lou, Billy. I'm going to be trying to find the person who killed that man you found down at the marina. Billy nodded and continued looking down at the ground. "I'm curious about whether you heard or saw somebody when you were walking to the marina or even to the spot where you were fishing?"

Billy said nothing; he simply shook his head negatively,

"Didn't see or hear anything?" Lou asked, hoping he'd open up a bit.

Again, a slow side-to-side shaking of his head indicated he had nothing to say.

"How about the two of us going for a motorcycle ride someday; would you like that?" Lou asked. Billy nodded positively.

"Well, Billy. I'll be on my way. Sorry you had to have that experience this morning. You did the right thing in calling 911 and helping the police. You're a brave young man. I'm proud of you. You know that?" Billy nodded and looked up into Lou's eyes, the first time he'd seemed to acknowledge his presence.

Lou put his hand out and they shook hands. Lou gave him a hug and patted him on the back. "I understand it's your birthday. I'll bring you a gift soon, Billy. You take care of yourself, son. You understand?"

Again he nodded. He had not said a word during Lou's visit, but that was fine. He had to do what was comfortable for him. Lou sensed that he wasn't hiding anything, just trying to keep from thinking about a horrible scene. Lou left to join Chuck in going back to Arcadia.

Chief McFadden had turned the investigation of the crime over to his Detective Sergeant Jerry Maguffin, a twelve-year veteran of the force. Jerry knew of Lou and Maggie and felt comfortable working with them to try and solve this murder.

Back at the police station on Maple Street, Chief McFadden called the mayor and the president of the city council to report the crime and to explain what procedures were being carried out so they would be assured all was being done according to department policy. He then transcribed a press release giving the news media all the information they would need to accurately report what had happened and to accompany news photos and video footage collected by news reporters and their media teams. The release was factual and brief. It identified the victim, explained, without detail, the condition of the body, time of discovery of the crime and a note to assure all citizens that a statewide alert was underway for the criminal. Once the news release was typed and reviewed by Mickey, it was given to the reporters on hand and immediately put onto the major news wires.

Chief McFadden knew that this would not satisfy the hungry reporters. He promised a news conference in an hour so that he'd appear accessible to the news media and all would see a cooperative police chief.

Once the calls had been made to follow protocol and once the press release had been dictated and approved, Chief McFadden then entered the complaint prepared by Detective Maguffin into the Automated Incident Capturing System or AICS database. This information would go to the State Police and be available to all others who chose to use the AICS to assist them with crime investigation.

He also began searching for similar crimes as this could be a serial. He added his information and at the same time studied the Law Enforcement Information Network or LEIN, a statewide system that also might alert him to similar crimes.

Lou called Maggie to bring her up to speed with the murder and to alert her that they'd be working on another case. Maggie, who lives in Battle Creek with her retired dentist husband Tom, said she'd join Lou in Grand Haven.

Next Lou called Carol and reported what she had already heard on CNN. Lou told her Maggie was coming to Grand Haven and they'd probably both arrive around the same time.

While Lou was driving south to Grand Haven, and Maggie was driving north to Grand Haven, Chief McFadden was holding a news conference on the steps of City Hall.

"Thank you for coming. My name is Chief of Police Mickey McFadden. I wish to begin by thanking each of you for your cooperation and what I expect to be fair and accurate reporting. I also wish to thank my staff for an immediate response to this crisis and the professional way in which the investigation is being handled. Detective Sergeant Maguffin is responsible for the investigation of this crime. We are grateful to have his expertise and professionalism. He'll coordinate his work with other law enforcement agencies as needed.

"I gave you a press release an hour ago. If you didn't get a copy, extras are on the table down there near the grass, my right, your left. If you have specific questions, I'll take them at this time." What followed were a series of questions asked by a variety of newspaper and television reporters. TV news cameras were capturing the news conference for evening news audiences around the country.

"Do you have any suspects?"

"No, we're searching our databases for information regarding similar crimes. But, we do not have a suspect at this time."

"Motive, do you have a motive?" a reporter shouted from the back of the crowd.

"No, all we have is a victim."

"Are any of the marina guests suspects? Are they free to go? Are any being detained?"

"All marina guests have been identified, interviewed and cleared. All are free to stay or go."

"What more can you tell us about the victim?"

"The victim is Dr. James Rothchild. He was a nationally recognized physician from Cadillac. He is survived by his wife and daughter. His family and staff are devastated by this tragedy as I'm sure you can understand. I don't know much more than that."

"What is the cause of death?"

"The cause of death has not been determined and I can't comment on that until I get an autopsy report and I don't expect that for a day or two."

"How did the doctor die?"

"As I said, we'll have to wait for the autopsy report."

"I heard he had a rope around his neck. Was he hanged?"

"Yes, there was a rope around his neck, but we don't know if hanging was the cause of death."

"Is it true that a little boy found the body?"

"Yes, he was fishing off a dock in the marina and saw the body. He called 911 and we immediately responded. He did a good job in a very stressful situation."

"How is the boy?"

"He is adjusting as well as any ten-year-old boy could given what he experienced."

"What is the boy's name?"

"I will not give you that information. The last thing he or the family needs, with all due respect, is all of you hammering away with questions. We will maintain confidentiality unless the family chooses to reveal information, but having talked with both parents, I doubt that will happen."

"Will the marina be closed for the time being?"

"I expect us to open the marina later today. We won't do so until we are assured that all evidence has been collected."

"I saw Lou Searing. Is he going to be involved?"

"Yes. Lou has a high degree of respect from me and Detective Maguffin. We are pleased that he and Mrs. McMillan will help us. They are nationally known investigators. I am confident that my staff can adequately solve this crime and my asking Mr. Searing to assist is not meant to show any disrespect for my staff but only to provide them with all of the resources to do a thorough investigation. To save you a little time and effort, Mr. Searing and Mrs. McMillan will direct any media questions they receive to Detective Maguffin, so don't waste their time or yours."

"Will the marina be patrolled in the foreseeable future?"

"Most definitely. Our citizens can feel safe and our guests at the marina will have around-the-clock police presence. Thank you for coming. I will hold a press conference daily at this time unless additional information warrants a change. You'll be informed if this should be the case. Thank you."

With that, Chief McFadden retreated to his office to answer calls from national media and to check for any responses to his search for serial killers or information that would help him and Detective Maguffin solve the crime.

✧

Once again Jake called Father Thomas Murphy.

"St. Joseph Rectory. May I help you?"

"May I speak to Father Murphy? This is an emergency."

"I'm sorry, but Father Murphy is not here. Would you like his voice mail?"

"When will he be back?"

"We expect him back late tomorrow. Would you like his voice mail?"

"Yes, please."

A few seconds later he heard, "Thank you for calling. I'm sorry I am not here to talk with you. Please leave your name and phone number, and if you wish, a short statement of your reason for calling. I will get back to you as soon as I can. God bless you." Beep.

"Father, bless me for I have sinned. The second has died."

✧

Father Thomas Murphy was in Texas participating in a demonstration against the death penalty. In the spring he carried a placard outside an abortion clinic in Wichita, Kansas. Life was very important to

Father Thomas Murphy. His attitudes about the sanctity of life were consistent with the teachings of his church. He had always been sensitive to life. His grandmother Murphy was the adult in his life who helped him form a very pro-life attitude. His belief was so strong that he became a vegetarian at a young age because he couldn't accept the slaughter of animals as a means of sustaining his own life. When Father Murphy became a priest there was no conflict with the Vatican in his thinking about abortion, euthanasia, suicide, or any kind of killing. He was a conscientious objector as well.

It was a steamy, hot afternoon in Houston as Father Murphy carried his placard, "Stop the Killing! Taking a Life is God's Decision, not yours!" He marched in a line of people from a variety of backgrounds. Talking to any of them was preaching to the choir, but for many outside of the ring of protestors, taking the lives of people who had killed others was a no-brainer. Why should a serial killer live after taking the lives of five women? Why should a young man live when he had killed his family?

Father Murphy stayed true to the teaching of Jesus or so he thought. There were many beliefs of his church that he could challenge or even debate, but any form of life-taking was not up for discussion. Anyone who knew Father Murphy well, knew this, including Jake Prescott.

Father Murphy believed that Jake and his family had been wronged. The dilemma was very evident. It would not go away. He loved Jake Prescott like the brother he never had, but he loved God and his church even more.

৵

Maggie entered the city of Grand Haven in her specially designed van about four-thirty in the afternoon. Carol had anticipated Maggie's arrival as she knew that Lou didn't investigate a complicated murder without Maggie's brilliant mind. Carol freshened up the guest bedroom and put some flowers from her garden in a vase hoping that Maggie would enjoy them.

THE MARINA MURDERS

The Searing home had one step up into the house so Lou and Carol would help Maggie negotiate that. Maggie was a good friend, so hopefully, she wouldn't mind giving a little of her independence to Carol. Lou and Carol had purchased a patient transferring and lifting system from their friend Rick Ingolia in Bloomfield Hills. The device came in handy when helping Maggie transfer from her chair to other places in the house.

〜〜

Maggie was an attractive woman in her mid-forties. She almost always wore slacks and during the summer, colorful blouses. Her warm smile made everyone who met her feel comfortable. Her brown hair was cut short and her sunglasses hid beautiful dark brown eyes. Maggie's use of technology was evident as she had a laptop attached to her chair, her cell phone at her side, and other technological gadgets in her saddle bags as she called them.

While Maggie was unpacking in the Searing home, Father Murphy was sitting in Hobby International Airport in Houston, Texas, listening to his voice messages. He would fly back to Michigan in an hour, but he wanted to know what he would face upon his arrival. Most were of little importance and could be handled when he got home.

When he heard the message from Jake, he felt he would become physically ill. He now knew that two murders had occurred. His conscious once again was flooded with guilt for not being able to interfere with this taking of a life. Two people had died who would be alive today if he had acted. His vows to the priesthood continued to lock him in crisis.

That afternoon, Father Murphy protested the state of Texas killing people who had killed others and yet at this moment he shouldered the murder of two people, two people who would have lived if Father Murphy could have or would have told the authorities of Jake's plan.

〜〜

Father Murphy was bound to secrecy. He felt helpless and realized that nothing he learned in the seminary could have prepared him for this feeling of helplessness. He hung up the phone, went over to a row of seats in the waiting area and hoped he wouldn't be approached by a stranger. He needed time to think and to pray. With Rosary in hand, he silently began the words that he had said daily for many years. He was about half way through the first set of beads when he realized that his mind was wandering. He had a—

> FLASHBACK: Jake is my best friend from my youth. He is for all practical purposes my brother. There is nothing I wouldn't do for Jake Prescott. We were on sports teams together, we shared our souls, we double-dated often. We served at hundreds of masses at St. Ann's.
>
> Six months ago, on a very cold February afternoon, it was almost dinner time when Jake appeared at the rectory. I welcomed him and invited him to stay for dinner. He seemed nervous and all he said was that he wanted to have the sacrament of confession and could I go to the confessional and he'd meet me there. I realized he was troubled, very troubled. I said, "Of course, Jake. I'll be right there."
>
> I quickly went to the confessional, put on my stole and waited for him to come in. As in the past he chose to confess face to face. He entered. "Father, bless me for I have sinned. My last confession was last Christmas. I am planning the murders of several people. I am doing this for Dad, Mom, and John as well as myself. My anger is an addiction and I can't free myself from knowing that I must seek the justice that escaped those who committed this terrible crime."
>
> "Jake," I said. "Has this just come over you? I know that you've thought about this as you've shared your anger before, but if I may ask, is your plan detailed and are you feeling compelled to carry it out?"

"Yes. I will carry it out."

"Jake, are you still seeing your psychiatrist?"

"No. It wasn't doing any good. We'd talk and talk and it wasn't helping, just taking a lot of time."

"Does the psychiatrist know of your plan to kill others?"

"No. I never told him. We spent all of our time talking about my feelings about losing Dad as a young boy. It was a waste of time."

"Can I do anything to turn you away from committing this sin, Jake?"

"My only sin is wanting to take the lives of other people. I have not killed anyone."

"Yes, you are correct."

"So, I am here to ask forgiveness."

"You will be absolved of your sin if you are truly sorry, but before absolving your sin, I am going to try and convince you not to carry out the plan, Jake. I've been your friend for years. I know the hurt, the pain, the anger and believe me, my family and I especially share that with you, your mother, and John. But, taking a life is inconsistent with the Lord's teaching and as a Catholic man, to do so would be a mortal sin and I beg you not to go ahead with this, Jake. Can I help you in any way? Maybe you would like to live with me at the rectory for awhile?"

"Thanks, Father. Maybe I'll change my mind. I know murder is a mortal sin and I expect to seek forgiveness for each sin I commit, but I will tell you right up front that while I may kill, it is only to take seriously the commandment to honor thy father and mother."

"I realize you think that, Jake, but breaking a commandment is not justified by adhering to another commandment. I'm sure you understand." Jake looked at the floor.

"Is there anything else you want to say?" Father Murphy said.

"No, Father. Please forgive me."

Jake, your sin is forgiven in the name of the Father, the Son, and the Holy Spirit. I again beg you to stay with your psychiatrist, trust that he knows what he is doing and can help you. I beg you not to act, but as your friend, I will tell you that whatever I hear in this confessional will never leave this room."

"Thank you. If you take care of my soul and intercede with God, I will do what I have to do to honor my father and mother."

"God bless you, Jake, and if there is anything I can do for you, and I mean anything, I will come to you in an instant if I can guide you away from sin."

"Thank you Father." Jake rose from his chair and walked from the room.

Father Murphy's attention drifted back to the Rosary and he was able to stay focused throughout his prayer. He sat still for a few minutes hoping some guidance would come from God. Soon his flight was announced and he boarded knowing that he was headed home to Michigan and to a very troubling situation for him and for Jake.

༘

That evening Carol made one of Lou's favorite meals, cabbage rolls. As the three of them enjoyed the meal, Carol told about her 4th of July trip to Chicago. From the sound of things, other than a sleepless night in the hotel, all had a marvelous time. Then the conversation turned to the marina murder in Manistee. The discussion was summarized by Carol when she said, "Looks like you two will be busy for a few days."

After dinner Carol and Lou took their evening walk along the beach while Maggie stayed inside to make some calls and to rest.

She had had a long day. Carol and Lou took Samm with them. She loved for them to toss pieces of driftwood for her to run after and return. It was her instinct and fun for them as well.

The cool waters of Lake Michigan lapped over their feet and onto their ankles as light waves came ashore. Carol and Lou walked hand in hand, talking about their children and grandchildren. They turned to face the lake, and with arms around each other, watched the yachts moving north and south far from the shore.

Lou couldn't help but think that anyone on those luxury boats could be the next victim in the marina murders. It was his passion to find the murderer and stop this sickness before further lives were lost.

As they turned and headed home, Lou said to Carol, "How could he pull that off?"

"Pull what off?" Carol said, shaking her head and smiling. "You always expect me to read your mind when you drop these short sentences on me."

"Sorry. How could someone get the body under a dock in the summertime when the place is teeming with people who are up all hours of the day or night. You'd think someone would hear or see something suspicious."

"You sure would," Carol replied.

"The problem with a possible serial killer is that you know he's going to hit again and with marinas in every city along the lakeshore, the potential for the next killing is immense and how do you anticipate where it will be?"

"I don't know, Lou," Carol said. "What's the motivation? Got any idea?"

"It doesn't seem to be sexual. I doubt the autopsy will show any sexual abuse."

"Robbery?"

"Don't think so; this guy's wallet was on him and contained several hundred dollars. His yacht didn't have anything missing, at least nothing that was obvious."

Lou and Carol washed the sand off their feet outside the back door and after drying them and putting on sandals, walked inside.

Maggie greeted them and said, "Chief of police in Manistee called you, Lou. He asked for you to call."

Lou picked up the phone and dialed Mickey's number. "Hello, Mickey. What do you need?"

"I've got some information for you, Lou."

"What've you got?"

"The doctor that was killed this morning? His daughter is missing."

"Hmmm."

"Yeah, she lives in Pentwater. Mrs. Rothchild called her to tell her about her father's death. The daughter, Penny's her name, told her mother she'd go to Manistee and then go to Cadillac. Mrs. Rothchild called me a couple of hours ago to see if she had arrived here because she was not in Cadillac."

"She probably stepped out and didn't tell anyone where she was going," Lou replied.

"No, she told her mother she was going to Manistee. She told a roommate that she tried to call her boyfriend but couldn't reach him. The roommate said she was very emotional. She said she gave her a hug and then she left with plans to come to Manistee. She hasn't been seen or heard from since."

"But that was only a few hours ago, "Lou responded.

"Nine hours actually, and it only takes an hour to get here."

"Maybe she went to some other friend's home or who knows where she could have gone?" Lou reasoned.

"Nothing would be as important to her as her father's death. You're right, lots of logical explanations. Fact is, she's not here and she's supposed to be. Just a part of the drama that I wanted you to know about."

"Thanks. What's happening at your end about this?" Lou asked.

"We've put out a 'be on the lookout' alert to the county sheriff and State Police. We're also asking for a vehicle to retrace her trip or at least the most direct route from Pentwater to here, looking for any tire marks going off the road or any area hard to see from the road."

"OK, thanks, Mickey. Please keep me posted."

"Will do."

When Lou hung up, Carol asked him to come to their back window. Since the front of their house faces Lake Michigan, the back of their home is a hundred or so feet away from the road between Holland and Grand Haven. "Someone in that car over there seems to be keeping an eye on us," Carol said.

Lou got his binoculars and trained them on the vehicle and driver.

Lou saw a person, but he couldn't tell if the driver was a man or woman. The person had a set of binoculars looking at the Searing home and obviously saw Lou looking at him or her. Within a minute the vehicle pulled away going toward Grand Haven. Before it was out of sight Lou was able to identify it as a red pickup. He kicked himself for standing at the window looking out. How stupid, he thought later. A discreet look from Maggie's bedroom window would have given him more time to identify the vehicle or call the Grand Haven Chief of Police Vern Bryant to request intervention. But, he did what he did, and consequences usually follow stupid decisions.

"One of our many admirers was out front, Maggie," Lou said as he hurried out of the house, got on his Harley, and took off faster than he thought he was able to move for his 60 years. Lou drove the bike toward Grand Haven going as fast as he could, barely stopping at stop signs. He rode seven miles to town but didn't see a red pickup except for one in a driveway on Sheldon Road, but that one had a tool box in the bed and the one he saw did not have that feature.

Lou continued to ride around hoping he'd come upon the vehicle but had no luck. He rode back home, up his driveway, and into the garage.

As Lou entered his home, the phone rang. It was Chief McFadden. "Lou, that murder in Traverse City was a marina murder and the right wrist was cut. The body was tied under a dock to one of the pilings. I'm going to meet with the chief of police in Traverse City to compare information. I thought I might also talk to the daughter's roommate and maybe her boyfriend. Do you and Maggie want to come along?"

"I think Maggie would want to go with you. I want to go to Cadillac and talk to Mrs. Rothchild if she can be interviewed."

"Good idea. Please ask Maggie if she'll drive since her van is accessible. I want to go up early in the morning and come right back. I've got a meeting late tomorrow afternoon."

"She'll be at the police station around 9:00 in the morning, is that OK?"

"Great. Thanks, Lou."

Lou asked Maggie to go, hoping his making decisions for her would be acceptable. They've worked so close for a long time that Lou thought he could commit her and she'd go along with it. She did.

CHAPTER FIVE

Tuesday, July 7
Traverse City, Pentwater,
and Cadillac, Michigan

Maggie and Chief McFadden were driving up U.S.31 for their scheduled ten o'clock meeting with Ted Beltzer, Chief of Police in Traverse City. The meeting was to take place at The Sandwich Shoppe, right downtown and easy to find. Lou had recommended this place as he had had an amazing bowl of chili there a year ago. The owner, Terry, had entered his recipe in the 2000 Chili Cook-off and won.

As they were driving through Beulah, Mickey said, "You and Lou are getting a great reputation for solving murders."

"I guess we deserve it. That's not being very humble, but with Lou's skill we seem to get the pieces of the puzzle to fit and the big picture often becomes clear."

"He seems to credit you with being the brains in the duo."

"Flattery gets him everywhere, Mickey. We're a good team, a combination of our skills usually gets the job done."

"That Bois Blanc murder was a feather in your caps."

"Yeah, a lot of it is having the perpetrators making a stupid mistake or two and then as was the case with the murder on Bois Blanc, a little or a lot of luck comes in handy."

"How did you get into this business? You always been a private investigator?"

"No. I was an insurance claims investigator and still am as a consultant. I didn't stay with the company I was working for after I got attacked by a guy that I turned in for fraud. Now I am a contracted claims investigator and I work with Lou. My husband is a retired oral surgeon so thankfully, we don't need the money to live comfortably, so I do what I want to do, and he does golf."

"Lou tells me you see the patterns in the crimes?"

"Yeah, I guess I get that attributed to me. I call it common sense, he calls it patterns. I seem to see what was going on before the murder. It's like going to a movie and watching the whole thing - eventually, you can see how it came to be and then all you need do is uncover the circumstances and you've got it solved."

"Well, I hope that happens with this investigation. I think we've got a serial killer and that means that every boater in a Michigan harbor is potentially a victim. We've got to catch this guy and soon."

"I'm hoping that we'll learn something from Ted that will shed some light on it."

꒱

Maggie and Mickey arrived at The Sandwich Shoppe. Maggie parked in a space reserved for drivers with disabilities. She activated the switch that would allow the ramp in her accessible van to lower her to the ground. Once down, she set the ramp in motion once again to retreat into the van and the door closed. Mickey walked alongside Maggie as she powered her chair toward the entrance to the restaurant. They went inside and met Chief Beltzer who had already arrived and was drinking his second cup of coffee.

The three greeted each other and then got down to business. There weren't many customers inside because it was between breakfast and lunch. The waitress brought hot coffee and some menus, but each said they only wanted coffee. Maggie would have loved to sample the famous chili, but she couldn't handle a bowl in mid-morning. She vowed to return to try the famous soup.

"Guess we've got the same problem, Ted." Mickey said.

"Yeah, I figured he might strike again and he did."

"When did the murder occur and who was the victim?" Mickey asked.

"Saturday, May 23, and the victim was Dr. Glenda Knoble. She was a surgeon. Her husband's also a doctor. They live in Gaylord. They moored a 40-foot Formula Super Sport in Traverse City. The name of their yacht was *Rx: Smooth Sailing*. Here, I've got some photos of the yacht, the couple before she died, and some photos of the victim when we found her under the dock."

Maggie and Mickey looked at each photo and found similarities to the crime scene in Manistee.

"The murderer is consistent. Everything I see here is identical to what I found in Manistee," Mickey said.

"Did your team find any clues to the murder?" Ted asked.

"No, nothing. We had no witnesses, no motive was learned, no evidence of any disturbance, struggle, nothing."

"Neither did we."

"Who found the victim?" Maggie asked.

"A collie was yapping near the end of the dock. This got an older man curious. He looked under the dock and there she was."

"What time was the body discovered?"

"Late morning."

"Did she have any known enemies?" Maggie asked.

"She was well-liked, but she did have a threat on her life. Apparently she made a mistake in surgery, everyone on the surgical team witnessed it. It led to the patient's death, something about ordering the wrong concentration of a powerful drug into a patient during surgery. She was written up, and the error went through the normal internal review and discipline procedures. But the media became involved and a family member of the deceased contacted her and threatened her."

"Recently?"

"About three months ago."

"Have you identified this person and interviewed him?" Chief McFadden asked.

"Yes. He had an alibi. We worked with his lawyer and arranged for a lie detector test. He passed it. I don't have any other leads."

The police chiefs conversed for a minute while Maggie listened.

"If this is a serial killer, did it begin in Traverse City?" Mickey asked.

"As far as I can tell, yes. I've looked in the LIEN and can't find any other killing like it. There have been some deaths in marinas around the country but they appear to be random killings and not a part of any serial activity. There is no common means of death, patterning, or victim profile. As far as strangulation, cut wrist and discovered under a marina dock, I think the first was in my backyard and the second was in yours, Mickey."

"Hard to find any evidence," Maggie said.

"Right, no fingerprints, no weapon, nothing to trace the killer, no shoe prints, no tire tracks, and our canine unit can't trace anything. The crime scene investigators from the State Police tell me the knife used to cut the wrist was more than a jackknife, probably like a 6-inch-long blade; guess they tell that by the width of the incision. They also said the marks on her throat were deep, indicating the murderer didn't strangle her, but apparently held the rope tight and jerked it around. Fibers from the rope were found well below the skin. There didn't appear to be any struggle. Material under her fingernails was normal, no skin from trying to scratch the attacker, no bruises on her body indicating any physical confrontation and there had been no sexual activity."

"No record of anyone contacting her?"

"Yeah, her answering service told us she received a call from the hospital here in Traverse City asking her to immediately report to the hospital for emergency surgery. Her car was found in the hospital parking lot."

"Luring her away from the marina?"

"In retrospect, I guess so."

"Was that call recorded?"

"No. The answering service doesn't record their calls."

"Is the husband a suspect?" Maggie asked.

"Initially, I thought so," Terry said. "As you know, we're all trained to suspect the spouse in these things and he initially fumbled around in answering questions about his activities that evening. I think it was his grief that caused him to stumble a bit."

"What do you mean, stumble?"

"We asked him where he was late that night. He said he was on their yacht working at his computer, but there was no computer on the yacht when we did our check of the craft and no laptop when we checked his car. He then said he must have been thinking about working at home and that he's been under a lot of stress at work and can't seem to remember from one evening to the next."

"And you believe him?" Mickey asked.

"Yeah, the guy lost his wife in a brutal murder. I didn't fault him for having a mind slip about working at a computer."

"But what was he doing, if not doing work at his computer?"

"Still don't know. There are no witnesses to confirm his story."

"So, you believe Glenda was on her yacht just before she was murdered?"

"Can't be sure. Time of death was early in the morning and we can't account for her presence between around one in the morning, when her husband said they went to bed, and when she was found under the dock in the marina, except that her car was found in the Munson Hospital parking lot."

"Her husband said she was gone when he woke up?" Maggie asked.

"He says he doesn't remember."

"Doesn't remember? Are you serious?" Maggie asked dumbfounded. "He can't remember seeing his wife in the morning, the morning of her murder?"

"That's what he says."

"Wait a minute. You mean he wakes up, and spends hours around the boat and the marina and then her body is found and he doesn't recall her being missing?"

"He claims he woke up to the sounds of sirens when his wife's body was found. He thinks he got up in the middle of the night, worked at his computer which he now thinks was a dream, had trouble sleeping, thinks Glenda was in bed all this time but can't be certain, finally goes to sleep around 4:30 or five according to the digital clock and then is awakened about 10:30 with all the police and ambulance vehicles arriving at the marina."

"This is fascinating. Sounds like we're going to have another sleepwalker murder here," Maggie said.

"But, we didn't find any evidence of wet clothes on the yacht, no wet towels in the cabin, nothing that was wet, no evidence that if he killed her that he could have gotten back onto his yacht and gotten into bed without leaving some water or damp clothes or towels somewhere. That's basically why I think he's innocent."

"Hmmm, good point. What was she wearing?" Mickey asked.

"She was wearing what her husband said she was wearing the evening before. He thinks she got up and put on the same clothes."

"Which were?"

"Well, you can see from the photos I showed you, slacks and a blouse."

"And, nobody saw her in the marina area the next morning or in town?"

"Guess not. No witnesses."

"Did you talk to other boaters?" Maggie asked.

"Interviewed everyone up and down the marina. No clue and I'm convinced everyone is innocent."

"Sounds like we need to suspect an alien craft coming down into the marina," Mickey said, shaking his head.

"You know, I'd almost come to believe that's what happened until I heard that he struck again down in Manistee. Once I heard that, I was convinced that somebody's out there who's very sick."

"Where was her husband when the Manistee murder occurred?" Mickey asked.

"You know, I don't know."

"We need to check that out," Maggie replied.

꩜

Before going to Cadillac, Lou stopped in Manistee at Billy Lorimer's home. He put a bow around a brand new Zebcor rod and reel and then penned a note, "I hope you catch a lot of fish with your new rod and reel." Billy smiled when Lou gave it to him so he thought Billy liked it. Mrs. Lorimer thanked Lou, offered him a cup of coffee, but he declined. He needed to be on his way to Cadillac.

کۍ

Anita Rothchild was well enough to talk with Lou. He took her to lunch. Actually it was her suggestion. Lou surmised that she thought she could control her emotions better out in public. They went to the Big Boy restaurant in Cadillac.

"I guess you can just ask me your questions, Mr. Searing," Anita said. "But, I've already told Detective Maguffin everything I know."

After sipping his coffee, Lou took his pen in hand and asked, "Was there anyone in your husband's life who could have done this, Mrs. Rothchild?"

"Like I told Mr. Maguffin, not that I can think of. I always said Jim never had an enemy in the world. Everybody liked him."

"Were there any lawsuits pending from his medical practice?"

"Not that I know of. Well, every once in a while there was a patient or family member who wasn't totally pleased with the outcome of his treatment, but I don't think anyone held a grudge against him."

"But there were some people who weren't pleased with procedures?"

"Well, yes, but people can't seem to accept that their loved one is about to die. Cancer is still a killer in spite of all that medical science is doing to cure it, and Jim did everything he could to save his patients. Sometimes the disease would win in spite of all of his heroics. But as I say, some folks can't seem to realize that cancer wins sometimes and they think it is only because the doctor doesn't do his job well."

"I understand. Was everybody on Jim's staff accepting of him?" Lou asked.

"Oh, yes, everyone loved working for and with him. His staff is as loyal as any staff can be. He gives all of them bonuses at Christmas and he was even voted 'nicest boss' for boss's day a couple of years ago."

"Can you give me the name of someone to talk with on his staff if I have some questions?"

"Sure, that'd be his head nurse, Shirley Lockyear. She'll help you in any way you ask. Tell her I told you she'd cooperate fully."

"Thanks. Talk to me about family. Is there anyone in the family who might hold a grudge or maybe even be mentally ill?"

"Oh, no, not in our family. We're blessed in that way. I can't think of anyone in our family, and I'm going to all branches of the family. I can't think of anyone who isn't loving."

"Everyone. No one has any aggressive tendencies?" Lou asked.

"No one, well, except for Mike, but he isn't in the family. At least not yet and I hope never, but you know young kids, you can't control 'em or make decisions for them."

"Mike. Who's he?"

"He's Penny's boyfriend. He's different and I wish Penny would leave him, but she stands by him every step of the way."

"Chief McFadden mentioned she is missing."

"Yes, but that doesn't surprise me. I called Chief McFadden to report her missing because of James' death and I feared more trouble, but she's more often missing than present. She always turns up and she will. I'm not worried. She's probably pretty upset about her father's death and has chosen her unorthodox way to deal with it, and Lord knows what that would be."

"Did Mike get along with your husband?"

"Mike doesn't get along with anyone, let me put it that way."

"Well, then, could he be involved in James' death?"

"Oh, I doubt it. He's different, all of his body parts are pierced and I mean all of them, navel, tongue, nose, ear, eyelid, nipples and Lord knows what else has some cheap diamond attached to it." Lou smiled and nodded while making a note of Anita's comment. "And, I don't think he has the ability to plan much let alone murder someone."

"Did he have any conflicts with your husband?"

"Oh sure, all the time. He was living with Penny. James was furious when he heard about it. I tried to tell him that this is what happens today, but James is kind of old-fashioned."

"Mike lives in Pentwater?"

"Yes."

"What else can you tell me about him?"

"He's rich. He inherited a lot of money from his parents who both died at a rather young age. He's into music, plays the guitar, he's a vegetarian, he's very intelligent, at least Penny tries to convince us of that. But, like I said, he has no gumption at all."

"OK, anything else."

"He likes to drive a speedboat."

"He keeps it docked in Pentwater?" Lou asked.

"No, he pulls it wherever he goes. He's got a big pickup. They all look alike to me, so I can't tell you the name of it."

"Ford or a Chevy?"

"Yeah, or a Dodge maybe. I don't know. Anyway, it's a big red vehicle and he pulls his boat wherever he goes, and he goes all over. He's a marina junkie if you ask me."

"Does Penny go with him?"

"Oh, sure. She loves speed too. Don't know where we went wrong with that girl. She was a model kid till high school and then she changed. She wasn't our daughter anymore. Lord knows we tried to put up with her but after a while, you simply tune out and then before you know it, she's gone and we're left shaking our heads."

"Are you sure you don't think Mike is involved with your husband's death? I see conflict all around this fella and the two of you."

"No, it wasn't Mike."

"Because?"

"Because he simply wouldn't kill Penny's father. No, I'm thinking that something happened a few years ago that is the reason Jim was murdered."

"Can you tell me about it?"

"Not now. If my hunch is right and the killer hears I've told the authorities, I could be next. And quite frankly, even with my grief of losing James, I'm still in love with life."

"I'll keep the information in confidence. You can trust me," Lou said.

"I'm not concerned about you. Lots of people interact with James. Why send you hunting for somebody when it could only anger the person and give another person reason to wreak havoc with my family or what is left of it.

"Actually, the more I think about it, I'm wrong. I was thinking it could be a couple that James befriended. Later James testified against the man in court and rumor always had it that James would one day pay for putting this guy in jail for a long time."

"What was the case?"

"Oh, it's been awhile, I think it was a hospital administrator who embezzled money or stole drugs. Something about a guy in the hospital's higher administration. I never liked the couple, not my type, or James' type either, so I did what I could to put them out of my mind."

"That does seem like a motive. Revenge is a strong emotion."

"Yes, but I don't think he'd kill James and besides he's still in jail and I think the gossip mill had the wife remarrying. Forget it, just my reaching back for a possible person to blame."

"Well, I'm going to look into it and I assure you, I'll keep all of what I learn to myself. I promise you."

Anita nodded without saying a word or looking Lou in the eye. She simply stared down at her salad bowl, wiped a tear, and said, "I really don't think I have any more information for you, Mr. Searing. May I leave now?"

"Of course. Here's my card, in case you want to talk with me again."

Anita took the card and said, "Thanks for lunch. I hope you find James' killer, Mr. Searing. Jim never should have died. It's such a loss of life, a loss of two skillful hands and a very loving heart."

"I'm sorry, Mrs. Rothchild. I'll do my best to solve it."

"I know you will," Anita said as she slowly, with head bowed, walked toward the door and out to her car.

THE MARINA MURDERS

Before Mickey and Maggie returned to Manistee, they stopped in Pentwater and tried to find Penny Rothchild and her boyfriend Mike, but had no luck. Penny's roommate said she'd not seen nor heard from her since she drove away yesterday afternoon with plans to go to Manistee.

They did see Mike's vehicle. The vehicle was a red Chevy Tahoe. It was parked in the driveway with a speedboat behind it. Mickey noted the vehicle number and license number. He also inspected it closely noting some mud under the rear panel. Other than that, there was nothing about the vehicle that caused him to take note. Mickey did glance in the driver's side window and on the seat was a Michigan Harbors Guide, but this didn't seem out of place for a man who has a boat and does a lot of boating around Michigan.

～♪

Since Lou was in Cadillac, he wanted to talk to Dr. Rothchild's head nurse, Shirley Lockyear. Lou called and she answered. Lou introduced himself and indicated that Mrs. Rothchild suggested he call and that she thought Nurse Lockyear would be willing to help.

"Please come to his office, Mr. Searing. I'm willing to talk with you."

"Thank you." Shirley gave Lou directions to the office and he drove over.

Shirley welcomed Lou. He noticed that the receptionist was in the office as well. Lou was introduced to her and was told that she was taking calls from sympathetic friends and colleagues who had gotten the news from the media. She also needed to cancel tens of appointments scheduled into next year and to try and find another specialist who would be willing to take over Dr. Rothchild's practice.

"First of all, I'm sorry for your loss in the death of Dr. Rothchild." Lou said.

"Thank you very much. We are all in a state of shock around here. The last thing any of us would expect would be to have Dr. Rothchild die and to die in such a brutal way. We're still in a state of denial and disbelief."

"I can certainly understand. Again, I'm very sorry."

"Thank you. What can I do for you?"

"Well, I guess my main reason for being here is to learn if you or any of his staff knows of any person that could have done this or of anyone who would have a motive for bringing such violence to the doctor?"

"Dr. Rothchild didn't lack for controversy. His patients were tough cases, people in near-death situations, people desperate for a cure, and when that didn't come he'd either be blamed, or if not blamed, at least thought of as a doctor who didn't do enough for the loved one."

"That makes sense, but did anyone hold a profound grudge or even take steps to sue him?"

"Yes, there were some difficult people. I can't imagine any of them killing or arranging to kill Dr. Rothchild. I can't give you their names or even allow you to see their files."

"I understand. Did you know of anyone in the doctor's personal life who was troublesome? Was he having an affair, did he have a problem with gambling, drugs, or anything dealing with unsavory characters?"

"Not a chance. He was a faithful husband, or at least as far as I know. He was a community leader. He is highly respected. He gave much to his alma mater, the University of Michigan Medical School."

"What do you mean, 'gave much'?"

"He gave money, he presented guest lectures, he served on a number of committees, he attended fund raisers, he went to a few sporting events and was on a first name basis with the head coaches of the major sports. I suspect he was a good alumnus when it came to contributing to the alumni association, providing scholarships for medical students, things like that."

"One more question. Was Dr. Rothchild right-or-left handed?"

"Right-handed. Why?"

"Just a question I was curious about. That's all. How can I get the names of difficult patients? Have any ideas?"

"I mentioned some names to the police. Maybe you can contact them and see what they're willing to share, but, as I said, I can't give you any information."

"I understand. Here's my card. If you think of anything else, please contact me."

"I will. Please excuse me, there's so much to do in the aftermath of this tragedy."

"Of course. Thanks for your time."

࿘

Maggie and Lou returned to Grand Haven arriving within a half hour of one another. That evening at dinner, Maggie and Lou compared notes as Carol listened and asked good questions. While eating apple slices for dessert, Maggie said, "The most important thing about this serial killing thing is predicting where the next strike will happen."

"Yeah, but we haven't got a clue where to begin with our predictions."

"I know, marinas are all up and down the Lake Michigan shoreline and who's to say the killer will limit his carnage to the Lake Michigan shore?"

"The two victims had jobs in medicine," Lou said.

"Right, and that seems to be the only link we've got at the moment."

"There's conflict with Dr. Rothchild and there's an unhappy family member of a patient who didn't survive surgery due to Dr. Knoble's mistake, but some nut isn't going to kill on behalf of disgruntled family members."

"Agree. While the Rothchilds seem to dislike Mike, I'm certain he is not our murderer. Even if he did kill James, why would he also kill a lady from Gaylord that he doesn't know?"

"You mean, as far as we know, he doesn't know her."

"Likewise, if the husband of the surgeon killed his wife, why would he then come down to Manistee and kill a fellow doctor, a man who as far as we know, he doesn't even know."

"Right. No patterns that would cause us to cover a specific marina to catch him, her, or them, red-handed."

The word had gone throughout the state. Chief McFadden made sure that police departments in every marina-based city in the Great Lakes knew about the possibility of being the next hit. Most passed out handbills telling their boaters of this crazed maniac and suggesting that people be extra cautious. The coast guard was out on alert, too. So, at least whoever the marina maniac is, he'll have to carry out his crime under the watchful eye of a lot of folks.

The phone rang. "Let's hope that isn't murder number three," Maggie said as Carol walked over to the wall phone.

"Hello"

"Carol, is Lou there?"

"Another marina murder, Mickey?"

"No, just got more information for him."

"Here he is."

Carol handed the phone to Lou. "Yeah, Mickey. What you got?"

"They found Penny Rothchild."

"Dead or alive?"

"Alive."

"You say 'they found'—who is 'they'?"

"Her mother called. I guess she went to visit a good friend in Ohio."

"Ohio?"

"Yeah, guess she wanted to be with a friend where she could just let off some emotion. She didn't contact her family as she figured her mom would be busy making funeral arrangements."

"Seems a daughter would go to family," Lou said.

"Yeah, but this isn't a typical young woman - very unorthodox in her ways, I guess."

"Well, glad she's been found. I was hoping that the murderer had not taken the life of another member of the Rothchild family."

"Right. Wanted you to know that this missing person has been found."

"Good news. Thanks."

"Where's Mike?"

"Who's Mike?"

"Her boyfriend, the walking jewelry store."

"Oh, yeah. He went over to be with Mrs. Rothchild."

"Really?"

"That's what Anita said. She just called to tell me."

"But Maggie said that his vehicle was in the driveway when you and Maggie stopped by early this afternoon."

"Yeah, but that was about 1:30. It only takes an hour to get from Manistee to Cadillac."

"So, now we know that Mike didn't kidnap Penny?" Lou asked.

"We're certain he did not."

"Thanks for the information."

"Sure. I'll let you know if anything else develops and you do the same."

Maggie wheeled her chair into the dining room of the Searing home having gone to her bedroom to get a sweater. "Lou, your admirer in the red pickup is out front again."

Lou immediately went to the phone and called Chief Vern Bryant. "Chief, I need some unmarked surveillance."

"Sure, what's the problem?"

"There's a red pickup across the road from my home. This is the second time in two days the vehicle has been there. Yesterday the driver was looking at the house with binoculars. I took off after it on my Harley, but couldn't locate it. Could you send one of your officers out here to look into this?"

"It's covered, Lou. I'll call you when I learn something."

"Thanks."

Lou wasn't about to make the same stupid mistake two days in a row. He discreetly glanced out the window by the door. It did seem to be the same vehicle with a lone driver. It didn't seem that the driver had any binoculars trained on the house.

Inside of a minute Lou noticed an unmarked car pull up to the vehicle. A man approached and talked with the driver for a couple of minutes. The officer returned to his vehicle and left. A minute later, the phone rang. It had to be Vern. Lou answered.

"Got that mystery solved, Lou."

"Who and why?"

"The mystery man is a Mr. Misner, picking up your neighbor's daughter for working in the Bookman Bookstore. Chuck Misner is a birder and seems that you might have a pileated woodpecker in some trees behind your home. He wasn't looking at you, but at a bird he needs for his life list. He was embarrassed to be questioned by an officer. All is fine."

"Well that has a good ending. Generally, I'm not paranoid."

"Chuck says he's using his boss's pickup this week. You'd probably recognize him in a Toyota, but his car is in the shop for some body work."

"Oh, yeah, we've seen a red Toyota often across the street. Well, sorry for the unnecessary alert."

"No apologies needed Lou. We can't be too careful. Call me anytime you're concerned about anything."

CHAPTER SIX

Wednesday, July 8
Grand Haven and South Haven, Michigan

The phone rang at 4:22 a.m. Carol turned on her bedside lamp, answered it and gently tried to awaken Lou, "Lou, wake up, Mickey McFadden is on the phone. There's been another murder."

It took him a few seconds to realize what was happening. Lou took the phone while still in a daze. "Yeah, Mickey. Another murder?"

"Marina murder number three, Lou—South Haven."

"Same cut wrist, noose around the neck, body tied to a piling under a marina dock?"

"Exactly. Except in this case the left wrist was cut, not the right. Don't ask me why."

"Was the body just found?"

"Yeah, about 45 minutes ago."

"Who discovered it?"

"Some guy on his yacht heard some splashing, was curious, went top side, looked around, didn't see anything. But, he couldn't get the splashing sound out of his mind thinking it had to come from somewhere. He took his flashlight and looked all around the water and there it was."

"Hmmm. Any other clues?"

"There is one good one, I think. The guy who found the body

noticed that there was no water on the dock in the vicinity of the dead body. There was also no blood on the dock."

"All that means is that the murderer didn't come up to the dock after securing the body to the piling."

"Correct, but it tells us that perhaps the body was brought to the dock from a spot away from the marina."

"Hmmm, good point, Mickey," Lou said. "I'll ask Carol to awaken Maggie and we'll get right on it. Are you going to South Haven?"

"No. I don't think I can be of much help. Detective Maguffin will stay in touch with their detective."

"Maggie and I want to get there as soon as possible."

"Good. I'll let the chief know that you'll be down. His name is Leon Babcock."

"Thanks. Tell me, was the victim in the medical field?"

"Don't know yet. All I know is that the serial killer hit again. I'll give you more details as I learn them, but if you're going down there, you'll learn much more about the case. Please brief me or Jerry when you get back, okay?"

"Definitely. Thanks for the heads up. We're practically on our way."

While Lou was on the phone, Carol was assisting Maggie who had heard the phone and figured it was news that wasn't pleasant. Carol then went to the kitchen to put some fruit out for an early morning breakfast before the two headed to South Haven.

Lou kissed Carol goodbye and hoped she'd be asleep before he and Maggie got to U.S.31 South. The two took Maggie's van so the accommodations would be helpful to her. The ride down gave them some time to talk about the case even though they had little information to go on and had already gone over the specifics.

"Do you think this killer is targeting marinas or people?" Lou asked.

"I've wondered that too. I've studied the marinas and there is nothing that seems to distinguish them. They're relatively small. Obviously each has immediate access to Lake Michigan and each is linked in some way to a river or lake. The first two victims were medical personnel. I'll be anxious to see if this South Haven victim is in the medical profession. If he or she is, that just about locks up the pattern and we can use that to help us predict where a future murder might occur."

"So far, the marinas are on the west side of Michigan and in the Lower Peninsula. I wonder if that will continue to be the pattern until we stop this maniac."

"Yeah, hard to tell."

"Thinking ahead if it is, I guess we'd have to try and learn about malpractice suits or conflicts along those lines."

Maggie and Lou stopped for a cup of coffee near Holland and then continued on to South Haven. They exited the expressway and drove down Phoenix Street and then onto Water Street where they could see, at the bottom of a slight hill, the South Haven Municipal Marina on the Black River. It was beginning to get light as they pulled up. There was not the throng of people at this scene that Lou had experienced in Manistee. Word had not gotten throughout the town as it was still quite early.

The two exited Maggie's van and approached the crime scene, Maggie in her power wheelchair and Lou on foot. They introduced themselves to Chief of Police Babcock. He said that Mickey had called and told him to anticipate their arrival and to feel confident about allowing them to work with him. Lou and Maggie appreciated Mickey's introduction.

"Has the victim been moved from under the dock?" Lou asked.

"Yeah, about a half hour ago."

"Has he or she been identified yet?" Maggie asked.

"Yes, his name is Peter Verduin."

"What do you know about him?" Maggie asked, expecting to hear that he's a doctor.

"One of the paramedics thought he was a lawyer in town, but couldn't be certain. We haven't confirmed any information about him."

"Does he have a yacht here in the marina?" Lou asked.

"Yes, over there," Leon said, pointing to a 42-foot Grand Banks Motor Yacht. On the back could be seen, *Malpractice Benefits* with "South Haven" under the name in bold gold letters. Maggie and Lou looked at each other as they instantly made the medical connection.

"I take it this guy, if he is an attorney, represented medical folks in malpractice suits?" Lou asked.

"Yes, the paramedic said he thinks this guy represented doctors all around the country. Pretty famous guy in his circle of expertise, I guess."

"Did you learn anymore from the guy who heard the splashing?" Maggie asked.

"Nothing more than that. He apparently heard some splashing, went looking for the source of the noise and eventually shined the light on Mr. Verduin and called 911. We were here inside of two minutes."

"Are there any security cameras fixed on the Black River or on the waters around the marina?" Maggie asked.

"No."

"Does the coast guard monitor boats going out into Lake Michigan?" Lou asked.

"You'll have to ask them, but I don't think so. They probably monitor the navigational radio channels, but I'm certain they don't communicate with or video every boat. On Saturday or Sunday, it would drive them nuts with all the traffic going to and from Lake Michigan."

Neither Maggie nor Lou noticed a red pickup on Water Street, outside of the yellow "Do Not Cross" tape. Inside was Jake, alone, and wearing dark glasses. Jake drove the pickup along slowly, parked for a few minutes and then left without drawing any attention to himself or to his vehicle.

ॐ

Father Murphy learned about the next murder via a radio news program while en route to a meeting in Charlevoix. As in Texas he almost became ill. He pulled off the road, bowed his head and prayed for the victim, for Jake, and for himself. "Lord, please forgive me for I feel that this man's death is of my doing. Please help me understand this tragic situation and guide me to be your servant here on earth. Amen."

Father Murphy took a few deep breaths and then continued on his way. He doubted he would be able to focus on the meeting topic, as his mind and emotions were consumed with this third murder. A murder that would never have happened if he could have alerted the authorities. Just outside the city limits of Charlevoix he had a—

FLASHBACK: Jake was my best friend in high school and remains so today. But he was not liked by many in school. Guys on the wrestling team said he wrestled to hurt others. It was never enough to win the points or the match, he had to cause pain. In a couple of instances, the coach and others had to literally pull him off competitors or even members of his own team in practices.

His girlfriend, Jenny, was the captain of her cheerleading club. Jenny loved Jake for his brilliant mind, his perfectly shaped body, his desire to become a doctor, but she told me privately one day that she thought Jake thought of her as property and that he often hurt her. She said that others would think his behavior as simply showing affection, but he almost seemed to enjoy hurting her. She told me recently that when she broke up with him, he taunted her for weeks.

I remember a few years ago in college. We were both home for the weekend and we were out drinking late at night. An animal, a dog or raccoon or some form of wildlife came onto the road up ahead and Jake said, "Watch me kill that thing up there." He sped up and didn't seem to pay attention to my pleading for him to let it live. Had I not reached over and steered the car away from the animal before impact, Jake would have fulfilled his desire to kill. I always found it odd that Jake didn't hunt.

He never hurt me, but he seemed to want me to share his need to be infatuated with death, inflicting pain, and the excitement it apparently brought to him. Most of the time I was repulsed because his thoughts and actions were so foreign to my attitude about life and our connectedness to all of life's forms. Whenever I was around, I tried to save life and to steer Jake away from doing something. I was always successful, but I had no idea what he was doing when I wasn't around.

꒷

A hot summer sun beat down on vacationers in St. Joseph, Michigan. The heat wave was brutal but it was July in Michigan and was to be expected. It was four o'clock in the afternoon when Jake pulled into the St. Joseph Marina on the St. Joseph River. Jake got out and walked along the dock, discreetly inspecting the pleasure craft docked there. He was dressed in a pair of dock shoes, Bermuda shorts, and a T-shirt with "MSU Spartans, 2000 National Champs" emblazoned across the front. He wore fashionable sunglasses under a Chicago White Sox baseball cap. Jake looked like he had come from a weight lifting gym with muscles predominantly displayed under his shirt.

Jake wasn't surprised to see a sign, "Warning. Three boaters have been killed in marinas. Authorities are warning all boaters and marina guests to use extreme caution and to report any strange persons or activity to the harbormaster or the police. Thank you."

Jake walked along with a styrofoam cooler hoping to give the impression that he was a boater bringing some food from town. He was looking for the yacht, *Bypassing Through*, owned by Dr. Will Harrison, a Chicago-based cardiac surgeon who, according to Jake's research, took a couple of weeks each summer to enjoy marina-hopping along the eastern shore of Lake Michigan.

꒷

Maggie and Lou spent the morning getting as much information as they could in South Haven. Unfortunately, about all they could do was study the murder scene, talk to marina personnel and boaters. As in Manistee, nobody had seen anything that would prove to be helpful.

They did learn more about the victim, Peter Verduin. The paramedic was right. He mainly represented doctors in malpractice lawsuits. His secretary, although quite shook up, was able to answer their questions.

"Did Mr. Verduin have a client, or a relative of a client, who was upset with him?" Lou asked.

"No, all of his clients were very pleased to have had him as their attorney. There are many people who would love to have had his services, but he was very particular about whom he represented. No, every one of his clients and their families are thankful and held him in high esteem."

"How about the other side of the coin," Maggie asked, "Is there anyone he was involved with in litigation who is exceptionally angry or capable of killing him?"

"Well, obviously the plaintiffs are not happy. In the first place, they've lost something; a life, mobility, or who knows what, so they're not happy. They knew Mr. Verduin was very good and was often so persuasive that they didn't receive a just settlement."

"That's what I'm thinking. Did he receive any threatening letters or calls or did he ever mention having a confrontation with someone away from the office?" Maggie asked.

"Yes, now that I've had some time to think about it. I'm not saying this person did it."

"You can trust us not to divulge our source," Lou said.

"Well, then I'd say, Billy Estes should be considered as a suspect."

"Mr. Estes?" Maggie repeated to be sure she got the name right.

"Yeah, he lost his wife about two months ago. Her doctor got some lab results confused with another patient, prescribed some medication that she was allergic to, she had a reaction to it, couldn't get any medical help, and died. Mr. Estes, who already has a psychiatric problem, came unglued, but his wrath wasn't directed at the physician and his family."

"Then why did you think he could have killed Mr. Verduin?" Maggie asked.

"Well, he stopped in one day and wanted to know if Mr. Verduin had decided to represent this physician. I didn't see any harm in answering his question. I did and I was reprimanded for it. I almost lost my job. Mr. Verduin was not at all happy that I said 'Yes.'"

"Something must have happened as a result of this?" Maggie implied.

"Yes, it did. Two days later, Mr. Verduin got a threatening letter from him and strangely enough it had to do with his boat. Mr. Estes called him arrogant for having a boat named *Malpractice Benefits* telling him that he was living the life of leisure from representing evil people who had taken other lives and that Mr. Verduin's money should go to the victims and not toward supporting his lavish lifestyle."

"What was the threat?" Lou asked.

"He said he'd blow up Mr. Verduin's boat if he lost his case."

"Did he lose?"

"Mr. Verduin never loses a case, Mr. Searing."

"I see. So, Mr. Estes lost a case to this doctor who then didn't have to pay for his mistake."

"Exactly."

"When did this case end?" Maggie asked.

"Last Friday."

"Did Mr. Verduin hear anything from this Mr. Estes between the verdict and this morning?"

"One phone call."

"The threat?"

"No. He said he wanted Mr. Verduin to represent him when he seeks his revenge."

"Hmmm. And what was Mr. Verduin's response?"

"Poor judgment in my opinion, and this is a rare mistake for this stoic and reserved man, but he laughed at him."

"Ouch."

"Ouch is right. Now I don't know if there's any connection to his murder, but if I were looking for a suspect, Billy Estes would be pretty high on my list."

"Well, I can assure you, we'll check him out. Have you got an address for him or a phone number?"

"Yes. We note all calls into the office and I have that in my data base. He lives in St. Joe, Michigan. The number is 555-9911."

"OK, thanks. Any other clients or potential clients who may have reason to be upset with Mr. Verduin?"

"Yeah, one more comes to mind. There was a woman who wanted Mr. Verduin to represent her in suing the U. of M. Medical School."

"Suing the med school?" Lou asked.

"As I understand it, her son or daughter was rejected for admittance to med school and she wanted Mr. Verduin to sue them or at least do what he could to have the decision overturned."

"And, did Mr. Verduin accept the job?" Maggie asked.

"No. The lady came here to meet with Mr. Verduin and there was loud talking. A client in the waiting area and I exchanged glances as the shouting seemed quite threatening."

"Then what happened?" Lou asked.

"It quieted. She left still a bit upset. I asked Mr. Verduin what had happened and he simply said that sometimes emotions get a bit out of control but it was only a reaction to being rejected. Being rejected by my boss is tantamount to potentially losing a case. If Mr. Verduin represents you, you win. His batting average is almost a thousand, but he carefully picks and chooses his cases."

"Do you have this woman's name and address?" Maggie asked.

"You know, I don't. She just showed up and demanded to see Mr. Verduin. He was free and so I asked if he could see her for a quick counsel. Mr. Verduin agreed to see her and they went into his office. She left just as quickly. So I don't know who she was."

"Could you describe her?"

"Attractive. That's the first thing I noticed, very attractive. Nice figure, brown hair, a plain dress. She didn't look affluent like most of Mr. Verduin's clients."

"Is that it as far as possible suspects go, Mr. Estes, and this upset mother of a rejected medical school applicant?" Maggie asked checking her notes.

"Well, yeah, but folks are upset all the time. Those are the only two to show some emotion. There are a lot of people unhappy with him."

"I understand. Thank you. You've been most helpful."

Maggie and Lou left Mr. Verduin's law office and headed for Maggie's van. "We've got to make two stops before going home."

"Two? I'll bet the first one is a chocolate shop," Maggie said with a chuckle knowing Lou's love of chocolate.

"Wrong! The first is to the KC Book Store on Eagle Street."

"What's special about KC Books?" Maggie asked.

"Cindy and Grayling, that's what special."

"Cindy and Grayling, like the city, Grayling?" Maggie asked puzzled.

"Grayling is my favorite cat in South Haven. I stopped in to see Cindy Maxwell awhile back to see how my books were selling. Grayling took a liking to me, which by the way, is rare. So, I don't want to be in South Haven without seeing Cindy and my cat friend, Grayling."

"OK, whatever you need to do. And, the second place?"

"The second place is Captain Nemo's."

"Some yacht owner I take it?"

"Nope, my South Haven ice cream place. They'll have my Mackinac Island Fudge, single dip waiting for me. They see me walking in and the dipper goes right for the tub of Mackinac Island Fudge. Ummm, good."

Maggie chuckled. "I knew chocolate would figure into one of your stops. OK, Cindy, Grayling, and Captain Nemo. Coming up."

⁂

While Lou was savoring a chunk of chocolate in rich vanilla ice cream, a doctor by the name of Philip Heyboer of Michigan City, Indiana, was reading his local newspaper. The article presented the two marina murders in Michigan.

Philip read with interest about the deaths of Glenda and James. He knew these people from his days at the University of Michigan. When he finished the article he sat in his chair and had a—

FLASHBACK: The meeting of the INVEST club was held in the early evening at the apartment of Glenda Davies. INVEST was an acronym for Investing In Very Exciting Stock Tips. When everyone had arrived, Glenda called the meeting to order. She said, "I've got some bad news. The investment in the Lake Huron Marina project of which this club contributed a few million is now defunct. We do have the land, but it is worthless unless it is developed, and right now there will be no development."

"Defunct?" James Harrison said. "You mean we've lost all of our money?"

"Not really, not totally anyway. We all knew it was a risk and the money would only be recouped when the condo lots and marina slips were sold. But, the developer caved in to a local citizen's anti-marina development project as well as pressure from a powerful environmental advocacy group. But, there is one chance to make the investment survive," Glenda said.

"What's that?" Edith Haire asked.

"We need to raise about three or four more million and if, and it is a big if, we can overcome public opinion with a public relations campaign, we may get our marina built."

"Why a PR campaign?" Sherry Tomsik asked.

"We need a PR firm to change people's opinions about this marina and the millions it can eventually bring to the community. We can do it, but it is like mounting a political campaign. As we all know, we can only get our money back or make money on our money if the marina is built and occupied. If this doesn't happen, we've paid millions for what would be useless land, at least at this time."

"I suggest we invite others in to give us more capital," Will Harrison said.

"That's a good idea, Will," said Cris Gallow. "How about allowing four more members to join us with an initial investment of a million a piece. This would allow us to hire an excellent PR firm and I think it would put us back on track."

"I say we do it." Cris said, enthusiastically "We can't lose our investment and if Glenda thinks we can survive, I say to grow and earmark the new money into a public relations effort as Glenda suggests."

"There is one more hurdle, but I don't think it's a problem," Glenda said.

"What's that?" Sherry asked.

"I found out that the developer had not conducted a study of the land in regard to its soil analysis."

"That's standard operating procedure," I said. "Why wasn't that done?"

"I think the developer saw this land as a gold mine and didn't care about any particulars. He was in a bidding war with other developers and he didn't care what condition the land was in; he only saw a tremendous investment and would use the land for a modern state of the art marina."

Philip set the paper aside and wondered if he had been targeted, and if he had, which bullet had his name on it.

کب

Meanwhile, about three o'clock in the afternoon, back at the St. Joseph Marina, Jake had located the *Bypassing Through*. He glanced at the boat, paid close attention to details, doors, curtains inside, position in the marina, and any people who may be on board.

As Jake walked toward Will, Will was coming out to wash down his deck. He nodded at the stranger in less than a sincere greeting. The nod was returned. Jake approached Will.

"Excuse me. Can you help me?"

"Yes, if I can. What do you need?"

"I've been here a few days. I'm docked a ways down there," Jake said, pointing toward the end of the dock. "I'm curious about places to shop for food here in St. Joe. I need to stock up on some groceries."

"I go to the IGA, it's about two blocks toward town."

"Thanks. Have a nice day."

"Yeah, looks like I picked a good week for my vacation."

"You with family?"

"Yeah, wife and our grandkids."

"You folks have a good time. I'll be leaving soon."

"Smooth sailing to you," Will said.

"By the way, good name for your boat. You must be a cardiologist or a doc that deals with the heart?" Jake asked.

"Cardiologist. Our son suggested that name, play on words. Our friends thought it appropriate, so we named her *Bypassing Through*."

"Won't keep you from your work. I'm off to town."

Will went back into his yacht and dialed the harbormaster. "Harbormaster?"

"Yes."

"This is Dr. Harrison."

"Yes, sir. What can I do for you?"

"There's a strange guy walking along the dock. I wanted to brief you about his presence."

"Can you describe him?"

"Muscular guy with a cooler. He should be coming up toward your office any second."

"What makes him strange?"

"I've been here for three days and never saw him before. He claims he is docked in the marina. He walked past, turned around, and came back to talk to me. He said he was heading to town to get some food, but he was walking toward the end of the dock, not walking toward town. Furthermore, that is a question he'd ask you or he would look at the community bulletin board. His behavior was odd."

"I'll confront him. I see him coming this way."

"Thanks. I'm on edge a bit with these killings going on and especially since they've been medical folks who've been killed."

"I understand. I see him coming this way. I'll handle this, sir." The harbormaster hung up, stepped out of his office and confronted Jake. "Excuse me. You got a boat here in the marina?"

Jake was startled and caught off guard. He stumbled with his response. "Looking for a friend is all. I didn't see him."

"I asked you if you've got a boat in this marina," the harbormaster said politely, yet sternly.

"No, as I said, I was looking for a friend. Something illegal about looking for a friend?" Jake snapped.

"This marina is off limits to everyone except those who have a registered boat or are a guest of a registered boater."

"You got some problem with me walking along the dock?" Jake said, raising his voice and acting testy.

"No trespassing allowed. Sorry."

Jake shook his head, mumbled some obscenity under his breath, turned and walked away with his empty cooler, wondering if Will Harrison had brought this trouble upon him.

The harbormaster returned to his office, noted the confrontation and wrote a description of the man with the styrofoam container. The thought crossed his mind, *if he didn't have a boat, why did he tell Will that he was docked in the marina?*

The phone rang in the harbormaster's office as a boater was wanting to rent a slip. After hanging up the phone, the harbormaster wondered if he should've called the police or questioned the trespasser further. *There had been no description of this killer, so perhaps this was just a summer tourist wanting to see the boats in the marina,* he thought.

⌇

Maggie and Lou drove back to Grand Haven in time to share dinner with Carol who had volunteered in the afternoon at the Ronald McDonald House. The three talked about what they'd learned and what their next steps would be. While Maggie, Carol and Lou were finishing their meal, Will Harrison told his wife Nikki and grandchildren Nicholas and Sherry, aged 10 and 12, that they'd be leaving soon.

"Really? I thought we'd be here for another day," Nikki replied.

"We need to leave."

"But, that wasn't our plan, I thought we were ..."

"It's our plan now," Will said, in a serious and forceful way. "If we leave now we can get up to Holland before dark. It should take a couple of hours. Once on the water, I'll call and see if they have a slip. If not, we'll keep going up the shore till we can find one."

"Are you okay, Will? This isn't like you," Nikki said quite concerned. "We set up an itinerary that had us here another day. I was going shopping down ..."

"Something happened today that makes me think we've got to be going."

"OK, but I don't underst ..."

Out of hearing range of the grandchildren Will said, "I talked to a strange man this afternoon. I think he's the marina killer and I think I'm next. If we stay here, I'd most likely be dead and under this dock by morning."

"Oh, Will. Tell me this is a bad dream. Are you sure?" Nikki said, distressed by what she had heard.

"This man asked me where he could do some shopping, but he gave me the impression that he really wasn't concerned with where to buy groceries, but was simply casing out our yacht."

"Will he follow us up the coast?" Nikki asked.

"I don't know. I just know that staying in this marina tonight is asking for trouble, and I can't risk it."

"I'll begin to untie the boat from the moorings," Nikki said. "You get the grandchildren settled and into their life jackets."

Unfortunately, Will didn't tell the harbormaster of his concerns and why he was leaving; he simply pulled away from his slip and headed out into the channel. Had he told the harbormaster of his fear and expressed his reasons for leaving, the harbormaster very well might have contacted the police.

Will couldn't see the killer up in the park above the marina. Jake was looking down at the *Bypassing Through* and noting the yacht's activity. Jake didn't know if they were going out for an evening cruise or moving to another marina. He watched the boat as it left the harbor, sailed into Lake Michigan, and then headed due north.

Jake would monitor its movements by listening to a ship-to-shore radio kept in his pickup.

As the yacht made its way to Holland, Michigan, Will had a—

FLASHBACK: INVEST voted to allow four doctors into the group. Each had heard of our success and really wanted in, so finding the four was not a problem. We only had to be assured of their commitment to invest at least a million per investor. We chose Dr. Wey, a cardiologist, Dr. Buillion, a pulmonary specialist, and Dr. Prescott, a young plastic surgeon with a bright future. He borrowed to get the million as he was just starting out in his practice, but he desperately wanted in. And, our final choice was Dr. Brenda Kanillopoolos, an anesthesiologist, whose father was a highly successful Greek architect. She simply had to ask Dad for the money. Mr. K , as we all called him, saw the loan like giving junior a quarter for a piece of bubble gum, so wealthy was his portfolio.

There was some discussion about allowing young Prescott in because of his lack of capital should the project fail. But, he so desperately saw this as a way to instantly pay for his sons' private schooling in a prestigious prep school in the east and to pay for his wife's education now that he had completed his studies. He practically begged to be let in, so we welcomed him.

Maggie powered her chair onto the porch and soaked in the magnificent view of the Lake. The Searing cats, Luba and Millie, jumped into her lap, their favorite warm spot whenever Maggie visited. Carol and Lou had gone for their evening walk along the shore of Lake Michigan. Maggie, with purring cats in her lap, decided to meditate for a few minutes while they were gone.

Samm pranced around waiting for Lou or Carol to toss her a piece of driftwood. Each of them obliged her.

"Very sad, Lou."

"What's sad? The murders?" Lou asked.

"Yes, this evil that lurks among us, always tugging at our souls, always nipping at our desire to experience absolute joy on earth," Carol said.

"It bothers me too."

"Seeing all of these yachts out on the Lake causes me to look forward to our next cruise," Carol said with a smile and an effort to change her negative thinking to positive thinking.

"I agree. Where are we going again?"

"I think we'd like a Scandinavian cruise."

"That's right. I think we're ready to go to Europe. We've sure enjoyed the few cruises we've taken in the Alaska Inside Passage and from New York to Montreal via Nova Scotia and the St. Lawrence Seaway. Last year we went to China for that trip of a lifetime."

"Good memories, Lou," Carol said with a smile and a squeeze of his hand.

"Definitely. Guess we'd better be thinking of dates and putting some dollars into the trip kitty."

"I'm looking forward to getting you away from a crime scene, Lou Searing. It would be just my luck to have death on the high seas and you'd pour your heart and soul into a case on the cruise ship."

"Not much chance of that happening," Lou replied. "People pay too much for the cruise to be killin' someone in a closed community like that."

"You seem to draw the cases to you, Lou. I'm simply going to hope that our cruise ship will be crime free."

By now, Lou and Carol had turned around and were headed back to their home. They looked ahead to see Maggie sitting peacefully, head back and enjoying the warm breeze that came ashore to caress her hair and fair skin. Samm ran up to her and begged a toss of driftwood. The cats decided that the action was too much for them and jumped down. Maggie threw a stick toward the Lake and Samm dutifully retrieved it for her. Samm had a friend for life, a good one at that.

Lou, Carol, and Maggie decided to go in the house and watch the sunset through the picture window in the den, which tonight promised to be a sky of orange and blue with a ball of yellow slowing disappearing into Wisconsin, or so it seemed.

꒰ꙫ꒱

Will radioed ahead to the Yacht Basin Marina in Lake Mackatawa on Channel 9.

"Yacht Basin Marina—Yacht Basin Marina—Yacht Basin Marina. This is *Bypassing Through* calling Yacht Basin Marina."

"This is the Yacht Basin Marina. Go to 68 please."

"This is the *Bypassing Through* on Channel 68."

"You have the Yacht Basin Marina dock master."

"Tom Denherder, is that you?"

"Yes, Doc, it is. All the help is busy. I'm workin' all the jobs this evening. Coming in, I hope?"

"I'm looking for a slip for a couple of days. As you know, I'm a 38-foot Sea Ray with a 12 foot beam, and about a 3-foot draw."

"You are in luck. I have a slip that's got your name on it. I was full, but a skipper left this afternoon. Give me a call back when you are 10 minutes out, Doc, and I'll have specific information for you."

"Roger. Oh, Tom, please tell Paul to keep the ship store open, I'll need a few supplies."

"For you, Doc, Paul will reopen if need be."

"Roger, this is the *Bypassing Through*, out on 68, switching back to Channel 9."

Not knowing exactly where Dr. Harrison would be docking, Jake drove to the DNR Boat Launch, just north of the marina. He stayed in his vehicle and monitored his ship-to-shore radio, and watched as *Bypassing Through* entered the marina and slid comfortably into the assigned slip.

Before going to bed Lou called Mickey McFadden to report that they were back and to suggest that Maggie and he share a conference call with him and Detective Maguffin around eight o'clock in the morning.

CHAPTER SEVEN

Thursday, July 9
Grand Haven and Cadillac, Michigan

Lou awoke and noticed that Carol was not in bed. He glanced at the clock and saw 6:23. It was rare that Lou slept in as he was usually up within the five o'clock hour. And, he always woke Carol and gave her an early morning back rub. It was strange that she wasn't in bed or in the bathroom.

Lou got up, put on his robe and went downstairs to find her. Carol wasn't in the house. The door to Maggie's bedroom was closed so Lou assumed she was still in her room and hopefully asleep. Lou noticed that Samm wasn't around either. He looked into the garage and both of their cars were there. Next he looked toward the Lake and there she was, standing on the shore practicing Tai Chi.

Lou poured a cup of coffee and quietly walked onto the porch and sat down to enjoy her graceful movements. She was a part of the moment. She didn't appear to be on the earth practicing an ancient art known to man for centuries. She seemed to be a part of the tapestry, a natural fixture in space, a mass of energy in tune with all around her. Her movements were synchronized with the movement of waves, the seagulls, and the grass swaying in the gentle breeze. Lou found himself meditating and leaving the cares of the physical world behind as he focused on her rhythmic movements. Samm was not running around, but was quietly resting on the cool sand and watching Carol as well.

About a half hour later, Carol walked back from the beach and saw Lou sitting on the porch sipping his cup of coffee.

"Good morning," Carol said with a smile.

"You are never up before seven; you had me concerned there," Lou replied.

"I guess I took a longer nap than usual last evening and I was up early. I stepped outside and the temperature was perfect for a Tai Chi session. So, I went to the water's edge to enjoy the setting. Samm wanted out so she came along."

"You are really an excellent Tai Chi student," Lou said with pride.

"Thanks, but it takes lifetimes to master it."

"I've heard that, but to me, you've got it down. I can't imagine you getting much better."

Carol smiled, "Well, stick with me for a few lifetimes and I think you'll see an improvement."

"I'm along for eternity, if you'll have me."

The peaceful moment was interrupted when the phone rang. "I hope that isn't murder number four," Carol said. She walked into the kitchen and answered the phone. "Lou, it's for you, Chief McFadden."

"Good morning, canceling our conference call or do we have another murder?"

"Neither. I got a call this morning from the chief of police in Holland. He told me he has a visitor in an area marina who has asked for police protection. The visitor thinks he's being targeting by the marina murderer."

"Is that so? What's the story?"

"We'll talk about it when we have our conference call. I do need to change the time which was the real reason for my call. I don't need to cancel, but I need to move it forward a half hour to eight-thirty. Is that OK?"

"Not a problem."

"Good, talk with you and Maggie at 8:30."

I turned to Carol, "Not a murder; Mickey needed to change our conference call time. Maybe the murders will stop. Whoever is doing this has to realize that everyone is on guard."

⌇

Maggie and Lou linked up with Chief McFadden and Jerry Maguffin.

"What did you learn in South Haven?" Mickey asked.

Maggie briefed them and mentioned Billy Estes.

"I didn't call him or ask to see him, Mickey. I wanted you to know about this possible suspect and then we'll take your lead. You may work with the police in South Haven or you may want Jerry to handle it. Your call."

"I'll call Chief Babcock. He may have information about this guy and he may want to follow the lead. I'll let you know what we decide."

"Maggie and I have been thinking about the technique of the killer. In South Haven, you noted there was no blood or water on the dock, and the guy who found the body heard some splashing. Autopsy reports for Dr. Knoble and Dr. Rothchild indicate that the cause of death was monoxide poisoning. They also found Midazolam in the tissue. It had been injected in the thigh. So, the victim is drugged and gassed on land. We think that in the middle of the night, the killer must swim underwater with scuba diving equipment to the marina dock. That's probably what happened in Manistee when Rose Crandall thought she saw a fish jumping and the break in the channel water.

"We think the darker than usual red marks around the neck and the fibers found deeper into the skin are because the killer is pulling and jerking the body behind him as he swims toward the dock. We think the body is weighted down a bit so as not to break the water surface but not be so heavy as to be difficult to pull the body along behind him. We think when he arrives, he ties the rope around the piling and then slits the victim's wrist and swims away."

Maggie added, "This is perfect for a killer because there is no evidence at the scene of the crime, no fingerprints, nothing is left behind. He swims underwater so no one sees him bringing the body to the dock where the body is tied."

"Sure makes a lot of sense," Chief McFadden replied. "Great minds are in sync because Maguffin mentioned most of your thinking to me this morning when I got in. We seem to be in agreement with the killer's MO."

"Good, all we've got is common sense intuition, and an 80-year-old woman's story about a fish jumping," Lou said.

"This won't surprise you, Mickey, but I think the serial killer is all about revenge for some medical mistakes," Maggie said. "All three victims are a doctor or a lawyer who defends medical folks in malpractice cases. So, that pattern exists."

"I agree, and how do we break that pattern?" Mickey asked.

"I think we need to get with the American Medical Association or at least some Michigan variation of this organization and try to learn of any outstanding cases that could cause a doctor to be threatened," Lou said.

"I agree, but these murders don't seem to be the result of some major dispute. They are situations that any doctor might face. Every doctor, nurse or medical person could be targeted."

"That's true," Maggie offered.

"But, by asking for difficult cases, it might give us a clue along the way."

"Fine, pursue it, by all means, I just don't think it will lead to anything," Chief McFadden reasoned. "What we've got here, it seems to me, is somebody contracted by an organization whose membership is made up of victims of medical malpractice. If it is not a copy cat killing, but the same guy doing it all, the guy doesn't pick off all of these folks just because he's been angered or personally affected by some decision, mistake, or inappropriate treatment. He must be hired to kill these people which is why I'm thinking it could be a contract from a victim's organization of some kind."

"Could very well be," Lou said, making note of Mickey's observation.

They talked about a few other ideas and possibilities and then brought the meeting to a close, promising to stay in touch.

‿〜

Lou had momentarily forgotten that today was the day of the funeral for James Rothchild. It would be in Cadillac at 1:00. Lou wanted to be there, because he's one of those few who think the killer might get some kick out of showing up at the funeral of his victim. The possibility was remote, but he didn't want to miss the chance to test his theory.

Maggie decided to go to Manistee and visit the Chalet West Apartments. She was curious about Rose Crandall and wanted to talk with her. She also agreed to call the U of M Medical School Admissions Office and see what she could learn.

‿〜

Lou arrived at the funeral home early so he stood around outside looking at everyone coming to the service. He didn't look conspicuous or at least he hoped he didn't. He was dressed in a plain dark suit as he stood quietly to one side of the entrance hoping he looked like one of the funeral home employees.

Once the service was about to begin, Lou sat in the back so he could see the crowd. He had no purpose in being at the funeral other than to look at people and to study reactions and movements. Of course Lou lowered his head during prayer and attended to the kind words spoken about the deceased. He was moved to realize the family was in agony, but his sole purpose was to solve the case and bring justice to the family in grief. He could only do that by being sharp in his observation skills.

Liz Crawford had been quietly sitting in one of the front pews during the service. She was distracted by a comment from one of the persons giving a eulogy when she had a—

FLASHBACK: The Crawford and Prescott boys were swimming in the lake by our cottage. My husband, Art, was mowing the lawn and I was working in my flower garden. I still can hear the shout of my son, Dick, "Dad, Herb's gone under! DAD!!!"

Art ran into the lake and then swam as quickly as he could to the raft which was about one hundred feet from shore. I went into the cottage to call 911. I didn't wait to see if it was necessary. I figured they may be needed so it was best to have them on the way.

Herb was the youngest son of the Hopkins, our neighbors a few cottages to the east. He wasn't a particularly good swimmer, but he could make it out to the raft and his parents allowed him to join the other kids from nearly cottages.

Art swam under the raft and found Herb's limp body. Apparently he got under the raft and couldn't make his way out, sort of like not finding a light switch in a dark room.

The scene for the next several hours was surreal. The tranquil row of cottages on the lake was transformed into a crime scene with officers, photographers, detectives all moving around doing their jobs, Fear gripped all those in the area. The one thing that was devastating to me and to Art was the rumor that our son had held Herb under water and that is what killed him. Our son, who is a good boy and who can be trusted, vehemently denied this.

By the end of the service Lou hadn't seen anything suspicious. He thought the trip was a waste of time. Lou didn't see any reason to go to the cemetery for the interment nor did he see any reason to go to the reception in the basement of the First Presbyterian Church. On the other hand, he was in Cadillac to see what he could learn, so he changed his mind and got in the procession to the cemetery.

Lou drove out of the church parking lot, and positioned himself behind a Jeep SUV. The ride took about ten minutes and Lou was surprised at the number of cars going to the cemetery. He exited his car and again stood near the back. He noticed a young couple with Mrs. Harrison and figured it must be Mike with Penny. If he was right, Mike looked pretty normal to Lou, but maybe he'd grown accustomed to youth expressing themselves with body piercing so it isn't the novelty it once was. Mike was wearing a suit and looked quite fashionably dressed for a young man. If the young woman was Penny, she looked nice as well and seemed to be a source of comfort to her mother.

Once the grave site service was underway Lou glanced around the cemetery. He noticed a red pickup. From the moment he spotted it, Lou paid more attention to that vehicle than he did to the graveside service. It was quite a distance away such that Lou really couldn't see anyone in the vehicle. A few minutes later the door opened and someone got out.

Lou definitely found it strange, because had the vehicle been in the cemetery for someone to pay respects, the person would have gone to the grave site. This person didn't get out of the vehicle for a good five minutes, and then when he or she did get out, the person didn't leave the truck. The person seemed to be looking at the people at the grave site service. Again, he or she was quite a distance and perhaps Lou was imagining things. The person could have been silently meditating during the whole time, but he doubted it. Lou couldn't get in his car and drive to the pickup because it was sandwiched in between the others.

The person got back in the pickup and drove away before the procession was ready to leave the cemetery and return to the church. Lou noted his observation once in his vehicle as he waited for the mourners to leave the cemetery. Back at the church, Lou had some refreshments, paid his respects to Mrs. Rothchild, introduced himself to Penny and Mike and began to leave.

When Lou got to the parking lot and was about to enter his car to drive back to Grand Haven he was approached by a woman who obviously had been at the services. "Excuse me, Mr. Searing?"

"Yes."

"I'm Mrs. Liz Crawford. I understand you're investigating James's murder?"

"Yes, that's right. I'm working with the Manistee Police to try and solve the crime."

"Well, I think I know who did it and I'd like to help."

"We'd like your help," Lou said, pen and notepad in hand. "What information do you have?"

"Well, it all goes back a few years. The Rothchild family and our family owned a cottage on Lake Missaukee. We all thought it would be great fun to co-own a cottage on a lake. Our children and grandchildren would enjoy the water and we were all getting on in years and thought a retreat spot would be wonderful. So, we did a lot of research and finally decided on a piece of property a little northeast of Cadillac.

"The first summer we were there, our children were playing on a raft. A neighbor boy, Herbie Hopkins swam out to the raft and something happened, something that I've never understood to this day and I suspect neither did Anita and James, but Herb drowned.

"The family of the boy strongly believes there was foul play on the part of our children. Herb's older brother, Rich had often been in trouble with the law and had spent time at a center for troubled youth. We always sensed that he would seek revenge in some way and I believe this is the revenge for Herbie's death."

"Thanks for sharing this. Can you give me information about this family?"

"Yes, the family name is Hopkins. Their address and phone number is 2456 Shoreline Avenue in Cadillac and their phone number is 555-8762." Lou wrote down the information and after thanking Mrs. Crawford, put the notepad on his front seat. He had written at the top of the page, "Suspect in Dr. Rothchild's death" followed by the name "Richard Hopkins," along with his address and phone number.

"I hope I can trust you, Mr. Searing. I really don't want anyone to find out about this conversation. You saw what happened to James and I don't want a similar fate to happen to me or my husband. We suffered enough always looking over our shoulder."

"You have my confidence, Mrs. Crawford. I thank you very much for sharing this information. It very well might lead to James's killer and the killer of the others as well."

Lou got into his car and headed for M-55 and the three-hour trip back to Grand Haven. Perhaps his spotting the red pickup and Mrs. Crawford's information made the trip worthwhile.

⸼

At dinner, Lou asked Maggie what she had learned during the day. "Well, on a personal note, having nothing to do with our case, Tom is about to head for Myrtle Beach for his annual vacation with his golfing buddies. He wishes us well in our investigation."

"Does Tom still practice his dentistry?" Carol asked, thinking he had fully retired.

"Well, the golf course is getting more and more of his attention. He is sort of a dentist on call for most of the Battle Creek dentists. He fills in on emergencies or if a dentist needs a vacation and can't find help in his or her absence. He keeps his hand in the profession, but to be honest, if he turned in his drill for a new putter, he'd be very happy."

"I'm a bit envious of Tom's heading to a golf vacation, but what did you learn today?" Lou asked.

"I called the state medical society and asked a lot of questions about their procedures to account for suits and major confrontations with patients. I learned practically nothing. All of their members have their own insurance and the Society collects no data that might help us."

"I wonder who the major insurance carrier is?"

"I asked that too and learned that it is Lifeline Associates. I called them and they cited confidentiality or pending court action as reasons they couldn't give me any information."

"I'll bet if it meant the information might help us save a few lives of their clients, they'd change their tune."

"I did bring that up, but they stuck to their policy of privacy."

"Anything else?"

"Chief McFadden called. He called Chief Babcock and they talked about Billy Estes. Apparently Billy Estes is cooperating fully with them. He had a good alibi plus he doesn't know how to swim. He's not a suspect, Lou. Mentally he's not very secure, but he's not the marina murderer. The police don't think so and I agree."

"OK, we'll drop him from our list."

"What did you learn in Cadillac?" Maggie asked.

"Two things happened. I saw a red pickup quite a ways from the grave site of James Rothchild. The occupant seemed to be watching us and then left. Second, a woman named Mrs. Crawford stopped me as I was about to leave the reception and told me of an event that happened a few years ago that might be the motive for having James murdered."

"I'm all ears."

"The Crawfords and Rothchilds bought a cottage on a lake near Cadillac. A neighbor boy, Herb Hopkins, joined their kids on a raft in the lake and drowned. The Hopkins family believes Herb died as a result of foul play and that the Crawford and Rothchild kids are responsible for the death of the young lad. The older Hopkins son, Rich, is a juvenile offender and is dangerous, or so I was led to believe. Mrs. Crawford thinks this Rich may have done this to avenge Herb's death."

"Logical."

Carol had been listening to all of this and didn't offer anything until she said, "The next call will be to tell you that Mrs. Crawford has been murdered."

"You think so, huh?" Lou asked.

"I sure hope not," Carol replied.

"I suppose you'd like to hear what I learned when I called the U. of M. Medical School?" Maggie asked.

"Definitely, but I bet you didn't learn anything all that helpful or you would have told me by now," Lou said.

"That's right. They said there are tens of rejections, far more are rejected as are accepted. The person I talked to said parents are often pretty upset if their son or daughter is rejected but the majority come to accept it and move on. Some call the president of the university and some even call legislators to try and have the decision overturned. They couldn't give me names because of confidentiality, but if they could, the list would be in the hundreds."

"Hmmm, makes sense," Lou replied. "I doubt the woman who visited Mr. Verduin is our killer. Why kill a bunch of people because a lawyer won't represent you. There are tens of lawyers hungry to represent a client. I don't doubt that this Verduin was good, but he was only one lawyer." Maggie and Carol nodded in agreement.

The dishes were cleared from the table. Lou rinsed them off and then Carol placed them in the dishwasher and wiped off the counters. While Carol and Lou took a short walk on the beach, Maggie watched "Wheel of Fortune."

CHAPTER EIGHT

Friday, July 10
Manistee and Holland, Michigan

Lou had nothing planned for the day. He thought about going with Maggie to Manistee but decided against it. He had some shopping to do and some correspondence to handle. The break for a day was welcomed.

Maggie left for Manistee very early in the morning. She arrived about 8:30 and wheeled her chair into the Chalet West Apartments. She asked to speak to the manager. The manager had heard that Maggie was a part of the investigation team and welcomed her.

"My guess is you're here to talk to Rose?"

"Yes. I understand she saw something the night of the murder."

"Nobody knows what, if anything, she saw. I'm sure you've been informed of Rose's storytelling obsession?"

"Oh, yes. I'm ready for an earful, but I might learn something."

"You and Rose can use our conference room here. Would you like some coffee or tea?"

"A glass of iced tea sounds good, if that wouldn't be any bother."

"Not at all." The manager paged Rose, told her Maggie wanted to interview her, and asked her to come to the conference room. She also phoned the kitchen and requested two glasses of iced tea.

About ten minutes later Rose slowly came around the corner with her walker, greeted Maggie, and sat down.

"It is a pleasure to meet you, Mrs. McMillan. I've read all of Mr. Searing's books and I so enjoy your work."

"Thank you, Mrs. Crandall. We've been lucky in some of our investigations."

"Hey, you solve 'em and it's nice to see some justice. We rarely see that in real life. Oh, and please call me Rose. May I call you Maggie?"

"By all means. Thanks for meeting with me."

"My pleasure. What do you need?" Rose asked.

"I want to know what you saw the other night, if anything."

"I couldn't sleep, it was around three in the morning. I opened my drapes and looked out as I always do when I can't sleep. I saw the lights of the harbor area and downtown. I saw a fish jump by the DNR boat near the west end of the marina."

"You sure it was a fish?"

"Had to be. Sort of like a big fish jumping out of the water."

"You saw this with your eyes?"

"Yeah, then I took my binoculars and I saw some form by the dock, but I couldn't tell what it was. When I had the binoculars, I saw a reflection of light from the moon on something in that same area."

"Could it have been a light?"

"No, it was a reflection."

"Now, I hear you are telling stories about a monster like the Loch Ness monster being in the channel, finding people to eat, and..."

"Oh, Maggie. Let me explain," Rose said with an embarrassed chuckle. "You see, people expect me to come up with these outlandish tales and so I do. They hang on every word. When I was a third grade teacher, I used to make up stories. The children would be enthralled. They loved it. These old folks are just like children, they like a good story. So, I tell them one. I'll take a minor thing like a fish jumping and before you know it Godzilla is cavorting around Manistee devouring people and crushing everything in its path." Both women smiled and chuckled.

"Humm, I was given the impression you sort of lived in a fantasy world, Rose."

"Naw, I'm a pretty normal old gal if you ask me. But, when I turn into my storytelling character, I get pretty carried away. If I'm ever considered for placement in a mental health hospital, I'll have to come clean. I'm OK, I just like to entertain and since the people seem to like it, who is harmed? Believe me, if it weren't for me and my stories, this place would be quite dull."

"Did you see anything else besides the fish jump down by the DNR ship?"

"I saw something surface in the middle of the channel. It could have been another fish or the same fish or some piece of wood, I don't know."

"Could it have been a swimmer or someone with scuba diving equipment?"

"Sure. By the time I focused on the break in the water and got my binoculars on the area, there were only a few ripples. I have no idea what it was."

"But you did see something break the water surface?"

"Oh, most definitely."

"One last question, Rose. Why didn't you tell the police officers the facts as you are telling me?"

"What? Lose my reputation with my boys in blue. They like a good story too. If I'd seen some crime I'd have leveled with them, but all I saw was a fish jump. No crime there - just an invitation to tell a whopping good story. They loved it, Maggie." Rose smiled so proud of her entertaining skills. Maggie smiled if only to enjoy the moment with an elderly lady who had her act totally together.

"But, you didn't tell me the same tale?" Maggie asked.

"Nope. I'm going to be in Lou's book and I want my descendants thinking I have my head on straight because I do, I really do."

"Oh, I see. Well, that does make sense."

Maggie thanked Rose for her help. The two women finished their tea while talking about grandchildren and life outside the Chalet West Apartments.

Call it a woman's intuition, but Maggie felt a need to get to Holland. She couldn't get her mind off the information from the

Holland police chief about the man in the marina who thought he was being targeted for death. It was only 9:30 in Manistee, so she got in her accessible van and headed south. Maggie's plan was to drive directly to the Holland police station.

ॐ

Will Harrison stepped from his yacht, *Bypassing Through*, and stretched toward the morning sun. Nikki and grandchildren had left to go to Holland with Assunta Magliocco, an old college friend who wanted to show Nikki the sites around Holland. Nikki thought the two grandchildren could use a break from the water so invited them to go along. Assunta is Italian for Sue and everyone called her Sue. They had left around eight-thirty and now Will began to plan how he'd spend the day.

Will liked Holland and had stayed in the Yacht Basin Marina on many occasions. So that he could get to the downtown Holland area, Will used his ten-foot Zodiac dinghy with an 8-horsepower Mercury motor. He'd take the dinghy across Lake Macatawa to Kollen Park where he'd dock and walk the six or so blocks to the downtown area.

Once downtown, he'd probably spend a portion of the day doing some window-shopping. He needed to get an anniversary gift for Nikki. He'd probably go to the library and read some back issues of the paper. While he enjoyed his escape from the stresses and strains of the everyday working world, he did remain curious with what was happening around the globe.

He'd be sure to eat lunch at the 84 East Restaurant, a favorite spot of many years. Finally, having a day to himself would be relaxing, that is, if he could get his mind off of the marina maniac.

Jake had other plans for Will Harrison. He had seen the car leave with Dr. Harrison's wife and grandchildren. He didn't know where they were going or for how long, but he did know that Will was alone and that his plan for murder was on track for success. Once again, he reviewed his briefing. He noted that when Will took the dinghy toward Holland he was heading for downtown because Dr. Harrison's mode of operation would be to dock the dinghy at Kollen Park and walk to town.

Before leaving the marina, Will stopped and chatted with Tom for a few minutes. He wanted to make sure his reservation was intact and he wanted Tom to know of his plans.

The trip across Lake Macatawa was uneventful. True to form, he docked the dinghy at Kollen Park and then headed to JP's for breakfast. This favorite breakfast spot in Holland was on the corner of 8th Street and College. Once inside he ordered two eggs over easy, whole wheat toast, bacon and regular coffee, no cream. He'd gotten used to the caffeine in med school when staying up all night got to be routine.

Will had picked up a copy of the *Holland Sentinel* in the newspaper dispenser. While waiting for his order, he noticed an update on the marina killer. The news was simply telling citizens that no new information had become available. Readers were asked to report anyone suspicious around the marina areas. Once again Will had a—

FLASHBACK: The INVEST group had an emergency meeting about a month after the new members were welcomed into the club. Glenda looked devastated and began to read a letter to the group. The gist of the letter was news from the county that the land that the club had bought with millions of dollars could not be developed without the removal of toxic materials. It had come to light that years and years ago this land was used by industries to dump their toxic material and in addition, close by had been a gas station back in the 1950s that had had extensive underground leakage.

Glenda summarized, "We have now lost it all. We invested our money with a developer who changed his mind about building a marina based on intense anger and criticism from the locals and a powerful environmental lobby who would never allow a zoning ordinance to be changed. We now own the land, paid a PR firm to lobby on its behalf, and obtained a land study report. The land study was completed and the land was determined to be full of toxic material. The marina investment was DEAD. The money we put into the project was gone." Anger, devastation, and a feeling of despair and a state of shock hung over the meeting room.

Glenda told all of us that she had checked with her lawyer prior to the meeting to see if they had any recourse. The attorney told her that standard procedure to is purchase land with a contingency clause meaning that the deal would only go through following a successful land analysis study, but the paperwork he had studied found no such contingency. After carefully reviewing all the papers, he declared the transactions legal. The INVEST risk was just that, a risk, and they lost their shirts. Pure and simple.

Jake was seated on a park bench in front of a sporting goods store across the street from JP's. He appeared to be reading a paper, but in reality he was watching for Will to exit.

Will ate his breakfast and kept looking at the paper. Back home he didn't have time to read most of the paper. He'd simply read headlines and if a topic caught his interest, he might read the first paragraph but never more than that. He set the paper down, picked up his coffee cup, and turned to his left to look out the window. There, across the street, was the profile of the man he'd talked with in St. Joe. The doctor was trained to be observant, usually observant of symptoms of disease, but observant none-the-less and he knew he had seen that profile. The marina murderer, in his opinion, was right across the street right here in Holland, early the morning of July 10.

Jake didn't know that there was a back entrance to JP's. The rear exit led to one of many municipal parking lots and was where most of the customers parked. Will knew of the back entrance and decided to take it and hopefully, if he was being stalked, he'd have a jump on getting away from this crazed maniac.

$$\backsim$$

As Maggie was beginning her drive to Holland, Will was planning to go to the police station. He knew the Holland Police department was about 6 blocks east of JP's. He thought it best to simply walk there, talk to the Chief and have this character followed or interviewed or whatever the police do when they suspect someone of murder.

Jake realized that Will had been in the restaurant long enough for breakfast and couldn't understand why he hadn't emerged. Jake got up from the park bench and headed back to the marina; if Will had gotten out of the restaurant without his knowing it, he would have to return to his yacht sooner or later. He drove to the marina parking lot, put on his sunglasses, and waited for Will to appear. He was in no hurry, the murder wouldn't occur until late that night.

A half hour later, a police car came up to the Yacht Basin Marina on Ottawa Beach Road. Will Harrison got out and went with the officer onto his craft. Jake watched carefully. This guy is either paranoid or he's bound and determined not to be my next victim, thought Jake.

The officer talked with Will and the two of them stayed around the boat and looked in all directions. By now, other boaters were curious about the presence of the patrol car and the word quickly traveled throughout the marina that perhaps there was another murder or at least some suspicion that the killer was in the area.

The police car left. Jake waited for more than an hour and then he thought he'd take a risk and walk to the marina. He sat down on a bench about 100 feet from Will's yacht and began to read *USA Today*. Occasionally he would lower the paper to see what Will was doing. It was a strange but exciting feeling. *It must be what a tiger feels while stalking his next dinner,* Jake thought.

Jake decided he had overdone his welcome at the small marina. Staying any longer would cause someone to question his hanging around for so long. Jake got in his pickup and headed back to Holland. He had no idea that one of the vans that whizzed past him going in the opposite direction was Maggie's.

***

Maggie drove into the small marina and exited her van. She drove her power chair up to *Bypassing Through* and called out, "Anybody home?"

Will came out, greeted her and said, "Hello. Who are you looking for?"

"You, if you're the owner of this beautiful yacht."

"Yes, I am, so I guess you're looking for me. What can I do for you?"

"My name is Maggie McMillan and I'm working with Lou Searing and the Manistee Police in investigating the marina murders. I gather from your boat's name that you're into hearts that don't work very well?"

"That's right. I'm a cardiovascular surgeon."

"I see. You staying here for the duration of your vacation?"

"No, we've been at a marina in St. Joe; now we're here obviously, and we'll move up the shoreline in the next few days."

"I understand you've talked to the Holland police?"

"Yes, I saw a guy when we were in St. Joe and he seemed out of place. Maybe I'm paranoid, but you can't blame me, being a doctor, staying in a marina and all."

"I understand. If I were you, Dr. Harrison, I'd go home," Maggie said seriously.

"You're probably right. I usually go with my instincts but this is our vacation and my wife and grandchildren deserve a good time. I'm probably just being overly cautious."

"Being in medicine and being in a marina is just asking for trouble. The stress has to be high for you and your family."

"Well, yes, I thought so too. I thought I ran into this marina killer down in St. Joe. The guy acted strange and obviously didn't belong in a marina because he didn't have a boat. I quickly left and came up here. This morning, I looked out of the window at JP's and saw him again. I went to the police station to report my concern and got a ride back down here with an officer.

"If I were you, I'd go home and plan an extended trip next summer when this case is solved," Maggie suggested.

"I appreciate your concern, but I think we'll be OK. I've asked the police to keep an eye on us. They'll work with the county Sheriff to stop by frequently. We'll leave this marina in a couple of days and head home."

"It's your life, but you can't be cautious enough. We really haven't a clue who this guy is. We know he'll hit again, and one thing is for certain, he'll hit someone in the medical field and someone who is or has been involved in some type of malpractice suit or at least is in conflict with a patient and which of you folks isn't."

"Thanks for your caring. And, good luck finding this maniac."

Maggie smiled, shook his hand and powered her chair to her van. She sensed that Dr. Harrison would not take her advice. The chances were high that she'd never see him again.

꒳

Around three o'clock, Will received a call from a man impersonating a Holland police officer. The caller said they had a suspect in the marina murders and wanted to have him see if he was the guy he had seen in St. Joe. He was told that an officer would pick him up. The officer would be driving his own vehicle, a red Ford pickup. He was assured that the man was with the police and would be wearing a police officer's uniform.

Will never doubted the authenticity of the call. He waited out in the marina parking lot and when the pickup arrived, he got in fully expecting to chat with a police officer, not with his killer.

The officer impersonator was wearing a disguise and a moustache so realistic that a barber would begin a trim and not know the facial hair was false. Will did not recognize the driver.

The pickup left the small marina and headed east. "Understand you have a suspect in the marina murders," Will said. Hope you've finally got this guy."

"Yeah, chances are good that he's the guy. All we need is a positive identification from you and we'll book him for murder."

The two men continued their drive toward Holland. A mile or two of silence was broken when Will said, "Can you arrange for me to get to Kollen Park when I'm finished? I need to bring my dinghy back to the marina."

"Not a problem. I'll handle it or if the chief has other plans for me, he'll get someone to take you there."

"Thanks."

A block later, Jake said, "Say, were you ever a part of an investment club? I've been asked to join one, but I'm not sure it's for me."

"Yeah, I was in one about 20 years ago when I was at the U of M."

"Did your group make any money?"

"Oh yeah, we were on a roll. The results of our investments were too good to be true and this was before the happy days of the 1990s."

"Never had a bad investment?" Jake said. "Man, you were one lucky club."

"Well, yeah, we did have one bad one. Very bad. We got taken to the cleaners."

"How's that?"

"A land deal went sour."

"What do you mean by that?"

"We put in a lot of bucks on a huge piece of land that was going to become a mega marina. The opportunity had each of us expecting a windfall. The county and some federal agency did a land analysis and found the area to be toxic so out went the marina idea and the place became a dump. We lost millions."

"Ouch!"

"Ouch is right. We invited some other doctors to join in to get money to hire a PR firm, but that contract was a wasted few million as well."

"Bet everyone was devastated. Especially those later doctors who joined you."

"Oh yeah, they blew it though."

"Blew it? How's that?" Jake asked.

"Well, anybody who is about to invest almost a million dollars should have enough common sense to check the thing out. If they are stupid enough to walk in under blind faith, they deserve to take a hit."

"Sounds like they trusted you guys though."

"Yeah, they did, but investing money and especially big money requires a careful look at the proposal. You need an attorney to check it out, you minimally need that."

"Sounds to me like you double-crossed them?"

"Depends how you look at it. That's one way to see it, another is to see them taking a blind risk with the rest of us. They did and they got hurt. We all got hurt."

"Yeah, don't know if I want to take the risk."

"Actually, one guy killed himself. Couldn't handle the loss. He was not a well-adjusted guy, obviously. I mean killing yourself over one bad investment?"

"The others adjusted, I take it?" Jake asked.

"Yeah, they all did well, shook it off and made some good investment decisions and climbed right back up."

"But one guy you said, took it so hard he killed himself?" Jake asked, shaking his head and feeling the anger once again surfacing in his mind.

"Yeah, but as I say, he was weak. Too bad."

"Well, meet his son," Jake said extending his hand in greeting.

Will just sat there stunned and within seconds he knew he would be dead.

ॐ

Nikki, her grandchildren Nicholas and Sherry, and Sue Magliocca pulled into the marina. It was three-thirty in the afternoon. Nikki thanked Sue for a day of shopping and for buying her lunch. They promised to see each other again and hopefully sooner than the year and a half that it had been since their last visit.

As Nikki and her grandchildren prepared to board their yacht, Tom DenHerder approached. "Excuse me, Mrs. Harrison, I've got a message for you. Doc called and asked me to give you this message." He handed her the slip of paper, she thanked him and read, "I got a call to assist with an emergency heart condition at the Holland Community Hospital. Don't know when I'll be back. Hope you and the children had a good day. Love, Will."

For some reason, Nikki got one of those rare premonitions that she'd never see Will again. She'd read of these premonitions in womens' magazines, but never thought she'd experience one.

She immediately went to the phone and called the hospital and asked to be put through to surgery.

"Hello, this is Nikki Harrison, wife of Dr. Harrison of Chicago. He's assisting with surgery. Can you tell me when he's expected to be finished?"

"Sorry. There's no Dr. Harrison here."

"Has the surgery been completed?"

"No surgery has occurred nor is any planned for today."

"This is the Holland Community Hospital, correct?"

"Yes."

"Is this the only place where heart surgery would be done?"

"The only place in Holland and only basic procedures would be done here. If the surgery is major, the patient would be transferred to Spectrum Hospital in Grand Rapids."

"Let me repeat, I'm looking for Dr. Will Harrison."

"I heard you, ma'am, I'm sorry but we've had no emergencies, no heart surgery today, we've no record of a doctor by that name being here or even asked to come here."

Nikki hung up and immediately called her friend whom she just left a few minutes ago. Sue answered her cell phone in her car. "Hello."

"Sue, this is Nikki. Would you please come back to the marina?"

"Sure. Is something wrong?"

"I think something has happened to Will and I need your help."

"I'll be right there."

"Thanks. I need you to take the grandchildren. If there is going to be a crisis around here, I don't want them to have it in their minds for the rest of their lifes."

"I've turned around and am heading there right now. You okay, Nikki?"

"Yes, but I had one of those premonitions and I'm afraid Will be the marina killer's next victim."

"Oh God, Nikki, I pray you're wrong."

"Me too,"

Sue arrived, gave Nikki a sympathetic hug, took Nicholas and Sherry to her car and told Nikki to call if there was anything she could do. She drove away telling the children how lucky she was to be able to spend some more time with them and that Grandma would be joining them soon.

ॐ

Nikki decided not to call the police just yet. She didn't want to be seen as a crazed person. After all, this could all be a big mistake in communication. Will could have gotten the message wrong, left the boat, and then realized his error and gone on to Grand Rapids. Lots of things could have happened.

Nikki had to do something. She couldn't just sit in her boat and wonder if her premonition was accurate. She decided to talk to Tom again. She was certain he'd understand.

"Excuse me, may I have a word with you, Tom?" Nikki asked.

"Certainly. How can I help you?"

"Will thought he encountered the marina killer down in St. Joe and we've been nervous about this ever since. This afternoon he called and left you a message which you gave to me so you know what it said. But, when I called the hospital, they had no knowledge of him and no surgery is going on nor had any been scheduled."

"He stopped in to see me before going to breakfast and he told me of that encounter down in St. Joe," Tom replied. "I've been watching this place like a hawk. I sure don't want a murder in my marina."

"Did you see Will leave this afternoon?"

"About 3:00 he waved at me. He appeared to be waiting for someone to pick him up. He seemed fine then."

"Did he have any kind of a briefcase or bag with him?"

"No, in fact, he looked more like he was going to the beach than to work."

"To the beach?"

"Yeah, summer clothes, shorts, T-shirt. You know, summer wear for a hot summer day."

"Hmmm. This is strange."

"Now, early in the afternoon, I saw him talking to Mrs. McMillan, the private investigator who is working on the marina murders case with Lou Searing."

"Mrs. McMillan? How long did they talk?"

"They chatted for a few minutes, shook hands and she drove her power chair to her van and drove away. I saw her leave. But, I didn't see your husband talk to anybody else."

"Did Will talk to you about his visit with Mrs. McMillan."

"No."

"As I said, he isn't where he said he was going and that isn't like him. I think when he appears we're going to just head back to Chicago and get away from all of this stress."

"Can't blame you, this isn't the time for medical folk to be visiting marinas."

"Thanks," Nikki said as she lowered her head and walked away looking quite disturbed and concerned.

～

When Will Harrison didn't show up for dinner, Nikki decided to call the police and report his strange disappearance. Chief Donald Vanderwall came to the marina to talk with her and Tom. Lou was invited to join them and met them at the marina.

After listening to Nikki and Tom, they decided to put into place a plan for coverage of the marina. In addition to a police bulletin asking for all to be on the lookout for Dr. Harrison, a message was sent to all police departments along the coast of Lake Michigan that a physician had possibly been abducted.

In addition, all harbormasters and dock masters on the Lake Michigan coast were put on alert that Dr. Harrison was missing and to be especially observant at their marinas for any strange behavior. They were asked to alert all boaters in their marinas to be vigilant and to report any strange noise or behavior to the local police.

Chief Vanderwall decided to request the Ottawa County Sheriff have a deputy present at the marina all night, to keep watch on the Harrison yacht and to periodically walk the dock and to watch the surrounding waters. Mrs. Harrison promised to call the police chief as soon as Will returned or called.

Nikki called Sue and asked if the grandchildren could spend the night with her. She said of course and that Nicholas and Sherry had many questions about what was going on, but all Sue told them was Grandma would either call or come over as soon as possible and that there was a problem that she was attending to. This seemed to calm them, but every few hours the same round of questions would surface and Sue would repeat her responses.

While Nikki worried and called family and friends to find some comfort, Will Harrison, dead from carbon monoxide poisoning, lay in the bed of the red pickup. Jake had driven half way across Michigan. An hour and a half after leaving Holland, he pulled into the rest area near Grand Ledge, west of Lansing. He went to the rest room, got some M&Ms from the vending machine and walked to a red pickup, but not his. Jake's brother, John sat behind the wheel of Jake's pickup. The two acknowledged one another and then as planned, John took over, backed out and continued on to Harbor Beach. Jake would head north to Harrison.

As John was pulling onto I-96, he had a—

FLASHBACK: I was not at home when Dad took his life. I was at the neighborhood ball field. I adjusted better than Jake because I didn't have to live with an image engraved in my mind. But I did live with a lot of anger, loneliness, depression, and the financial hardship Dad's death brought to our family.

I guess I am not at all surprised that Jake asked me to help murder the members of the investment group. After all we are brothers and family needs to support family. I did realize that my medical career at Michigan State was threatened if we got caught, but Jake assured me we wouldn't get caught. He's very bright, pays much attention to detail, and has done a lot of work to research all of these killings. In a sense it isn't a whole lot different than killing the animals in the biology lab at school. My therapist sees this to be a big problem for me, but with his help and some medication I have the obsession to kill under control. I told Jake, I'd help, but I didn't want to do any killing. This means so much to Jake, this revenge for Dad's death and for not letting him in the medical school at U of M. I've got to be there for him and I will be.

John was Jake's identical twin brother. They spent much time in the weight room so were muscular. They had the same underwater exploring hobby. They also had the same psychopathic personality. John was in therapy and was making good progress in dealing with his problems. In fact, getting therapy was the basis upon which John was admitted to medical school at MSU.

With a dead Dr. Harrison in the back of Jake's covered pickup, John continued along the expressway making his way along I-69, north of Lansing and on toward Flint and eventually to the marina in Harbor Beach.

As John Pulled into Harbor Beach he had a—

FLASHBACK: Dad married Mom while he was still in medical school. Once graduated, Mom and Dad moved to Harbor Beach where Dad set up a practice with an older doctor who needed some help and who planned to pass along his patients to Dad when he retired in about 10 years or so.

Jake and I were born soon after Mom and Dad settled in Harbor Beach and we were raised near the water. We loved to go to the marina to look at the big boats and to play in the sand along the beach. Life was good in this town. Things got worse in Chelsea, but the formative years in Harbor Beach were special to every member of my family. I guess Jake wants this marina to be the site for a final resting place for one of the INVEST victims. I will honor his request.

That evening as John was about to enter the quiet village of Harbor Beach, Jake was calling Father Thomas Murphy. "Hello, St. Joseph Rectory. How can I help you?"

"Father Murphy, please. This is an emergency."

"I'm sorry, Father Murphy is not here. Would you like to leave a message or can I give you his voice mail?"

"Simply tell him that Jake called to tell him about number four."

"I will give him your message."

"Thanks."

CHAPTER NINE

Saturday, July 11
Harbor Beach, Michigan

It was two o'clock in the morning when John, carrying the dead body of Will Harrison, entered the water. Wearing a wet suit and with a tank full of oxygen, John descended into the water and swam with Will, a rope around his neck, in tow. He swam the 150 yards across the channel, tied the body to a piling, deeply cut the right wrist, and swam back in the quiet of night.

John wasn't clear about why the wrist had to be cut, but Jake told him to do it and so he followed instructions. He knew the noose symbolized his Dad's hanging.

John put all of his equipment in Jake's red pickup and drove into the marina parking lot to await the excitement and confusion once the body was discovered.

༄

The sun rose that morning in Holland on a quiet, sleeping town. There was still no sign of Dr. Harrison, no call, but no body either.

Nikki called Sue and said she'd like to come over and reassure the children that she was okay and to explain as best she could why they weren't staying on their yacht. Sue said she'd pick her up in a half hour and asked her to plan to have some breakfast with her and the children.

Needless to say, Nicholas and Sherry were glad to see their grandmother. They could tell that she had not gotten much sleep and seemed quite upset. Nikki told the children that they would have to go home to Chicago, and that their parents would greet them at O'Hare Airport. Sue would take them to Grand Rapids and put them on a direct flight to Chicago. Nikki told the children that there was a problem with their grandfather, but not to worry.

While the children were packing their things, Sue said she'd come down to the marina to be with Nikki once the plane carrying the children was safely in the air and out over the Lake.

"You're a great friend, Sue. I don't know what I'd do without you."

"You'd do the same for me, Nikki. I'm glad I can help."

"I just know Will is dead. I can feel it. He's obviously not in Holland, but he's dead. Whenever I try to be hopeful, or to think a positive thought, I immediately go back to my premonition, and I know he's dead," Nikki said, breaking down. Nicholas came into the room and saw Nikki crying.

"Something's happened to Grandpa," Nicholas stated with seriousness.

"We don't know where he is, honey. Yes, something might have happened to him, but we're hoping he is fine."

⌇

Preeti Gadola was moving toward the Harbor Beach marina. She had taken her kayak out into Lake Huron for an early morning ride. The third largest of the five Great Lakes was calm and the summer morning was a good time to get some exercise and to enjoy her favorite pastime.

As she approached the marina she saw something moving under one of the docks. She couldn't figure out what it was. It looked like a dead deer floating and swaying slightly with the movement of water.

Preeti decided to satisfy her curiosity so she paddled her kayak closer to the dock. As she got closer she knew this was a body, a dead body. She didn't move any closer, but directed her kayak toward the marina office. She beached the kayak, got out, pulled it up out of the water and calmly, yet feeling a bit nauseous because of what she had seen, walked up to the harbormaster.

"You don't want to hear this, but you've got a dead body tied to a piling out in the marina."

The harbormaster's reaction was not verbal, but only to look at Preeti and to replay in his mind what he had just heard. Finally, he said, "You sure?"

"Yeah. I was kayaking and saw something under the dock. I went just close enough to see it was a body. Looked like a man and it seemed he was tied to the dock. But I didn't stay, just headed for the marina."

"Did you call the police, or am I the first person you've told?"

"Came right to you."

The harbormaster lifted the phone and called the police. "Got a report of a dead body here at the Harbor Beach Marina. Body is tied to a piling under the dock."

Sirens could be heard in the distance shortly after he hung up. The emergency vehicles came into the marina. People came out of their boats while curious townsfolk and tourists with nothing to do filed in behind the police and ambulance.

John got out of his red pickup and approached two attractive women. "What's going on?"

"Some kind of accident or something down at the dock, I guess," one of the women replied.

"Somebody hurt?" John asked.

"I don't know."

The other woman looked admiringly at John's bulging muscles. "Where'd you order that body from, fella?"

John smiled, "Didn't order it from anywhere. It's homemade."

"You've got one fantastic body. Here let me take your picture with my friend."

"Naw, no pictures," John said.

"Oh, come on. We're on vacation up here. We want to impress our friends down in Kentucky. Let us have a little fun."

"Can't harm anything, I guess."

"Put your arm around her. They won't believe we hooked up with a stud like you. Smile like you like her." John put his arm around her, smiled and allowed his ego to enjoy two good-looking women admiring the body he had worked months to build.

"Thanks. They won't believe this when they see Trisha with you."

"Oh, stop it," Trisha said embarrassed. "This is all so phony. We're not going to show a picture to anyone and you know it."

"Nice meeting you ladies. I'm on my way. This place is going to fill up with the curious wondering how the guy died. He probably committed suicide. That's usually the case with a slit wrist. Maybe I'll see you again."

"Hey, if you're ever in Kentucky and need a date, I'm your woman! My name is Boots."

"OK, you got a deal, Boots" John said, as he climbed into his truck.

The marina did fill up, the police were doing all they could do to control the crowd, handle the media, and remove the body following the medical examiner's work. The police were interviewing other boaters, Preeti Gadola, and the harbormaster.

The authorities had no idea who the victim was. There was no identification on the body. They would enter a description into the victim database and see if a match could be made.

⌁

Chief Vanderwall was the first person in Holland to learn about Will Harrison's death. He called Harbor Beach and asked for a description of the man they found. Of course he couldn't be 100 percent certain until Mrs. Harrison positively identified the body, but the description sounded like Will Harrison.

Mickey called Lou to report the discovery of the body. "Lou, murder number four, over on the Lake Huron shore, Harbor Beach. Victim resembles Dr. Harrison. I think somebody needs to get to Harbor Beach and start asking questions. I should go, but I don't want to be away at this time. Detective Maguffin is involved in another crisis we had during the night. Can you go?"

"Sure can."

"OK, thanks. The chief's name in Harbor Beach is Jeremy Billings. He's easy to work with and will be expecting you."

Chief of Police Vanderwall got ready to go to the marina and talk with Mrs. Harrison. He turned to a rookie officer he had asked to accompany him. "This is the worst part of the job, talking to relatives of victims. I'm pretty sure she's expecting some bad news, but hearing it and dealing with the aftermath is going to be difficult."

Maggie fully expected the killer to tie Will Harrison to a piling at the Yacht Basin Marina. She didn't plan on him choosing a marina on the other side of the state. Now that it happened that way, Maggie saw that it was all so predictable. No murderer in his right mind would attempt to kill someone with the police covering marinas like a warm blanket on a cold Michigan night. But, why drive to a marina about five hours away? It made no sense. If simply tying the victim to a piling in a marina is the killer's mode of operation, there are a lot of marinas closer than five hours from the site of abduction.

While Lou was driving to Harbor Beach, those two attractive young women from Kentucky were in Smalley's Bar talking about the murder and the strange way in which the body was tied to the dock and how he was killed. They listened with interest to the TV in the bar: The newsman got their attention when he said, "We have an update on the murdered victim at the Harbor Beach Marina. As you may have heard and as we reported earlier, the body was found this morning by a kayaker coming into the harbor from a morning ride on Lake Huron. The victim was found with a rope around his neck and the rope was tied to the piling. There was no identification on him, but Police Chief Jeremy Billings has informed us that he has matched the description of the victim to a man currently listed in the database of missing persons and believes he knows the identity of the victim. No name is being released at this time.

"The victim also had a cut wrist and the pathologist says the knife was rather large. The medical examiner and the police agree that the victim was murdered. If you have any information about this murder, please call the police department. Their number appears on your television screen. You will not have to leave your name."

It was Trisha who spoke first. "You know, something's been on my mind all day about this murder."

"What's that?"

"Well, remember when we were at the marina watching all the action, and this muscular guy said, 'What's going on?'"

"Yeah."

"We responded that there was some kind of accident at the dock."

"Yeah."

"Do you recall what all he said?"

"Not really, I was just stuck on the guy, thinking about taking his picture with you."

"He said something about a dead guy and a cut wrist being a sure sign of suicide."

"Yeah. So?"

"So, how did he know the wrist was slit? How did he know it was a guy?" Trisha wondered.

"I don't know, maybe he had a police scanner at home or in his truck, or maybe he talked to the person who found the body before coming over to us."

"OK, but then why would he say, 'What's going on?'"

"I don't know. Maybe just a way to hit on us. You're taking this much too seriously."

"Don't think so, Boots. I've got to let the police know about this. I read a book once where the murderer got a kick out of seeing lots of people responding to his actions."

"No way."

"No way what?"

"No way we're going to the police."

"I think we should. We even got a photo of him. That could help."

"Listen, we're up here for some sun and fun and if we get

involved, this isn't going to be sun and fun. We'll have to be in court maybe and we'll be pissing off this hunk and we don't need to be looking over our shoulders for the next several years wondering if today is the day he gets his revenge."

"Guess you're right."

"Order us a couple more beers and I'll order a Smalley Burger for us to share. You start thinking about something else for a change, like that cute guy over there."

☞

Police Chief Vanderwall and one of his officers arrived at the Yacht Basin Marina. Sue Magliocco was with Nikki. Nikki saw the two officers walking up to *Bypassing Through*. She invited them aboard their yacht. Once inside the cabin, Nikki broke down and cried hysterically. She had heard of families who saw two people from the Army coming to the door in wartime or peacetime. She knew Will was dead, just as she knew it yesterday when she had the premonition. Sue held her and let her cry.

Chief Vanderwall told Nikki that a body matching Will's description had been found in Harbor Beach. He was sorry he had to tell her, but the police confirmed that the clothing matched what Will was wearing when Tom saw him yesterday afternoon. The body also fit the physical description.

Nikki continued to cry and to release emotions that had been lodged in her petite frame for the last several hours. She was thankful that she had the presence of mind to send Nicholas and Sherry back to Chicago.

After a few minutes she felt a bit better. Chief Vanderwall said that she'd need to identify the body. He said that he knew a private pilot who donates his time to helping victims in emergencies and that he'd be willing to fly the two of them to Harbor Beach.

Nikki agreed to this but wanted to call their daughter Harriet in Waukegan, Illinois. Harriet was a grief counselor with Hospice in Waukegan and although she'd now be the one in grief, she was also a rock in these kinds of situations.

While Nikki was adjusting to this news, Lou was arriving in Harbor Beach and introducing himself to Chief Billings. Just like South Haven, there was nothing to note except the cut wrist and the rope around the neck. Lou looked around and thought of Maggie's theory that the body was put in place by someone using scuba gear. He glanced left and right wondering where the land point was where the killer probably entered the water.

Lou joined Jeremy in interviewing some of the boaters and as in Manistee and South Haven, they didn't see or hear anything. Nobody was in the marina area that had been acting strangely or recognized as anyone who shouldn't be there.

Lou thought he'd made a long trip for no good reason. He was tired and didn't want to drive all the way back to Grand Haven that evening. He checked into the State Street Inn. Lou was not usually a bed and breakfast type person, but this quaint place seemed to call his name.

That evening Lou ate at Al's Restaurant. He returned to the Inn and called Carol to talk with her about their day. When they finished, Carol put Maggie on the line and Lou talked with her about what he had done. Maggie and Lou took a moment to discuss the case and realized they hadn't a clue about who was doing this and other than patterns of marina and medical people, they were a long way from solving this mess.

CHAPTER TEN

Sunday, July 12
Grand Haven and Harbor Beach, Michigan

Maggie planned to go to South Haven for a memorial service for Peter Verduin. She would drive there for the 1:30 service and then go home to Battle Creek. She had been away from home long enough. She enjoyed being with Carol and Lou, but like anyone, she missed the familiarity of her own home. She wanted to do some laundry, check her mail and be with her husband Tom who was expected back from a golf outing.

⌇

After enjoying a delicious breakfast at the State Street Inn, Lou went to church. He then picked up a copy of the Free Press and read it from cover to cover. The account of the murder was all old information to him, but it may be new to some readers.

Before heading back to Grand Haven, Lou decided to take one last trip to the marina to see if by chance he could pick up a clue of some sort. He wanted to make the trip to Harbor Beach worthwhile.

Trisha and Boots were back in their motel room. Trisha opened the *Detroit Free Press* to read the article about the murder in Harbor

Beach. She read it with much interest and noted that the police had no suspects but that the murder was very similar to those which had occurred in Manistee, Traverse City and South Haven.

Boots yawned and said, "All that late night partying wiped me out. I think I'll take a nap."

"Yeah, I'm kinda tired myself. Our late night living is taking its toll."

Boots fell asleep quite easily. Trisha jotted a note, "Have gone to town. Be back soon."

Trisha was happy that her friend had gone to sleep, as she was about to get involved in the marina murder.

⌒

After inspecting the marina area and finding nothing helpful, Lou decided to go to the Harbor Beach police station to express his appreciation to Chief of Police Billings before heading back to Grand Haven. While the two were talking, Lou glanced out the window and saw an attractive young woman jogging toward the front door. "Looks like you've got a visitor," Lou said.

"Yeah, and she looks concerned. Probably some domestic dispute. I hate these things. People sure do whatever they can to mess up other people's lives."

Trisha entered a bit out of breath.

"What's the problem?" Chief Billings asked.

"I've got to talk to someone about the marina murder."

"We're the right ones to talk to. I'm Jeremy Billings, chief of police here, and this is Lou Searing, a private investigator who is working with us."

"I sense I might be getting in this deep and I don't even want to be in it at all. I'm just in your town with an office friend and ...."

"Here, relax, take a deep breath, you're a stressed young woman. Sit down here. You want some coffee?"

"No thanks," Trisha said as she sat on the chair, crossing her legs.

"Now, slow down and tell us what you can," Chief Billings said.

"I think I know who the marina killer is."

"We sure want to know what you know," Lou said, taking a pen and paper from his pocket.

"I mean, I don't know his name, but he talked to my friend and me yesterday down at the marina when you guys found the body under the dock."

"He talked to you?" Jeremy asked.

"Yeah, and that's why I think he killed the guy."

"Because of something he said?"

"Yeah, he said, 'what's goin' on?' I said, 'Some kind of an accident at the dock in the marina.'

"Later he said, 'Yeah, a slit wrist is a sure sign of suicide. And, he knew it was a guy.' My friend and I didn't think anything of it. My friend embarrassed me by asking him to have his picture taken with me. She was flirting with him. He's got a great looking upper body, muscles bulging out of his shirt."

"You've got a picture of this guy?" Jeremy asked.

"Yeah. It's on the roll in the camera."

"Can we have that roll?" Chief Billings asked.

"Well, my friend is the problem in all of this. She didn't want me talking to you guys. Once she learns that I've been here, she'll have a cow."

"Well, I assure you, we appreciate it," Lou said.

"I was brought up to try and help out in situations like this."

"As Lou said, we appreciate it. Can we get that photo?" Jeremy asked again.

"My friend owns the camera and I don't know how she'll feel about it."

"Can't you develop the film? We'll pay for it," Chief Billings said. "Could you get doubles down at the One-hour Photo in town?"

"That's okay with me, but I don't think she'll go for it."

"This is a great tip and you could help us save other lives if we could see this guy," Lou said.

"I'll tell you what I'll do; I'll go back, finish the roll, offer to go to town to one hour. I'll get doubles and I'll see that you get the photo."

"Thanks, fine. For our information, what's your name?" Jeremy asked.

"I'm willing to help, but I think I'm going to listen to my friend on this. I really don't want to get involved any more than what I've told you. I don't mind telling you what we heard, and giving you a print of the photo of the guy, but I don't want to be in any court and speaking against this maniac. So, no name, just my story and a photo when I get it. Give me your business cards and I promise you'll get a photo."

Jeremy let her go after thanking her for the information and the promise of a photo. He pleaded once again for a way to contact her, but Trisha wouldn't share the information. Jeremy didn't press it because he felt he could learn about her from the motel when they checked out.

As Trisha left, Jeremy said, "Follow her, will you, Lou? I'm concerned about this and I don't want anything happening to her."

"Sure."

Lou immediately left and got in his car and pulled out trying to keep her in his sight as he pulled onto Route 142. He had to step on it a bit as she pushed it to the floor. A red light ahead allowed Lou to get a little closer. She approached the Huron Motel and pulled in. Lou stayed far enough back but he did see her enter the last room on the first floor. Lou took down her license number.

Trisha was pleased to see Boots still sleeping. She wound the film up, opened the camera, took the roll out and put in a new roll. Now she was free to have the set of prints developed. She'd have a set for Boots and she'd give the photo of the suspect to the police.

❦

Lou glanced at his watch and saw that it was early in the afternoon. He wondered what Maggie was experiencing at the memorial service for Mr. Verduin in South Haven.

Maggie parked her van in one of the slots reserved for people with disabilities. She remained in the parking lot area looking around realizing that she didn't need to get inside to get a seat, she was in it, and an usher would wheel her to any area in the funeral home that she wanted. It was probably because she was looking for a red pickup that she didn't see one. She was certain that it would appear. It had to be a pattern and since that is what Lou saw in Cadillac, that is what she expected. However, there wasn't to be any cemetery service. This was simply a memorial service. The body had been cremated. This memorial service was stipulated in Peter Verduin's will. To see that his wishes were followed, and to provide an opportunity for friends and family to gather to pay their respects, the service was scheduled for Sunday afternoon.

She glanced at her watch and saw that the service was about to begin. Most mourners were inside except for a few people hurrying along from the back of the funeral home parking lot. Maggie went into the funeral home and as predicted, the usher asked where she'd like to sit. "Near the back on the left side, please."

Maggie was positioned so she could see the entire group of people. Her chair put her a couple of inches higher than those seated so she really had a good view of all present.

The minister of the Hope Reformed Church rose to open the service with a prayer and a hymn. When it came time for comments from friends and relatives, Maggie noticed that a man from his yacht club got up and spoke eloquently of Peter's love of sailing and especially sailing on Lake Michigan. He made fun of the name of the boat, *Malpractice Benefits,* noting that over the years, he'd defended doctors and took more in fees than the total awards given to the plaintiffs.

He had just finished this thought when Maggie decided to leave the service and look at the guest book. She turned her wheelchair around and quietly left the mourners. She took the book down from the stand and glanced at each name. Not one name struck a chord with her but she didn't expect any name to have meaning. Studying the guest book was something she felt she should do while she was there. The perfect time to do this was when the service was going on as no one was around to sign it and no one would be curious why she would be carefully reviewing the book. Maggie's eyes went right over the name "Sara Prescott."

❧

Meanwhile back in Harbor Beach, Lou kept an eye on the motel room where Trisha entered. He called Chief of Police Billings to let him know that he was at the motel and that there was no activity. Jeremy told Lou that he had heard from Chief Vanderwall and that the small aircraft, piloted by Tom Howard, bringing Mrs. Harrison and himself to Harbor Beach was about a half-hour away. The plan was for Nikki to identify the body and then return to Holland.

Lou told Jeremy that he would monitor the motel room till something happened and then he'd be on his way to Grand Haven and to tell Manistee Chief of Police McFadden that he'd see him tomorrow. He said he'd deliver the message.

About five minutes later, the door opened and two women emerged from Room 34 at the Huron Motel. They got in their car and drove away, turning south on U.S. 25. Lou called Jeremy and told him what he had observed. He thanked Lou for his help. A few minutes later Lou pulled away and drove toward Grand Haven.

While Lou was on his way home, John drove Jake's pickup to Harrison where he dropped it off and picked up his own vehicle. The brothers shared a drink and discussed past success and future plans to murder the remaining members of the investment club. John was tired so he pulled out of town and headed for his home in Grand Ledge, a small town west of Lansing.

❧

Lou continued his journey to Grand Haven. He would be home in time to take a walk on the beach with Carol. As Lou drove along I-69, he tried to go over the past week in his mind. What a week it had been, three people dead, no solid clues except a red pickup, a muscular guy, and a photo in a camera yet to be developed and delivered. Lou made a mental note to follow up on Rich Hopkins, the young man in Cadillac who Mrs. Crawford said was unstable and might be involved. Actually, Lou realized that he should have looked into this earlier, but didn't.

Lou called Maggie on the car phone. She was safely in Battle Creek. She told Lou that she learned nothing at the memorial service. Lou thanked her for going anyway. He told her of the blond woman's belief that she had talked with the killer and that she had a photo of him.

Lou was tired when he pulled into his driveway at about 8 p.m. Carol greeted him with a kiss and a hug. She said that she had taken a walk with Samm along the shore's edge and missed him.

Lou and Carol sat down to a glass of iced tea and talked about their weekend. It was good to be together. They enjoyed having Maggie with them, but it was special just being together. They valued the time and were thankful for every minute they were in each other's presence. Lou wanted to walk on the beach, so Carol joined him. Under a half moon they walked arm in arm to the water's edge to take a deep breath, hold each other tight, and enjoy being together. It was a nice way to end the day.

CHAPTER ELEVEN

July 13, Monday
Grand Haven, Manistee
and Escanaba, Michigan

Lou was always up around 5:30, give or take 15 minutes, but this morning was different. Lou didn't wake up until almost eight and for once in quite a while felt he had a restful sleep. Lou smelled the coffee downstairs. Carol was not a coffee drinker but she would often brew a pot for Lou on those rare occasions when she awoke and went downstairs before he got up.

Lou put on his robe and went downstairs to greet Carol with a kiss, hug, and a back rub. Samm wanted a pet or two and the cats seemed to linger about his feet wanting to rub their cheeks on his feet. Having greeted all of the loves in his life, Lou sat down to some All-Bran cereal and toast. He picked up the paper and noted the lead stories. There was not much new as he had listened to a news station on the radio on his way home from Harbor Beach last evening.

"We've gotten two calls this morning."

"Chief McFadden?" Lou asked.

"No. Close. Detective Maguffin."

"Oh, what did he have to say?"

"He wanted me to tell you that Mrs. Harrison positively identified the body as being her husband. They flew back last evening. He also told me to tell you that they've set up a task force to try and solve these murders. I wrote down who is involved: you and Maggie, the Coast Guard, the Marina Association, the Chiefs of Police Association, the State Police and one or two other groups will be represented. They are going to have a think-tank meeting this afternoon at 2:00 in Manistee. He'd like it if you and Maggie, or at least you, could be there."

"Did you commit me or am I to call?"

"I committed you. I know we rarely do that for each other, but I couldn't imagine your saying 'No thanks.'"

"You're right. Good decision. I'll be there. I'll call Maggie and see if she wants to come up. My guess is she'll suggest I attend and let her know what happened."

"I already called her and briefed her and you're right, that's what she told me, you go and brief her later."

"Oh, you called?"

"Yes."

"Thanks, it's one less call I have to make. Did Maggie have anything else to say?"

"She was glad you were sleeping in. She hoped the extra winks would give you some grand idea for solving this mess."

"Don't I wish. Nothing came to me in a dream, if that's what she hoped. OK, the second call?"

"The second call was from Lora McComb in Manistee. She and Roy have invited us to stay with them."

"That's nice of them."

"She heard you were working on the murder investigation and thought we could visit. It would allow you to be closer to the case and they'd like to share their cottage. Roy rides a Gold Wing so you two could get lost in your motorcycle riding passions. Lora and I could talk about our days of teaching youngsters in East Lansing."

"Sounds like a good idea. Do you agree?" Lou asked.

"Sure. I like Lora and Roy and it would give us an opportunity to see their home."

"Let's accept with thanks and head up there."

"OK, I'll call her back and begin packing."

The phone rang. It had that ring that caused both to think, *this is going to be bad news*. Both Carol and Lou quickly looked at each other anticipating something very negative. Lou moved toward the phone and saw Carol shaking her head as if saying no to whatever he was about to hear.

"Hello. This is Lou Searing."

"Good morning, Lou! I was hoping to wake you up with this call. Nobody should sleep the day away."

"Hello, Maggie! You got good news or bad news?"

"Neutral, why did you ask?"

"Carol and I heard the phone and we had a feeling that we'd get some bad news."

"Sorry to disappoint you two. Listen, that task force that's meeting today. I've got some information for you."

"Shoot."

"Well, I called every public marina bordering the lakes on both sides of Michigan."

"Every marina," Lou asked, surprised because that would be quite an effort.

"Yeah, on Lakes Michigan and Huron. I got the list on the Internet along with phone numbers and times the harbormasters would be on duty."

"Why did you call them?"

"Well, it seemed to me that the only way to stop this killer is to identify all the potential victims so I asked each harbormaster to try and identify all the medical people currently staying in their marina and if any of them had plans to go, to tell me their next port of call."

"What did you learn?"

"There is no way a harbormaster can tell the occupation of a boater, but many knew people who came into their marinas frequently and by getting to know them, they learned that several are doctors. I'm faxing my report, but in summary, there are a lot of medical folks staying in marinas."

"Where, Maggie?"

"They're scattered throughout, no patterns there, but there are several marinas where they are not staying, so I think we've been able to narrow the number of possible places for a murder."

"Great, but remember, Will wasn't staying in Harbor Beach, he was taken there."

"Yes, but he was abducted in Holland."

"Correct."

"And, I'm now convinced that the red pickup is definitely involved. So, I suggest that every city that has a marina and every marina be on the lookout for a red Ford Ranger and stop every one that moves. The police should check out the driver and the contents of the vehicle, at least to the extent they can do this within the law. I'm predicting they'd find a wet suit, oxygen tank, face mask and snorkel inside, and maybe a list of future victims."

"Good work, Maggie."

"Well, the patterns, weak as they are, are these: marinas, medical folks, and a red pickup, so we simply have to narrow the field."

"I'll report and praise you at the meeting this afternoon."

"Good. Praise isn't necessary, but thanks."

"Sure you don't want to come up and give the report yourself?"

"No. I'm staying put for awhile. I love being with you and Carol, but living out of a suitcase and away from my universally designed house, well, it's simply a lot more comfortable for me to be in my own home, as I'm sure you can imagine."

"I understand. We've got phones, faxes and e-mail to keep in touch. We've got to have your mind in solving this Maggie, you know that."

"You're kind."

"Thanks, I'll look for the fax. Thanks a lot, Maggie. Oh, Carol and I are going to be visiting with friends up in Manistee for a few days. I'll call later with their phone number."

"Thanks."

The fax arrived before Lou and Carol left for Manistee. Lou took a Michigan map and a magic marker and highlighted the marinas where Maggie found medical folks. Lou copied enough for the number of people coming to the meeting and put all of the papers in his attaché case.

As Carol and Lou were on their way to Manistee, Jake and John were having a telephone conversation. "It's time to ditch the red pickup," John said with conviction. "As I told you yesterday, I may have been seen in Harbor Beach."

"The phony license plates should have confused anyone who's looking for the vehicle's owner," Jake said.

"Yeah, but pulling into a town in this vehicle is just carrying around a bull's eye in an archery contest. Gotta ditch it," John said with conviction.

"OK, not a problem."

"Will all the scuba diving equipment fit in whatever you're going to drive, Jake?"

"Not a problem. I'll be driving a white Silverado. My friend said he won't be needing it for awhile. The equipment will be in the bed of the truck with a tarp over it and well tied down."

"Does your friend suspect anything?"

"Of course not. No one will ever know we're behind the murders and my friend will have his truck returned without ever knowing what I used it for."

"Good!"

"Hey, while we're on the phone, we've got to change our tactics," Jake said.

"Change our tactics?" his brother responded, a bit puzzled.

"Yeah, the cops have got to be covering these marinas. It's time to quit using the downstate marinas. If I were a good investigator I'd have a lot of surveillance in place. These cops and investigators are sharp and we need to stay one step ahead of them."

"Now what?" John asked.

"My research tells me that Dr. Mihalik will be coming into Escanaba soon. I'm heading there and I'll be in touch. I'll need you to take the body to Alpena." As Jake hung up the phone he had a—

FLASHBACK: Alpena was the last place our family went on a vacation together. We rented a boat and lived on it for a week. My dad was always busy but Mom convinced him to take a week off and get away from the grind of being a young physician. We stayed in the marina there and had a great time. About the only fond memory I have of us as a family before Dad died was that vacation in Alpena. Now, I wanted a lasting memory of one of my victims floating in the marina.

※

Carol and Lou pulled up to the McComb cottage located in a relatively new development of condos and cottages between downtown Manistee and Lake Michigan. It was a beautiful place and close to the Lake Michigan beach on the north side of the channel. The channel is a short walk away and an ideal place for watching the freighters coming and going. The McCombs showed the Searings their home and made them feel very comfortable. Lou made it clear that he may be getting calls in the middle of the night, and that he may have to leave on a moment's notice. The McCombs understood that Lou's first priority was solving the crimes.

To celebrate their arrival, Lora McComb had made an apple pie using apples from the twenty or so apple trees growing in their complex. The pie was out of this world especially with a ball of vanilla ice cream sitting on the side. They all enjoyed the pie and coffee while they caught up on each other's lives.

※

Lou learned that Will's funeral would be held in Chicago mid-week. He decided not to attend. It might be a mistake, but the distance and other activities going on in Michigan led him to want to be close in case something broke. Will's son-in-law would take *Bypassing Through* back to Chicago once the police released it.

The task force meeting was a good think-tank type of meeting. Chief McFadden was clearly the leader. Statistics were presented and all evidence put forth. Mickey asked Lou to share what he knew and so he did, probably giving them more detail than they wanted or expected. Lou gave them the information from Maggie which they found extremely helpful.

The meeting ended with plans for each to continue information sharing and alerting every marina, posting signs, pulling over every suspicious red Ford Ranger in marina cities or elsewhere.

Mickey thanked all for coming and expressed the belief that the case would be wrapped up soon.

⌇

In Horse Cave, Kentucky, Trisha took the roll of film to a One-hour Photo Processing Center. She asked for doubles and waited for the film to be developed. She took the photo of the muscular guy and herself and put it in an envelope addressed to Chief of Police, Jeremy Billings in Harbor Beach, Michigan. She affixed a sticky note which read, "Here is the photo I promised to send you." There was no return address on the envelope. She dropped it into the mail box and felt that she had fulfilled her commitment to send the photo. The photo had the date and the time it was taken printed in the lower right corner.

⌇

In Escanaba, a community on the shores of Little Bay De Noc in the southern part of Michigan's beautiful Upper Peninsula, Dr. Sherry Mihalik, a pulmonary specialist and her husband Frank were pulling into the Escanaba Municipal Marina. They were on their way to Milwaukee from an enjoyable few days in the Les Chenaux Island area, a bit north and east of Mackinac Island. The couple enjoyed boating and were on their honeymoon. Sherry had been under a lot of stress recently due to the wedding planning and a malpractice suit. A patient believed Sherry had misread a chest X-ray, telling the family there was no sign of cancer when in fact the lung was cancerous.

Sherry had documented proof that she had advised the patient that the test results indicated the potential for a problem and immediately scheduled a biopsy. The family couldn't accept this potentially deadly diagnosis and refused to have the lesion biopsied. Eventually the patient was coughing up blood. Her family took her to the hospital but it was too late. The cancer had spread, and she could not be saved.

Sherry was innocent and most realized it, but she became the target of a law suit. The family contacted one of those attorneys who specialize in filing accident claims.

Sherry's yacht was named *Breathing Easy* and was a 40-foot Catalina sailboat. She and her husband had recently purchased the new boat and this was their maiden voyage, a chance to start anew; a new husband, a new pleasure craft and a new summer day to make it almost perfect.

Sherry had heard about the marina murders as most everyone had. By now, it was common knowledge all around the Great Lakes. People were on the lookout. Calls came into the command center in Manistee from people who were thinking that anyone they didn't know must be the killer. There was a lot of paranoia, but with good reason given the brutal murders that had occurred with no end in sight.

It was Sherry who caught on to what was happening. She knew the victims to date. She had lost touch with all of them over the past fifteen years but it was Sherry who saw a pattern and the pattern was the investment club. She didn't know who was doing the killing, but she thought that revenge could be a motive. With that thought in mind, she tried to reach Edith Haire in Indiana, Cris Gallow in Bay City, and Philip Heyboer in Michigan City, but didn't have any luck. She didn't leave a message, only made a mental note to try and reach them later. But, if she were right, she needed to be very cautious and she promised herself to be just that.

Sherry and Frank Mihalik had called the harbormaster on Channel 68 to request a slip for two nights. Their request had been granted. When they checked in at the marina the harbormaster reminded them of the problems downstate and asked them to be extra cautious. "We're not expecting any problem," the harbormaster said. "All of the murders have occurred downstate and nothing leads me to believe we'll have any problems, but to be on the safe side, please be extra cautious and let me or the police know of any suspicious persons or activities."

"We sure will. This is terrible," Sherry said, full of compassion for her medical colleagues who had been murdered. "It always amazes me that something like this can go on in a day and age when we've got such technology and skilled means of apprehending these people."

"I know, but apparently this killer is very shrewd and uncaring. Nothing will happen here, but please be cautious. Welcome to Escanaba. If you need any directions or anything, just ask me."

"Thanks for the warm welcome. We like Escanaba. I was here when I was a little girl. We'll have a good couple of days here."

Sherry and Frank returned to *Breathing Easy,* having no idea that the killer was on Aronson Island directly across from the marina, focusing high-powered binoculars on them.

Meanwhile, the Mackinac Bridge Authority had been advised to be on the lookout for a red pickup. Jake easily went through the Bridge toll booth in his white Silverado. No one suspected that Jake had moved into Michigan's Upper Peninsula.

ॐ

It was mid-afternoon and Lou felt the time was right to look up this young man named Richard Hopkins in Cadillac. Lou didn't want to make the trip to Cadillac, so he went to the Manistee police department and asked Mickey to contact the chief of police in Cadillac and to allow him to ask a few questions. He did so and the Police Chief, Ron Abbott was on the line in a matter of seconds.

"Chief Abbott, as Mickey has told you, we're looking into the marina murders. I have a tip that a young man in your community may be a potential suspect."

"Who's that?"

"His name is Richard Hopkins."

"Yeah, Rich. He's a suspect in most anything that happens. He's been a problem in our town for years. How did his name come up?"

"I was in Cadillac for the funeral for James Rothchild and while talking to a local citizen, his name came up. Apparently, the Hopkins and their neighbors had not been on good terms since the younger Hopkins boy drowned."

"That's right. Rich never recovered from that tragedy. In fact, most think it had quite a bit to do with his personality and his being somewhat rebellious. Others think it is in his hormones or in his genes. We'll never know."

"What can you tell me about this guy, Chief?"

"Well, his file is pretty thick."

"Serious crimes?"

"We've arrested Richard for drunk driving, petty theft, extortion, and assault and battery. He works out at the local YMCA and is all caught up in the muscle beach crowd, you know, always gotta have a bigger bicep."

"Does he drive a red pickup?" Lou asked.

"Yeah, he's got a pickup. Tarp over the back."

"Does he scuba dive?"

"Can't help you with that. Never heard of him doing that, but I suppose he could. The Hopkins have that cottage on the lake, as you know. They have a lot of money, Lou. Kid always had a silver spoon in his mouth."

"Can you track this guy for me for a few days?"

"Sure we can do that. You want him questioned?"

"No, I just want to know if he is in town and what he's been up to."

"I know for a fact that he's gone now and has been for awhile."

"You know where?"

"No, he hangs out at a bar when he's in town and I go in there often, got some informants there, and I'll often see Rich, but I haven't seen him in a week or so, and that means he's out of town."

"OK; well, for now, I'd like to know when you see Rich."

"I'll handle it, Lou. I'll call you when I learn anything."

"Good. Thanks for your help, Chief."

"You're welcome."

THE MARINA MURDERS

Lou called Maggie to report his conversation with Chief Abbott in Cadillac. Maggie said she would try to see how much of Lou's information would fit with the patterns. She didn't see anything at the moment, but perhaps the information would turn into something helpful.

Their day ended with Carol and Lou walking to town with the McCombs for an ice cream cone. The four of them had taken a beach walk and enjoyed the quiet and the cool breeze coming off the Lake. While resting on the McComb porch, Lou's cell phone rang. It was their son Scott in Grand Rapids. He was asking about coming over with his family to enjoy the beach on Saturday. The grand boys loved the water, of course, and the fishing from shore was always fun although fish rarely if ever met the worm. Lou and Carol would be back in Grand Haven by then and would look forward to seeing Scott, Patti, and their sons Ben, Nick, and Jack.

CHAPTER TWELVE

Tuesday, July 14
Escanaba, Manistee, and
St. Ignace, Michigan

Sherry and Frank Mihalik awoke to a warm summer day in Escanaba. Sherry wanted to go to some shops to find a birthday present for her mother. She also needed to do some laundry. The laundry facility at the marina was closed for repairs so the harbormaster offered to drive Sherry down to the Econ-o-Wash on Ludington Street. Frank planned to read following a long jog. He was a runner and while he loved the life on the water, he longed for a long run on terra firma. The marina area at Escanaba was perfect for it with at least a mile of bike path around the water treatment plant and over to Aronson Island.

The two enjoyed breakfast on their yacht and discussed how they would spend the day. They agreed to go their separate ways and meet at the Downtowner for lunch.

Sherry gathered up the clothes that needed to be washed. While she walked to the marina office, Jake was parked a hundred feet away with his binoculars fixed on her. If she was going to do laundry, the closest place was the Econ-o-Wash and he'd plan on meeting her there.

Before accepting the harbormaster's invitation for a ride to the laundromat, she purchased a *USA Today* at the marina office so she'd have something to read while the clothes went around and around in a dryer.

Frank stretched for a few minutes and then prepared for his long run. As he was putting on his Nike's and making sure his ID tag was around his neck, Sherry was putting clothes in the washer. Jake walked into the laundromat with a basket of clothes. He set it down in front of a washer three down from Sherry. He methodically went through procedures, placing clothes in the washer, putting in a cup of soap, and feeding the machine with quarters. He looked over at Sherry and said, "Good morning."

"Hi."

"You'd think we could find better things to do with our time than washing clothes," Jake said with a smile.

"I agree, but it's a job that needs to be done."

"You look like you might be a visitor?" Jake asked.

"Yes, a marina visitor."

"You folks bring us a lot of cash and it helps our economy. Thanks for coming into port. We're a friendly community."

"Oh, I know, I used to come up here from Milwaukee as a child with my parents. I still come back. I like this place, feel connected to it, if you can understand that."

"Yeah, I feel that way about some places, too."

"Hope you get to enjoy the day outside of this hot and noisy laundromat."

"I plan to. Thanks."

The two smiled. Sherry took a seat and picked up the *USA Today*. Jake went out to his truck and drove to the T and T Hardware Store only to return with a hunting knife which he put under the seat in his truck. He was gone about ten minutes.

Jake sat down three seats to the right of Sherry. He picked up an old *Popular Science* magazine and waited for the washer to finish its cycle.

Ironically Sherry was reading an article about Michigan's serial killer who was terrorizing boaters all along the Michigan shoreline. The article noted a muscular suspect driving a red pickup. The guy nearby was quite muscular. She saw him leave and noted that he was not driving a red pickup so it couldn't be him and she need not worry. Little did she know that she was sitting a few feet away from a man who was planning to kill her. While Jake was reading *Popular Science,* he had a—

> FLASHBACK: My mom had said that the leader of the investment club was a young medical student named Sherry Tomsik. Her father was a stockbroker and taught her everything she knew. Mom said that Dad told her that it was Will Harrison who came up with the idea to bring other doctors into the club to cut their losses once they discovered they had lost millions on the marina land development project. Sherry was in full support of the suggestion.

Jake turned toward Sherry and said, "You wouldn't happen to know of a doctor in town being a visitor and all, would you?"

"What's the matter?"

"My wife's really sick. We can't afford to pay a doctor or go to a hospital. I'm out of work right now and we're having a rough time of it. My friend let me borrow his pickup to do some laundry. But, back to my wife, her fever is bad and she seems kind of hysterical."

"I'm sure if you take her to emergency, they'll treat her. They have plans to help people who don't have resources."

"Yeah, but she won't go, afraid she'll die, she says."

"I just thought if you knew of some doctor, I could convince him to stop in and just take a look at her. I do some remodeling when I can find work and I could return the favor by helping him at his home or something."

"Where do you live?"

"Two streets over."

"Is she alone now?"

"Well, yeah, but my four-year-old is there."

"This wash cycle will take awhile. You drive me over and I'll look at her."

"Are you a doctor?" Jake asked.

"Yes."

"Really? Oh, my God. This is great. Thanks a lot."

"I can't treat her, but maybe I can give you some advice as to what to do next."

"Oh, thanks a lot. Imagine that, doing my wash right next to a doctor who can help my wife."

Sherry got in the cab of the pickup. Jake entered, pushed down the all-door lock and once again, a fly was stuck in the sticky web of his trap.

⌇

The Escanaba Marina harbormaster read the new alert advising all medical personnel with yachts to be contacted and advised of this crisis. He knew he had to contact Dr. Sherry Mihalik and Dr. Randy Wisner, a plastic surgeon. Randy was sleeping in his yacht *Nip and Tuck,* but Sherry was not on board *Breathing Easy*.

The harbormaster recalled taking Sherry to town. He called the Escanaba police and told them to check the Econ-o-Wash Laundromat.

The police car pulled up to the laundromat and two officers exited the cruiser. They entered and looked around, but didn't see anyone who fit the description of Dr. Mihalik. They did see a *USA Today* newspaper beside a chair and a *Popular Science* magazine opened and sitting by the newspaper. Across from the two chairs were empty plastic baskets and when they opened the washers they found two with clothes in them, three washers apart. But, there was no evidence of anyone in or near the laundromat. They called for an officer to monitor the comings and goings of people but after an hour, no one came to claim the laundry or the baskets or the *USA Today*.

During the investigation at the laundromat the forensic technicians did find a hair sample in both laundry baskets. They also heard from an older man who said he saw a lady doing some laundry and talking to a muscular guy also doing laundry. He said the guy left in a white pickup and returned about fifteen minutes later. He saw the two go out to the pickup and that's the last he saw of either of them.

The police put out a be on the lookout bulletin for a white pickup, make or size unknown and two people, muscular man and a woman, middle-aged, brown hair. The State Police made sure the Mackinac Bridge Authority received the BOL bulletin.

⌁

When Frank returned from his jog, his heart skipped a beat when he saw the harbormaster and Escanaba's Chief of Police Loren Haskins standing near his yacht. He had a feeling that his life was about to change. He stopped jogging and walked up to the men, bracing his emotions for what might be coming.

"Dr. Mihalik?"

"Yes. What's the problem?"

"Sorry to tell you, sir, we think your wife is missing," Chief Haskins said.

"Missing? She just went to the laundromat."

"Yes, and we've been there. We found a laundry basket and clothes in the washing machine. We'll need you to identify the clothes, but we think they belong to the two of you."

"I'm sure there is some explanation for this. Maybe she went into town fully expecting to come back and finish the work."

"We sure hope so, Dr. Mihalik, and maybe that's what we'll find, but we want you to know that this doesn't look good."

Frank went onto *Breathing Easy,* changed his clothes and with the police headed for town for questioning and to see if he could recognize the clothes at the laundromat.

As would be expected, the police suspected Frank in this kidnapping. But, after talking with him for quite awhile and finding him to be very cooperative, the police were convinced that Frank was not a suspect in the disappearance of his wife. He promised to be available at any time he would be needed and that he would report any information that may come to his attention. He was free to go.

Intense guilt engulfed him as well. Sherry had suggested on Mackinac Island that they go home to Milwaukee. There would be many more sailing opportunities. But, Frank thought leaving a honeymoon because of a few unfortunate murders downstate was acting out of fear instead of staying the course. Had he followed Sherry's instinct they would be happily married in Milwaukee right now.

Of course, there was the possibility that Sherry was alive. His gut seemed to tell him to hold onto hope, but he had to accept the probable reality that Sherry would soon be found with a rope around her neck, her wrist slit and tied to a piling under a dock in some marina.

Frank eventually reached a point when the reality hit him like a bomb. Sherry, his bride of only a week, was the latest victim in the marina murders. He stood on the edge of the dock in the marina and fought intense anger and sadness. He sat down and burst forth with uncontrollable sobbing and disbelief.

ॐ

It was 1:15 p.m. when the white pickup approached the toll booth on the St. Ignace side of the Mackinac Bridge, the five-mile bridge linking the Lower and Upper Peninsulas of Michigan.

The toll booth worker glanced at the BOL alert and then saw the white pickup five vehicles away. White pickups are a dime a dozen so she waited to get a better look. As the vehicle came alongside her booth she noted that no woman was inside but the man was muscular and so most of the BOL was in place. She picked up the phone and said, "I've got a white pickup in my line with a single male occupant. You may want this checked out."

"I'll call the State Police. Get the license number as it pulls through," her supervisor replied.

"Will do."

The white pickup pulled to a stop. A muscular arm with two one-dollar bills was outstretched.

"Hello," the toll booth worker said, taking the money.

"Hi."

"Have a good day," the toll taker said, as she dropped two quarters into Jake's hand. She looked to her left as Jake pulled ahead and noted an Illinois license plate, QWA-4569.

Within seconds a State Trooper pulled out of the post and entered the flow of traffic heading over the Bridge. The dispatcher sent word to the Mackinaw City police on the south side of the Bridge asking for a backup.

The State Trooper wouldn't pull over the vehicle on the Bridge. It would back up traffic and cause a lot of congestion which would hamper back up if it was needed. A Trooper would pull him over in Mackinaw City or shortly down I-75.

Jake looked in the rearview mirror and there was the blue Michigan State Police vehicle with a red flashing light. He pulled over and took a deep breath. He knew he had to be quick and clear in responding to the Trooper's questions. Jake knew that his fake license, registration and plates would pass scrutiny. His only fear was stammering on a Trooper's question or giving any clue that he wasn't Jim Simmons from Illinois.

The Trooper approached the vehicle as a backup patrol officer from the Mackinaw City Police pulled up behind the State Police vehicle. The officer stood behind the white pickup ready to respond to any quick movement or aggression by the driver.

"Mornin' officer. Speeding on the Bridge? Is that it?"

"No, we're on the lookout for a vehicle and occupant and you match the description of the driver."

"On the lookout for what?" Jake asked.

"A vehicle that matches the description of this pickup. It was involved in an incident in the Upper Peninsula. I need to see your license, registration, and proof of insurance."

Jake handed the documents to the officer. So far, the confrontation was playing itself out just as planned and rehearsed. Now all he had to do was play a good Jim Simmons from Joliet, Illinois.

The Trooper checked the vehicle license plate and registration and found his license was up to date and the computer indicated that Mr. Simmons was a citizen with a clean record. It appeared that the white pickup with Mr. Simmons was definitely not involved in the kidnapping of the woman in Escanaba.

The Trooper was experienced and had dealt with a lot of crafty individuals and because the BOL spoke of a white pickup and a muscular man and because it had been in the Upper Peninsula, the Trooper decided to question Jake.

"Where you coming from, Mr. Simmons."

"Sault Ste. Marie."

"What were you doing there?"

"I was gambling at the casino."

"Who were you with?"

"Nobody. Just taking a vacation in your beautiful state."

"A lot of casinos between Joliet and the Soo. Why that one?"

"Oh, yeah, well, I didn't come up here just to gamble. My old man used to work on freighters and often told me about the locks and I wanted to see 'em so I took a trip up here."

"Would it be okay if I took a look in the bed of your pickup?" the Trooper asked.

"Sure. Want me to unsnap the covering?"

"Yeah."

Jake got out and unsnapped some of the covering. The Trooper looked in and saw nothing and that concerned him. Why would a guy on vacation not have a suitcase or some type of luggage? the Trooper thought. He did not see any luggage in the front seat either. But there was nothing of note in the bed of the pickup.

Jake returned to the cab of his pickup. "What did the guy you're lookin' for do, Officer?"

"Missing person incident. How come you've got no luggage?" the officer asked, carefully watching Jake to see how he responded.

"I drove up yesterday and am going back today. I gambled most of the night, took a few catnaps in the lounge. You can see that I didn't shave. I had no need for any luggage."

"Have you been to Escanaba at any point in your trip?"

"Escawhat?"

"Escanaba. West of here a few hours."

"Never heard of the place to be honest. Nope. Up 75 to the Soo and back down is all."

"Have you ever heard of a Doctor Mihalik?"

"No, sir. Never heard of her."

"You are free to go, Mr. Simmons. Thank you for answering my questions."

"Hope you find whoever you're looking for," Jake said, very relieved that he had passed the test.

"Have a good day, Mr. Simmons."

The Trooper walked back and thanked the Mackinaw City officer for the backup. The two chatted for a few minutes before each went their separate ways. The Trooper knew that there was no way that this guy from Illinois would know that Dr. Mihalik was a woman, but he had no reason to hold him, so let him go.

Once free to go, Jake drove back over the Bridge and went directly to the hunting cabin to get the dead body of Sherry Mihalik and return to the Lower Peninsula, going through the same toll booth so that this time there would be no report and a pull-over. Or at least he hoped that is what would happen.

⚜

While Jake, masqueraded as Jim Simmons from Illinois, was on his way to the Mackinac Bridge, a call came into the Mackinac County sheriff's office.

"I'm callin' to report something I seen that has me concerned."

"What's that?"

"I'm kind of a hermit, living out in the woods. I came into the gas station to make this call."

"What you got for me?"

"I seen a pickup truck come down this road near my place and it pulled up to a deer huntin' cabin on my road. The cabin belongs to a priest downstate. It wasn't him. I watched this guy movin' stuff into the cabin. He'd have no idea I was lookin' at him."

"What'd you see?"

"I seen him take stuff out of a white pickup, looked like diving underwater stuff. You know, them fins, air tank, stuff like that. Then it looked like he took a body into the cabin. I can't be sure about that, but it sure looked like a body."

"Did you go to the cabin when the guy left in the pickup?"

"No, sir. Thought I'd call you guys, just to make sure. I'd want the priest to call you if someone came into my place."

"Where's this cabin?"

"It's on Gamble Road near East Lake."

"Can I have your name?"

"Cliff Feess."

"Thanks, Cliff. Can you guide a deputy into your area?"

"Yeah, I can do that."

"Where are you now?"

"I'm in Brevort at the Mobil gas station."

"OK, you stay there till I can get a deputy sheriff dispatched to that gas station. Then we'd appreciate it if you would lead the officer to that cabin."

"OK, will do."

"Thanks, Mr. Feess."

⚮

All was relatively quiet in Manistee. Lou had not heard about the missing Sherry Mihalik yet. He took the opportunity for some peace around the investigation to write more of his book. The joy in writing was wonderful. Telling the story of the previous case gave him time to reflect on what he and Maggie did that was right and what they did that was wrong. It was sort of like playing eighteen holes of golf in his mind knowing that an eight-iron would have given him ten yards and put the ball on the green back on the seventh hole.

Maggie was working behind the scenes. This was a strange case in that the murders were happening all over Michigan and as yet they couldn't predict where the killer would strike next. She was content to be at home in Battle Creek and to put her intelligence toward discovering the pattern, the motive, and the way to get out in front of the case and allow the criminal to come to them.

When Lou needed a break from writing at home, he'd get up, usually disturb Samm or one of the cats, Luba and Millie, and walk to the bay windows in his second floor writing studio. As he looked out the windows, he saw Lake Michigan and the yachts moving up and down the Lake. The scenic view before him in the summer would give him a relaxing view of a world that always held fascination and intrigue.

Lou did the same as a guest at the McComb cottage. He couldn't look out of bay windows, but he stepped outside and after a short walk was on the warm sandy beach looking out onto beautiful Lake Michigan.

Lou's cell phone rang. It was Harbor Beach Police Chief Jeremy Billings.

"The photo arrived from the lady in Kentucky."

"That's good. What do you have?"

"Good looking guy, mid-twenties, looks to be a weight lifter."

"Finally, a solid lead. Can I get a copy of the photo?"

"It's being faxed to you as we talk. I'm also sending a copy to Chief McFadden and I expect him to distribute it however he thinks best."

"Wait, I almost forgot, I'm not home. I'm visiting friends in Manistee. I'll go into town and get a copy from Chief McFadden and then I'll send it on to Maggie."

"OK. I've got a feeling this is going to bring us close to nailing this guy."

"Yup, first big clue. Mickey will see that this gets to every marina and every law enforcement office by the end of the day. Thanks and I guess we've got to thank the lady in Kentucky. Wish we knew who she was."

"I do," Chief Billings replied. I tracked her down with her car license plate number. I'm keeping it to myself because she wanted her privacy. She was nice enough to give us a photo, I don't want her harassed."

"Thanks for the call, Jeremy."

THE MARINA MURDERS

The deputy sheriff's cruiser pulled up to the Mobil station in Brevort. The deputy greeted Cliff Feess and then followed him about fourteen miles over the back roads of Mackinaw County. After what seemed to be an eternity, the two cars pulled into Cliff's driveway. Cliff got out of his old car and approached the deputy who also had exited his car.

"That's the place where I seen the guy taking stuff from his pickup and goin' inside," Cliff said, pointing to a cabin a hundred yards or so down the road.

"Thanks, Cliff. I'll take a look."

The deputy backed out of the driveway and slowly approached the cabin. He parked out on the side of the road. He looked all about him thinking that someone could have a deer rifle trained on him. It was deathly quiet and the deputy was convinced that no one was in the area. There was no vehicle and no movement of any kind.

The deputy approached the cabin, choosing first to walk around it again making sure he wouldn't be surprised by anyone hiding out back or in a shed, for example. Nothing but quiet.

The door was open and he went in and found an empty cabin. There were signs that someone had been there in the last few hours. Footprints were here and there and the dusty floor had several areas where it looked like something had either been placed on the floor or dragged across it. The place was dirty with mice droppings in the kitchen area.

The deputy returned to the outside and saw wide tire marks and some footprints in the driveway. Someone had stopped by within the past few hours. The deputy sat in his cruiser and wrote out a report providing detail of what he had observed. He then stopped briefly to talk to Cliff, letting him know that he had not seen any evidence of any underwater diving equipment, a body, or anything.

"That's strange. I'm gettin' up there in years, but I wasn't dreamin', sheriff. I seen a guy cartin' stuff into that cabin."

"I don't doubt it, Mr. Feess. The place is vacant now, that's all."

"Very strange."

"Listen, please keep an eye on the place and let us know if you see any more activity there, will you?"

"Yeah."

"We appreciate it. Thanks for taking the time to drive into town and report this."

Cliff shook his head a bit embarrassed for bothering the police to come all the way out there to find nothing.

❧

As Lou had predicted, Mickey did see that the photo got out to every marina and law enforcement office by nightfall. Almost every marina put the picture on a flyer with a plea to be on the lookout for this person and if seen, to report the sighting to the police.

Frank Mihalik looked at the flyer and instantly before him was the man suspected of taking the life of his bride, an incredibly gifted physician.

Frank was emotionally a wreck. He thought he should stay in Escanaba in case Sherry would be found or miraculously appear. On the other hand, he believed that his bride was not in the area or she would have contacted him. Frank's comfort; friends, family, and familiar surroundings, were in Milwaukee. If Sherry was found, he would fly to Escanaba and be there within an hour. He wanted to go home and so he chose to leave.

Frank went outside and untied the yacht from its pilings, started the engine, and slowly exited. As he pulled out, Frank got on the radio, hailed the Escanaba marina harbormaster. When he got finished with the correct contact procedures, Frank said, "I've got to get out of here. I can't take being where Sherry was kidnapped. The memory of us being on this boat and now being alone, we've got to leave. Thanks."

"I'm sorry, Dr. Mihalik," the harbormaster replied. "Have a safe journey."

The harbormaster recorded the call. It wasn't normal procedure, but with all of the murders and with someone missing from his marina he felt it best to have a recording of any calls coming in. There may be some confidentiality and ethical questions in the practice, but it was a precaution and one he felt he could justify.

Several hours before *Breathing Easy* headed south to Milwaukee, Jake had returned to the cabin near the home of Cliff Feess, and put the diving equipment back in the bed of the pickup. He also returned the body of Sherry Mihalik to the back of the pickup, pulled the tarpon up and snapped it clear around the perimeter of the bed. He made sure there was no evidence of his being in the cabin and then left. He decided not to go back toward U.S.2 thinking he might pass some cop car that may be patrolling the main highway between the Bridge and Escanaba.

He made his way over to I-75 and then headed south to the Bridge making sure he stayed in the lane where he was spotted before. If the shifts hadn't changed, he'd be recognized by the toll worker who brought him to the attention of the authorities. This time he had no problem. He paid his $1.50 fee and proceeded south over the Bridge.

When he got to the other side, he pulled into the Shell station at the first exit. He got out of his white pickup, put in fifteen dollars worth of gas, then went inside to buy a bag of M&Ms. Then John got into the vehicle and proceeded east with the destination being the Alpena marina at the entrance to the Thunder Bay River Channel. Jake, in John's truck continued south on I-75 to Harrison.

ॐ

Jake decided not to call Father Murphy to seek forgiveness. Not being forgiven previously was a slap in the face. If he wasn't given forgiveness for killing others, he wouldn't be forgiven for killing Dr. Mihalik. But, for some reason he wanted his friend to know that he was being successful. He called and once again, Father Murphy was not in. The housekeeper at the rectory said that he had been gone for a couple of days and she didn't know where he was or when he would be back. Jake left a message on his answering machine. "Bless me Father, for I have sinned. Number five is no longer with us." Tuesday slowly became Wednesday.

CHAPTER THIRTEEN

Wednesday, July 15
Alpena and Grand Haven, Michigan
Michigan City, Indiana

In the middle of the night, wearing a wet suit, fins and a snorkeled mask and with a scuba diving tank on his back, John slipped into the water and began his swim to the Alpena marina with Sherry Mihalik in tow. As the others before her, she was submerged by vest weights and she also had the buoyancy compensator so she wouldn't sink more than a foot under the surface of the water. For some reason only a few boats were moored in the marina on this mid-week night.

John swam under the water and quietly approached the dock. When he arrived at the dock, he took the rope and tied Sherry's body to a piling. He took the knife Jake bought in Escanaba and slit Sherry's right wrist. Once again, Jake told John to do this. He couldn't figure out why, but Jake was very smart and there had to be some logical explanation.

Satisfied that his work was complete with the body being secured to the piling, John looked in the direction of his truck and saw no evidence of life. He silently swam to shore. He got out of the water and quickly put his equipment in the bed of the pickup. He put on his clothes and left the marina area. He reached into the glove compartment and took out a notebook and a pen. He opened the spiral notebook and beside the name Sherry Mihalik, *Breathing Easy,*

Escanaba, he put a check mark. At the same time he looked at the sixth name, Dr. Edith Haire, *Skinny Dippin',* Oscoda, Michigan. He also used his cell phone to call Jake. When he answered John simply said, "She's floating."

ᴄ⌒

The sun came up in Alpena. It would be a warm one and tourists would enjoy a day of boating, fishing, swimming, and merchants hoped that folks would be in a shopping mood as motorists made their way up and down the coast of eastern Michigan.

John had spent the night sleeping for a few hours in Jake's borrowed Silverado in the MICH-E-KE-WIS Park that thankfully had no ordinance prohibiting overnight parking. He was not alone. A few other campers were in the park as well. All the slots had been taken at area campgrounds so the overflow went to the city park and while there was no water or electricity, the vehicles could park there and campers could sleep.

John awoke, used the public bathroom to splash water on his face and to urinate. As he was walking out of the bathroom, he looked into the face of a middle-aged man who had been sleeping in one of the campers in the park. The first thing that the man thought was, *I've seen that face before. Maybe it was on TV, maybe in a restaurant, maybe while walking through town last evening after dinner.* The image stayed with the man.

It continued to bother him as to where he had seen the face. But, the more he tried to recall it, nothing came to him.

John realized that he had forgotten to put on his disguise when he wandered into the restroom. John left the city park and drove to the marina to look over at the dock, under which floated the body of Sherry Mihalik. He got out of his pickup, disguise in place, and walked along the marina until he saw a poster warning boaters of the marina maniac and there for the first time he saw the photo that had been taken in Harbor Beach. He realized he could be instantly spotted so he immediately turned and went back to the white pickup.

John decided to leave town immediately. He'd not get to enjoy the community reaction to his work, but with his picture around the marina, he couldn't afford to be anywhere near the victim.

As John was driving south on U.S.23, the man who passed him leaving the bathroom, realized that he'd seen the man in the poster of the marina maniac. He was sitting in his camper with his wife when it occurred to him. "That marina killer was in the bathroom here at the park this morning."

"A killer here in the park," his wife said, finding her husband's claim a shock.

"I'm sure of it. I looked right at him and he was a big muscular guy. He looked just like the guy in the poster we seen all around town."

"You calling the cops?"

"Yeah, I think I've got to."

"You could drive over there. We're ready to pull out. Or, I think the state police post is on the edge of town. You could go to them."

"Yeah, let's do that as we leave town."

"I wouldn't take too much time though. Every minute we wait that murderer could be getting away."

"Yeah, let's go now."

The camper pulled away from the city park and headed to the state police post. They arrived at the intersection of U.S.23 and Ripley and parked their camper in the visitor parking area. The man walked inside.

"Can I help you?"

"Yeah, I'm pretty sure I saw the guy whose been killing' those folks in the marinas."

"Where did you see him?"

"In the bathroom of the city park."

"About what time?"

"I'm not sure. I didn't pay any attention. Sun was up, it was about an hour ago."

The officer was taking down information and continuing to ask questions. "Did you see his vehicle?"

"No, I was going into the bathroom and he was on his way out. I thought I'd seen that face, but it took me almost a half hour to recall where I'd seen it and then it hit me, I'd seen him on the posters around town and down at the marina."

"Did you see him leave the city park?"

"No, I did not."

"OK, we'd like your name and address. Could you put that on this report form?"

"Sure." He wrote, Tom Wildrom, 1123 High St., Niles, Michigan, 48555.

The officer looked at Tom's name, "Thank you, Mr. Wildrom. We'll put out a bulletin and try to apprehend him. He can only go south or north on 23 or turn west on 33."

"Hope you catch up to the guy. Terrible to have him killin' good people, you know."

"You've been most helpful, Mr. Wildrom. How can we reach you if we need any more help in the next few days?"

"We're on vacation, sort of trying to get into state parks along this here east side of the state. We've no car phone or pager. Guess you could only check in with some state parks and see if we're registered."

"Thanks. I've got to get this information out."

Before Tom had started up his camper, the state police had broadcast an alert to be on the lookout for the marina maniac sighted this morning in Alpena.

$$\mathcal{J}$$

Mickey McFadden had arranged for a conference call between Detective Maguffin, Maggie, Lou and himself. Mickey began, "Things are happening quite quickly and I'm beginning to think that this case might be solved fairly soon. So we can all be on the same page, I wanted you to know what I know. If we can predict where he might hit, we'll be ready to solve this case.

"First of all, we have a picture of the suspect, as you both know. This photo has been copied extensively and distributed all over the state and on the Internet. A law enforcement officer in every Michigan community has been asked to take the photo to any health club in their area and see if anyone can identify this guy. We've got the picture in every marina. We've got it in police cars all over the state. So, I'm hopeful someone will recognize the guy sometime today at the latest."

"This is the guy who described the victim before the body was taken from the water in Harbor Beach?" Maggie asked.

"Right. OK, we know that a doctor, Sherry Mihalik, was kidnapped from a laundromat yesterday in Escanaba. She's from Milwaukee. She and her husband were staying in the Escanaba marina. She went into town and never came back. The police found clean clothes in a washer, an empty plastic basket by the washer, and a *USA Today* newspaper across from the washer.

"She has not appeared under any marina dock as of this minute as far as I know. Now, I've heard from the state police post in St. Ignace and they gave me a copy of a report that said that they stopped and questioned a man in a white pickup by the name of Jim Simmons with a valid Illinois driver's license. There was nothing found in the bed of the pickup. He was released. All seemed above board until I did a check on Jim Simmons. There is no such person at that address in Joliet. The license and registration are phony."

"So, that could be our guy."

"Did they compare that photo to the one you're circulating?" Maggie asked.

"Haven't had that confirmed. Good point. I'll get that info when I get back to the office."

"If it is the same guy, it means he was in the Upper Peninsula and might explain the disappearance of Sherry Mihalik," Lou concluded.

"Yes, that's right."

"The last bit of information I have for you is this. I got a call from the harbormaster and the police in Escanaba. Actually it wasn't a call, it was a faxed report. It indicated that the husband of the missing Dr. Mihalik left the Escanaba marina at 8:15 p.m. and a voice transmission with the harbormaster occurred. He basically says Sherry's husband is leaving for Milwaukee but what is a bit strange is that he uses the pronoun 'we' and it could be that he is not alone.

"Who might be on the boat with him? Do they have children or a guest?" Maggie asked.

"No, as far as I was led to believe earlier in the day, the couple was on their honeymoon. Only the two of them."

"Then who's 'we' leaving the marina?" Lou asked.

"I don't know. The guy was a mental wreck all day apparently, which is understandable, but maybe he's still living as if his wife is alive."

"Or, maybe she is on the yacht and is okay?" Maggie asked.

"Or, maybe the killer is on the yacht with or without Dr. Mihalik?" Lou added.

"Hmmm, hadn't thought of that angle. Could be," Mickey said.

"I think that yacht needs to be monitored or definitely under surveillance when it comes into the Milwaukee marina or wherever it is going to dock," Lou suggested.

"Yes, we'll do that. Good idea, Lou."

"Anything else?" Lou asked.

"That's it, unless you've got something?"

"Nothing to add," Lou said, looking at his notes. "I do think we're getting close, Mickey. The photo sure helps and following up on that boat heading to Milwaukee should yield some information."

"I agree. Well, I've got to call the St. Ignace state police post and see if that's the guy they stopped. Talk with you later."

"Thanks for setting up the call and the information," Lou said.

"Sure. Just want all of us on the same page."

ぐ

Dr. Philip Heyboer was scared. He knew he was on the list and at any moment could be duped into being with the killer and found floating in his marina or any marina for that matter. Philip made arrangements to talk to his good friend, Molly Crowe. After Philip's wife died of cancer, Molly became a good friend. They enjoyed each other's company, but had not considered marriage.

He called Molly and asked her to meet him for dinner at the

Fern's at Creekwood Inn a short distance outside of Michigan City, Indiana. As Philip hung up the phone, he had a—

FLASHBACK: Brad Prescott had called me before making a decision to join the investment club. He wanted to know if joining was taking a calculated risk. He knew it was a risk, but he wanted assurance that it would be a relatively safe risk. I explained all that I knew, that the land was perfect for a huge marina and with boating being so popular on the Great Lakes and the economic forecast being good and in another ten years all the baby boomers would begin to retire, the investment in a huge marina had dollar signs all over it. I was honest with him and said that there were problems and spoke briefly about the environmentalists and the citizens in the area being against it. But, I told Brad that change is difficult for folks and any time something major is proposed there is opposition. It would pass. I also told him a land analysis would have to be done, but expected that to be a matter of routine. In sum, the PR folks should set the stage for acceptance, the analysis should be positive for proceeding, and then it would simply be a matter of watching the millions of dollars come in as the wealthy made plans for buying condos, cottages, and slips. My last words were, "Any time you invest a buck, it's a risk, but I really don't see how you can go wrong. I'm in because I'm expecting to make millions."

Brad took me into his confidence and said he was putting all his savings into this club. I guess I should have known how big a risk this was for him when he said, "But if I lose this, I don't think I can face my family. They've dedicated their lives to getting me through medical school and they trust me to give them a good life. So, if I lose this, I really couldn't live with myself." He then told me he was going to get insurance for every member of the family because if anything should happen to anyone, they would be out of money and would need some money to survive.

Philip and Molly were seated in the fashionable Creekwood Inn. After ordering and asking each other about their day, Philip said, "I want to take you into my confidence, Molly. I'm going to tell you something I haven't told anyone else, but I need to talk to someone."

"I'm glad you feel comfortable talking with me, Philip. What is it?"

"Eighteen years ago I was in an investment club when I was on staff at the U of M Medical School. We were having fun and enjoying much success until we invested in a land development project. We put in a lot of money to capture this huge chance to make millions of dollars. We signed a contract with a developer and became the owners of a large tract of land that we envisioned being perfect for a huge marina.

"We ran into opposition from the community and an environmental group. We thought a public relations firm would be helpful to change the attitudes of the community and the environmentalists. That was beginning to show signs of success when we had our required land analysis conducted by two firms, an independent firm and a government firm. Both reports hit us hard with much evidence of soil contamination. The projected costs of cleaning it up before building a marina were astronomical. In the meantime we had invited four more doctors into our club for one million dollars each. This was to cover the cost of the PR firm which did the job, but left us with a wasteland.

"One of the four doctors who we let into our club for one million dollars was a plastic surgeon by the name of Brad Prescott. He was beginning a practice in Harbor Beach. He had a wife Sara and twin sons Jake and John. Once the news got to Brad that his million was gone we heard that he sought mental health treatment, went into severe depression, his practice began to suffer and then something happened that nobody knows about but me, and now, you. Brad Prescott arranged for his family to be killed."

"Oh, my God. That's terrible," Molly quietly exclaimed.

"Yes, it is, and the reason, in my opinion, is that it was to be his only escape. He wouldn't have to face them for the rest of his life, and he'd have insurance money to get back on a healthy fiscal track."

"What happened?" Molly asked.

"I was a specialist in drug interactions. I've always believed that Brad's plan was to have two different drugs prescribed for his family but only he knew which drugs would be deadly in combination, based of course, on information he would get from me. In a sense I became a part of his intended crime. A pharmacist by the name of Dennis Burden, when he filled the prescription for Prozac, called Mrs. Prescott and told her that this drug was okay for her and the boys but must never be taken with the drug Anafranil or Deseryl. If the two were taken together, death was possible and especially with high doses. She asked why the drugs were prescribed and the pharmacist told her that they had been prescribed by Dr. Wills, for symptoms of psychotic behavior.

"Mr. Burden told her it wasn't his practice to call customers about drug warnings, but he cared for Sara and the boys so he told her he felt it best to call.

"When Sara was given Anafranil from her husband with instructions to take them with the medication prescribed by Dr. Wills, Sara realized that Brad was attempting to kill her and the boys.

"What I surmised is that Sara Prescott called her husband the day he died and asked him to come home. She confronted him on what she knew and accused him of wanting to murder the family and that she had no choice but to go to protective services.

"That afternoon, he killed himself."

"How is it that only you knew this?"

"The pharmacist, Dennis Burden, is my son-in-law, Marcia's husband. He told me of the call to Sara. Brad had called me earlier in the day and said, 'I'm thinking of prescribing some Anafranil for a patient and I want to know if there will be any complications if the patient is also taking Prozac or any drug that has a powerful effect upon serotonin.' I told him the combination would lead to serotonin syndrome and mixing the two drugs, especially in high doses, could be fatal. The police report notes that bottles for a prescription for Sara and boys for Prozac was on the kitchen counter and so was a bottle of high dose Anafranil not prescribed but having the fingerprints of Brad Prescott on the bottle. I put two and two together and kept it all to myself until now."

"That's quite a story, but I still don't see how I come into this?" Molly asked.

"Five people in the investment club have been murdered. There are three of us remaining. I am certain that the members are being killed by someone paid to do so and/or a member of one or more of the four families we took into the club. And, the logical murderer is one of the Prescott boys, most likely Jake, because they not only lost out on the money via their father's investment gone bad, but they also lost a father and my guess is that they would blame the club and not realize that their father's decision was not a good one and that there was no intent to bring others in to steal their money. At the time Brad Prescott joined our club, we all believed we still had a fortune by the tail. It was the soil analysis report that did all of us in."

"So, you are being targeted by the murderer."

"Yes, I'm certain of it."

"We must leave or you must leave, now."

"Yes, I think so, but I also think that there is nowhere I can go to where I won't be tracked and hunted down."

"Oh, Phil, this is terrible," Molly said shaking her head, taking his cold hand, and looking down.

"Yes, and I wanted you to know this, because if I do die, someone needs to know what really happened."

"Have you gone to the police for protection or to tell them you suspect Jake?"

"No. I can't do that."

"Why not? You might stop the killing."

"I am the godfather for Jake and John Prescott. There is no way I can turn them in."

"Can't you try to reach them and explain to them what you

explained to me?"

"They would not accept what I would tell them. Jake is a sick man. He has been mentally ill all of his life. Sara has done a great job of keeping this from the public over these many years. But, sooner or later, it will surface, it has to, it always does."

"But, just as you can't tell the police about them, how could they kill their godfather?"

"I said that Jake is a sick young man. The sickness defies common sense, Molly."

"What do we do?"

"Nothing but be cautious, live our lives and hope that whoever is doing this will be caught before three others lose their lives."

"Did you call the others to alert them, Phil?"

"Edith Haire agrees with me, but thinks she is sharp enough to keep herself out of harm's way. Cris Gallow, an otologist, seemed to welcome the challenge, strange but that's the impression I was given."

"I've lost my appetite, Phil. I'm very frightened for you."

"I'm sorry, Molly. But another person must know what I know and what I believe, for if I die, the truth must survive."

❧

Chief McFadden had called the Milwaukee police and explained that he would like them to intercept the yacht *Breathing Easy* when it came into the Milwaukee harbor. He went on to explain the reasons why and to describe the boat and who was on it. If the only person on board was Frank Mihalik, Mickey wanted to know that, but if anyone else was on board they needed to ask some questions and to report to Mickey what they learned.

The Milwaukee police promised to look into it and to report back. Within three hours Mickey got a call. The boat did arrive and the only person on board was Frank Mihalik. No one else was spotted. He was greeted by members of his family and some friends.

❧

THE MARINA MURDERS

With the possible sighting of the killer in Alpena, the Alpena police were thinking that a body was tied to a piling under the marina dock. Trying not to call a lot of attention to themselves, a pair of officers was sent to the marina to inspect the area for the body of Dr. Sherry Mihalik. A marine unit was also dispatched to look under the dock.

After an initial inspection, the marine unit and the officers on foot reported to the Chief of Police Mark Sabin that no body was found. The police chief couldn't understand why the killer was spotted in Alpena. There was nobody using the marina who was in the medical profession and there was no dead body under the marina dock. He was thinking the man in the camper in the city park was simply seeing things, looking for attention, or had over reacted to someone who might have born a resemblance to the man in the photo, but who undoubtedly was not the killer.

ༀ

Mickey McFadden called to say that the state police believed that the photo of the killer was, in fact, the man who they stopped yesterday south of the Mackinac Bridge. They had not gotten the photo when the alert was issued. Mickey and Maggie were now beginning to trace this killer. He'd been in Escanaba, Brevort, St. Ignace, and Alpena.

Maggie remained in Battle Creek. She had her mind on several different initiatives in her life. She was a consultant to insurance claims folks. The insurance companies found that the illegal side of insurance claims was big business. Maggie was an investigator with almost twenty years of experience investigating claims and finding those guilty of deception or fraud. She was one of the best, so even after she became a paraplegic, she continued to be a resource for a variety of insurance companies.

She also had found a new hobby in ceramics. She had discovered this talent in high school about thirty years ago. In fact, her art teacher thought she had such a future that he sought a scholarship for her at a prestigious university in the east. Maggie was in love with a guy who got a football scholarship to Western Michigan University and she simply couldn't imagine living away from him. She followed him to WMU and did take a class or two in ceramics but thought a more practical major would be pre-law. She graduated and married Tom who pursued a career in dentistry once he realized that running past huge offensive linemen was not something he'd be doing in the NFL. Maggie went to work for an insurance company, heading up the claims investigation office.

Maggie and Tom were married while he was in dental school in Minneapolis. A child, John Howard, came along within a year and baby John took all of Maggie's time. She loved being a full-time mom. So, with being a mother to John, and a wife to Tom, she put her knack for ceramics on hold. But, after the attack by a disgruntled and mentally ill customer for the insurance firm that employed Maggie, she took up ceramics as therapy.

Maggie enrolled in an adult education class in Battle Creek and the flare for this hobby took off. Tom made her a studio as an addition to their home in Battle Creek. Ceramics provided an expression for her creativity and her lack of mobility made this hobby a natural for Maggie.

In the past few years the demand for Maggie's pottery grew significantly. She displayed her work at a number of crafts fairs. Tom also made a display case for her awards and they were a source of pride for her. She soon realized that this could be a full-time job. Right now, it was turning a profit and was not only fun but therapy. It took her mind off her paralysis and put it fully onto transforming a hunk of clay into a beautiful plate, bowl, cup, or serving dish.

In spite of the joy of being a craftsman, the joy in solving murders with Lou was the highest mission in her life. Justice was something that had become a passion to Maggie. She couldn't stand to see someone robbing another of their freedom, their loved ones having their life ripped apart by some selfless act of passion or by some carefully planned interruption to another's life. Sure, a ceramics award was satisfying and having people love her work and want it in their homes was satisfying, but bringing closure to a major crime by having the perpetrator taken out of society gave her immense satisfaction.

So, when Lou called with a case, the ceramic business was put on hold. Or, if there was a gap in an investigation, Maggie could turn to her potter's wheel and on occasion, an important thought would hit her as the wet clay spun around her magical and creative hands.

Such was the case the afternoon of July 15. She was making a bowl, which would be in a set of dishes for John and his growing family, when the idea hit. The answer to this serial killer's identify lay in the motivation for the murders. The revelation was so strong that she literally stopped the potter's wheel, cleaned her hands, and moved her chair to another table and began writing.

She wrote, "I've been concentrating on all of the actions of the killer and looking for patterns of cities, victim profiles, and trying to identify the killer by physical attributes. The solution is in the motivation of the killer. Once I can figure out why this is happening, the killer or killers will surface."

Writing notes to herself was not uncommon for Maggie. She found it her way to clearly put forth her thoughts and ideas. She sat back and read it slowly and the common sense of her note was astounding. "Why had I not thought of this before?" she wondered aloud.

Because she would often get inspiration and ideas during her time at the potter's wheel she returned to her bowl while thinking of her new means to solve the crime. It would turn out that she would never forget the thought that hit her in making this bowl. In fact, she singled the bowl out for the trophy case because she believed it would be her memory for successfully solving this case.

She vowed from this point forward that her energies would be centered on the motive believing that once a motive was established, the rest of the case would fall together. And, so as the wheel spun before her and her hands created form from the mass of clay, her mind was into motive. Why would someone kill all of these people? she thought over and over.

One of her first thoughts was that it was not for personal revenge. Nobody would have rage for five different physicians from around the Midwest. She thought that it was undoubtedly a contractual relationship, a murder for hire situation, but that only led her thinking to who would want all of these people killed. She was back to motive once again. Maggie finished forming the bowl and decided that she needed to do some critical thinking and writing.

She cleaned up and pulled her wheelchair up to her kitchen table. With a fresh cup of tea next to her, she put pen to the legal pad. This was the first time she put onto paper what had been swimming around in her mind for days. She made lists as Lou often did in the midst of an investigation. Column one had the names of the victims; Glenda Knoble, James Rothchild, Peter Verduin, Will Harrison, and while not yet found but presumed to be dead, Sherry Mihalik. No pattern there with names. She noted the sex of the victims: woman, man, man, man, and a woman; not a real pattern there. Place of residence: Gaylord, Cadillac, South Haven, Chicago, Milwaukee. No pattern there. Medical specialty: surgeon, cancer, malpractice lawyer, heart, and lung, No pattern there. Hobby: sailing, sailing, sailing, sailing, and sailing. A definite pattern, but that was obvious. Marinas where abducted: Traverse City, Manistee, South Haven, Holland, Escanaba. No pattern there. Site of death: Traverse City, Manistee, South Haven, Harbor Beach, and one to be determined if Dr. Mihalik is found dead.

Maggie looked at the chart and the only pattern was the obvious, the hobby of sailing. *Another pattern, those who had been killed were all involved in a law suit. There is something about having a yacht. It is the only common denominator. What is it about owning a boat that would lead to their deaths?* Maggie thought.

Maggie knew that she needed to talk to medical folks who had completed a law suit and who owned a yacht. Maybe in talking to them, a pattern would emerge. She'd ask a few to participate in a conference call.

ॐ

Chief McFadden was very good about contacting Lou with information, but Lou couldn't wait for a call so he phoned him.

"Mickey, this is Lou Searing with a question. Sorry if I'm interrupting your dinner."

"No, just finished. What do you need?"

"Has anyone reported seeing the marina maniac?"

"Nothing, Lou. I'll be told as soon as the suspect is apprehended and I've received no word as yet."

"OK, no sighting of Sherry's body?"

"Negative, Lou. Like you, I'm certain she's under a dock in a marina, but no body has been found."

"OK, did anyone call and identify the guy as a result of going to health clubs?"

"Not with a positive identification. I did get a call from Ron Abbott in Cadillac, the photo is not of Rich Hopkins. That is news for you. Sorry not to call as soon as I learned that, but ..."

"No problem, Mickey. Thanks for sharing that piece of information. Guess we can drop him from the short list of possible suspects."

"Oh, I wouldn't drop him. All we know is that he's not the guy in the photo. We can't be certain that the guy in the photo is the killer. I'm sure he knows some significant information, but we don't know who he talked to before meeting with those women. I'd keep that Hopkins guy on the list. You never know."

"That's right. Will do. For your information, I talked to Maggie recently; she's putting all of her energy into the motive. She's thinking we need to try to discover what is going on behind the scenes and to find out why the pattern of sailing is so dominant. She's brilliant, Mickey. My guess is that she'll hit upon something that will lead to solving this thing."

"Hope so. Listen, Lou. I'm sorry, but I've an important call I need to take."

"Thanks, Mickey. I'm finished. Talk to you later."

✌

Carol and Lora were planning a day of shopping along the west Michigan coast and Lou was writing more of his novel into a laptop as the sun set into Lake Michigan. Lou was writing a mystery from a past investigation and trying to keep his head in the current investigation. He was finding it a bit difficult to keep the two cases straight. Lou realized he should put the novel to bed for awhile, at least until this case was solved. But, Lou was enjoying writing the story and at the same time trying to make sense of the reality of the marina murders.

CHAPTER FOURTEEN

Thursday, July 16
Manistee, Battle Creek and Alpena,
Michigan

Maggie was able to reach two doctors who fit her description of possible victims, Dr. Tamara Liddell from Ann Arbor and Dr. Elliott Eisensmith of Detroit. Because of the seriousness of the situation, both Tammy and Elliott were willing to participate in a 9:30 conference call.

Maggie began, "Thank you for dropping all of your important work and getting on the phone on such short notice. As you are probably aware, we're investigating the marina murders and the perpetrator seems to be targeting medical people who have yachts. They also seem to be medical people who had recently completed malpractice suits. Through my research I've been able to locate doctors who meet that set of characteristics and hence my contacting you two. I'll try to be quick so you can get back to your work. First of all, you two know that four and probably five doctors have been murdered. Am I correct?"

"Yes, and first of all, on behalf of all of us, Maggie, we appreciate your working on this terrible series of murders. We will do anything we can to assist you," Dr. Eisensmith said sincerely.

"I ditto Elliott's comments, Maggie. Thank you very much. We appreciate it, and please convey our appreciation to Mr. Searing as well."

"I will."

"The reason for wanting to talk to you is a shift in my attention to find a motive. I'm trying to discover why the man is doing this. So, instead of trying to tie evidence to a person or persons, I'm taking a different fork in the road and working to get into the mind of the killer and trying to discover what has led to this killing, and why people are on a list and if I can discover that, I can get out in front of him and perhaps we can stop the killing."

"Makes sense. What do you need from us?" Tammy asked.

"Your thoughts, if you have any, relative to motive."

Elliott began. "You know Maggie, maybe this doesn't fit, but I don't think the motive is related to the malpractice suits."

"Why?" Maggie asked.

"We're all heavily insured. We all have disgruntled clients. It's a rare doctor who isn't in conflict with some people. People blame us because we didn't do enough or didn't act quickly enough, or didn't suggest a different course of treatment or didn't do it soon enough."

Tamara interjected. "I would agree with Elliott. I think the key is the yachts. The one common thing beyond our being medical practitioners is sailing."

"OK, but let me go back to Elliott's comment a minute. How do we explain the death of the lawyer who represents many of you in high profile cases? That's what led us to think he was on the list because he defended doctors. After all, the pattern was broken when he was killed because he's not a medical person."

"Yes, he is, Maggie," Elliott interjected. "Pete Verduin was a doctor and as a result of an unjust accusation that he killed a patient, he went into law because he felt so strongly that we need good lawyers to defend us. He felt there was a void there. So, Peter was first a doctor and second a lawyer."

"Hmmm, didn't know that. Thanks. Good information," Maggie said, writing down Elliott's comment.

"OK, back to Tammy thinking the common denominator is sailing. If that's true, then why would medical folks be killed because of an interest in sailing?" There was silence.

Maggie continued, "Is it the company that sells the boats or a competitor who loses sales to this company? Is it an insurance carrier?"

"None of those, in my opinion," Elliott said.

"We might be targeted because of our environmental concerns," Tammy said matter of factly.

"What do you mean?"

"Some of us belong to an organization that works to protect our environment."

"Do you and Elliott belong?"

"Yes, but there are hundreds of us who belong, and it is only one of many organizations that have our attention."

"That's a good point, Tammy," Elliott replied. "We do take a variety of unpopular stands. That advocacy could generate some hostility, but I really don't think our conflicts would lead to murder."

"You don't?" Maggie asked.

"No, I don't. I think we've got a very sick and crazed man who has something against doctors and who is randomly killing to feed his sickness. You're the investigator, Mrs. McMillan, but to me, when all is said and done, we'll learn that this guy is mentally ill and has no pattern to his killing."

"You may be right, Elliott. That's certainly possible and has crossed our minds as well."

"I'm not as willing to link this environmental organization to these terrible killings."

"What's the name of this organization, Tammy?"

"Great Lakes Doctors Fighting for Our Land and Water."

"Do you have a typical organization structure? You know, president, vice president et cetera. You all pay dues, get a newsletter and have committees, a typical organization?"

"Yes, all of that," Elliott said.

"Are either of you leaders in this organization?"

"I'm president-elect, meaning I will be president next year," Tamara said.

"Elliott, are you involved?" Maggie asked.

"I'm only a dues paying member. I support it but my heart is in a number of other charities and causes."

"I see."

"Tammy, are any of the victims to date, involved in the organization?"

"I don't know. I'm relatively new to the organization."

"But, you're president-elect."

"Yes, but they pass the presidency around the Great Lakes and it's Michigan's turn and as is often the case, I'm probably the only one willing to say OK to the nominating committee. It's a lot of work and most doctors don't have the time or don't want to give it the time. I said OK to placing my name on the ballot, but I really don't know our leaders and I don't pay attention to who is who in the organization, but I guess I'm going to have to begin doing that."

Elliott said, "Again, I think we only have a crazed man here. But, if I were to come up with a motive beyond that, I wouldn't say it is our organization advocating for the environment, I'd say it is the work of an organization that supports the victims of crimes or in our case of mistakes folks in our professions have made. Revenge could be the motive, Maggie. Revenge brings a lot of emotions to the table. I can see a victim's organization paying a hit man to do to us what the courts didn't do, give them what they perceive to be justice or a pay back for a mistake. So, if you don't buy the crazed man theory, look at a victim's organization using their funds to pay to have justice their way and not through court decisions."

Maggie noted his comments and Tammy added, "Good point, Elliott. I can't argue with that."

Maggie appreciated Tammy and Elliott sharing their thoughts. "I realize that you both are very busy so I thank you for taking the time to talk with me. We'll be in touch."

"Not a problem. Thanks, Maggie," Tammy said.

"Are you two going to get any sailing in this summer?"

"I doubt it. My wife and kids live on the yacht and I try to get there on occasion, but I'm not doing a very good job of it this summer."

"And you, Tammy?"

"Every weekend. I sail out of the Elizabeth Park Marina on the Detroit River. We like to go into Lake Erie as well as Lake St. Clair."

"Well, thanks again. We'll be in touch."

Lou was concerned that they had not discovered Sherry Mihalik's body so he decided to go to Alpena, where the suspected killer was last seen.

When Lou got there, he encountered quite a bit of resistance from the police. Lou knew about law enforcement attitudes about private investigators, but to date, he had not encountered any hostility. In Alpena, Lou was almost told to get out of town. He surely was not wanted as they felt they had the situation in control. The last thing they needed was some private eye looking over their shoulder and causing doubt and conflicts.

Lou tried to explain that he was not a threat to them, but that didn't go over very well. Lou almost gave in and drove home, but then decided that he should be persistent. There was a good reason for his trip to Alpena and he wanted to see his mission complete.

Lou called Chief McFadden and explained that he was not welcome in town and could the Chief talk some sense into the authorities there. Chief McFadden said he'd call and see what he could do. He called back and said "I couldn't change his mind. I'm calling you home and sending Detective Maguffin over. You tell Jerry what you want done and he'll be your shadow over there."

"This isn't making any sense, Mickey."

"Lou, drop it. The Chief can do what he's doing. There is no law that says a police chief has to work with a private eye. He probably had a bad experience somewhere along the line. We're not going to win this one and I'm not going to push the agenda. Come on home. I'm sorry for your waste of time, but you'll have Maguffin to do what you'd like done."

"I don't like it, but I guess I have no choice. Is that what you're saying?"

"Exactly."

"OK, Chief. Can you put Jerry on the phone?"

"He's right here."

"Jerry, when you get to Alpena, I want a scuba diver to search below every piling under the dock at the marina. My hunch is that Sherry Mihalik's body is under the dock and I'd like my gut feeling followed on this one."

"Not a problem, Lou. I agree and will see that it happens."

Before leaving town Lou decided to eat at The Thunderbird Restaurant. It was a favorite of his. He also decided to stop at Adam's Bookstore. He recalled going there often when Adam Ludwig was still alive. Adam could find any book a person was looking for. Seeing him and chatting with him was worth a visit to his bookstore.

After enjoying a meal, trying to forget about being rebuffed, and browsing in Adam's Bookstore, Lou drove to the marina. He glanced at the Lanny Kingsury Rock. Lanny was a boat fan who offered much support for the harbor. Lanny would have let Lou investigate, but Lou wanted to follow protocol.

Lou drove south of U.S. 23 heading for home. He couldn't shake feeling a sense of frustration for not accomplishing his mission.

چ۔

Once Detective Maguffin arrived in Alpena, he made a case for a more through underwater search. He was sent out in the sheriff's boat and directed the diver. Detective Maguffin felt like a movie producer directing actors. He wanted each piling inspected and not simply a visual sighting at water level, but below water level, as low as the diver could go, all the way to the bottom, if possible.

It was on the study of the fourth piling from the end of the dock when the diver came up with a thumbs up signaling that he had found something. When he surfaced, he had a long knife in hand. Detective Maguffin had a plastic bag and opened it so the diver could place the knife in the bag.

The diver held onto the boat, removed his mask and said, "The body's down there. She's tied to the piling, but a weight pulled her body down. I can see a slit wrist. The body looks like it's been down there awhile."

The Alpena officer in the boat called in the finding and requested an ambulance and a crime investigation team from the state police. The police obviously didn't want the dock swamped with gawkers, but they had little choice; people follow ambulances and the police, and with all the hype around the marina murders, it was bound to happen.

Detective Maguffin called in the discovery to Chief McFadden who in turn called to tell Lou the body had been found and to compliment him on the suggestion to do a more thorough check. Lou then called Maggie to tell her. Chief McFadden also said he would contact the Milwaukee police and ask them to contact Frank Mihalik, inform him of the finding, and request that he come to Michigan to identify the body.

The ambulance arrived. The marina was closed to anyone except police and medical personnel. The medical examiner was quick to arrive. There weren't many boaters in the marina as most boaters arrived on Friday.

The procedure was routine. The body was raised from under the dock, placed in a body bag and taken from the marina to Alpena General Hospital for an autopsy. A reporter and photographer from *The Alpena News* were on hand to capture in word and picture the drama that descended on this small community on the northern Lake Huron shore.

The marina remained closed for most of the day and evening so that the police could do their investigation: taking photographs, interviewing marina guests and just trying to keep people from walking out onto the dock to gawk at the spot where a murdered woman had been found.

The police and hospital would handle all procedures and Detective Maguffin would represent Chief of Police McFadden who was the head of the task force.

Maggie went to the Internet and typed in www.GLDPLW.org. She wasn't certain this was their ULR but it was a good place to start. Bingo, up came the website for the organization Tammy had mentioned.

The web page was attractive and had some nice photos of the Great Lakes area. There were several pages to explore—Mission, Board of Directors, Committees, Policies, Links, and a Contact Us icon.

Maggie first entered the Mission page. She read, "It is the Mission of GLDPLW to preserve our natural resources and to advocate for cessation of land use for marinas, forest use for lumbering, and river use for anything other than limited fishing and canoeing. It is our belief that the corporate use of our land, the recreational use of our waterways, and the pollution caused by man will slowly but surely erode our natural resources. Therefore, our goals and objectives are to advocate for the land and water in the Great Lakes. We encourage you, a visitor to our website, to join us in protecting and preserving our land and water. Thank you."

She then went to the Board of Directors and saw names: There among the officers was the name of James Rothchild. He was the recording secretary of the organization. She clicked on the icon by his name to look at his profile. This is what she read: "Dr. Rothchild has been an internationally known proctologist for the past quarter century. He lives in Cadillac, Michigan, and has a strong connection to his alma mater, the University of Michigan. James can be seen at most home games of the Wolverines. He is a member of the Alumni Association and has held most offices in this organization. Dr. Rothchild dedicates much time to the U of M Medical School. He serves as a guest lecturer, participates in the mentoring program, and serves as a member of the admissions committee. Dr. Rothchild enjoys sailing the Great Lakes. He is married to his wife Anita and has a daughter Penny."

Maggie didn't recognize the names of any of the other board members and therefore concluded that this organization was not being targeted. She printed a profile of Dr. Rothchild. She already knew most of this information, but thought it a piece of information to add to the investigation file.

As the day progressed, Maggie kept thinking of Dr. Rothchild and his connection to the University of Michigan. She began to think of the other victims and where they lived. She recalled the disgruntled woman who wanted Mr. Verduin to sue the University of Michigan because her son or daughter's application was rejected for admittance. Maybe there is some connection to these murders. Maybe the serial killer is a guy who has been routinely denied admittance to a variety of medical schools, Maggie thought. And, if this is the case, then the victims are all members of the admissions committee. If I'm right, I have no clue who among hundreds of students may be a killer nor do I know the schools where the killer has applied so we can predict who else might be a potential victim.

⌇

Dr. Edith Haire was moving her yacht *Skinny Dippin'* closer to Oscoda. Edith Haire was a nationally recognized dermatologist. In addition to her love of sailing on the Great Lakes, she was one of those many folks who had a fascination for lighthouses and had visited about 90% of the lighthouses in Michigan. She would dock her boat in a marina then seek transportation to the lighthouse, take a photograph for her album and make notes of her observations. She then enjoyed giving programs on lighthouses of the Great Lakes to various service organizations and church groups during the fall, winter and spring.

Edith Haire at 62 had been sailing the Great Lakes with her friend Elaine Derby, a dermatologist in Indiana for almost thirty years. For a dermatologist, one would think Edith would have been more cautious in the sun. Her skin was tanned, weathered and looked as if she'd not seen a tube of sun screen in her life. She was an outdoors woman. She liked to hike, and up until the last few years, was the woman's masters running champion in Indiana. Edith was on her way to be included in the Indiana Woman's Hall of Fame. She had done it all, scholar, humanitarian, community leader, advocate for children, the environment, and perhaps was the most famous alumnus of the University of Saint Francis.

She and Elaine had called the Main Pier Marina and reserved a slip through the weekend. The marina was along the AuSable River and close by was the Charboneaus Restaurant, a favorite eating spot for them and other boaters in the Oscoda area.

She'd be sure to see the lighthouse, one of several she had visited during her summer travels in all of the five Great Lakes.

Elaine had come down with some virus and wanted to go to a doctor's office when they docked in the marina. Her fever was around 102 degrees and the two women thought that an internist needed to take a look at her.

As *Skinny Dippin'* entered the AuSable River, Jake sat in a white pickup in a highway scenic pull off. He had his binoculars trained on the beautiful 38-foot Sea Ray Sundancer. Like a hunter watching his prey, he kept watching the boat as it made its way into the marina. All was happening according to plan.

CHAPTER FIFTEEN

Friday, July 17
Oscoda, Michigan

Edith and Elaine began Friday in Oscoda by inquiring with the harbormaster about the availability of a doctor. The harbormaster said he would be glad to transport Elaine to the Oscoda Health Center. That was fine with both women.

On the way to the health center, the harbormaster warned Edith and Elaine of the dangers to each of them in that the marina maniac was targeting physicians who were staying in marinas. He said that they should report anything suspicious to him or to the police. "Actually, I'd rather that you two simply get on back to Indiana. I'm serious, ladies, this is not a time to be in our marina. Please get some help here at our clinic and be on your way."

"Listen, young man, if I ran from every person wanting to confront me about something, I'd never stop running," Edith said. "It's the nature of being a doctor to constantly be in demand and to have people praising you or attacking you. Sure, we'll be cautious, but we'll do what we planned to do and live as if we'll have unending tomorrows." Elaine nodded in agreement.

The doctor was able to see Elaine and gave her special attention in that she was a doctor as well. "I imagine you have self-diagnosed yourself and am surprised you took the time to visit with us."

"I'm sure it is a virus of some kind, but to be on the safe side, and being on the Lakes and away from medical care, I wanted you to confirm my diagnosis and offer whatever treatment you think appropriate," Elaine said.

"I would say it's a virus. I'm concerned about this fever. It's higher than it should be. I'm sure it's nothing, but I'd like you to consider spending the night in the health center and let us run a battery of tests. I'd like to keep you under observation overnight."

"You really think it requires that much attention? These days you are only kept overnight for the most serious illnesses. Do you folks in Michigan have more lenient standards?"

"No, we're under the same standards, but I think an analysis of your blood and some other lab tests would put us on the safe side. You are free to return to your yacht as you know, but I think a room in the hospital would be more comfortable, give you a change of scenery from your yacht and give us your full attention in case we feel we need to run some additional tests. I don't think this is a simple case of the flu or a bad cold. As you know, you lack some cold and flu symptoms which is why I'm a bit concerned. Your call, go on back or stay with us. I should have a diagnosis by tomorrow morning either way."

"Well, if you think staying in the hospital is helpful to you, I'll gladly stay."

"A good decision. Thanks. A nurse will assist you with intake procedures."

Elaine explained to Edith her decision to stay in the hospital and encouraged Edith to spend her day as she had planned with an evening visit to the hospital.

Edith was concerned for her friend and thought the course of action was best. She'd go back to the marina, do what she had planned and would return to the health center in the late afternoon or evening with Elaine's toiletries and a change of clothes for tomorrow. She'd also plan on having dinner at the health center and would spend the evening with Elaine watching TV or playing some backgammon, their favorite game while in the marinas.

Inside the hospital, an intern or an orderly seemed to be overly concerned with Elaine. He was of medium height, very muscular, and wore a short white jacket with the traditional stethoscope draped around his neck. Elaine thought it odd that he seemed to be constantly looking into her room, but she shook it off as a curious staff member getting word of a new patient.

ᘔ

Edith unlocked her bike from the bike rack at the marina and set out for town. She wanted to go to a bookstore and pick up a good book for Elaine, who was not a TV fan. She can only handle so many games of backgammon. She wheeled her bike into town and stopped at The Page Turner Bookstore, run by Brett Turner and his wife Page.

Edith and Elaine always stopped in the book store when they were in town. It was a warm and cozy place to enjoy looking for that perfect book. She parked her bike out front, walked in and was surprised that Brett remembered her. "Hi Edith, good to see you back."

"My goodness, I had no idea you would remember me," Edith said, pleasantly surprised.

"Remember you? We could never forget you. You and Elaine are a couple of our favorite summer customers."

"Really? Well, that's nice. I'm here to get a book for Elaine."

"Yes, I was just about to ask you how she was and why she wasn't with you."

"She's got a fever and the doctors wanted her kept in the health center overnight. They want to see if they can isolate the problem and having her around for tests made more sense than bunking her on our boat and going back and forth, especially since her fever is kind of high."

"Hope she'll be OK."

"Oh, yes, I'm certain she will be. I can't imagine it is more than a virus running its course and the fever is simply the body doing all it can to win the war, and it will."

"What kind of book are you looking for? Have you got an idea or are you just browsing?"

"I think just browsing, unless you've got a recommendation of the month or something?"

"No, not really. We're so busy in the summer, thank goodness, it's the only way we can make it. But, I don't get much reading time. So, I can't help much, but people are buying up high profile books, you know, books recommended by talk show hosts, *New York Times* best seller's list books, and a few local authors are selling well."

"OK, I'll just take my time and see what I can find. So good to see you, Brett. My regards to Page. I'll leave you to your customers."

As with the other murders, Jake had created a detailed outline on how to lure his victim. Every detail must be followed for the perfect crime and in return for his allegiance to his plan, there would be no chance of discovery - nothing was left to chance. Nothing.

So far all was going according to plan. Edith had gone into the book store. He knew if he watched her closely she would provide him with a way to execute this kidnapping. Quickly looking up the book store's phone number in the directory he had taken from a phone booth, he picked up his cell phone and dialed.

"Brett Turner. How can I help you?"

"Mr. Turner. This is an emergency. Would Dr. Haire be in your store?"

"Yes, she is."

"Please tell her that one of our security officers is coming to pick her up and take her to the health center. Her friend Elaine has taken a turn for the worse. It is critical that Dr. Haire come to her bedside immediately. Please give her this message."

"Oh, this is not good news. I'll tell her, thank you."

"Our security officer should be there any second."

Brett replaced the phone in the cradle and went to Dr. Haire. "The health center called. They're sending security to pick you up. Your friend is critical and needs you at her bedside."

"Thank you," Edith said, as she hurried to the front door. She spotted a man with a security looking outfit and immediately went to him, got in his white pickup and like a fly in a spider's net, was now in the control of a very strong and determined killer.

Call it instinct, or woman's intuition but Edith sensed that she had walked into a trap. She also realized that she was the next in the investment club of eight who were destined to die.

"What do you need from me, young man? Money? Drugs?"

"Don't need anything from you, Dr. Haire."

"OK, can you at least tell me where I'm going?"

"As far as I'm concerned, you are going to hell."

Edith reached over and jerked the wheel sending the pickup off the road and toward a ditch. Jake quickly recovered and got the pickup back on the road. In doing so, he took Edith's arm and snapped it from the wheel, breaking her wrist.

"We won't be trying anymore of that, Dr. Haire. Am I clear?"

Edith nodded. Her left wrist was in a great deal of pain.

"This is about your father's death, isn't it young man?"

"You got that right. Seventeen years is a long time to be looking over your shoulder, Doc, but today, it all comes back to roost."

"For what it's worth, the invitation to allow others to join us was a compliment and an opportunity for others to earn a lot of money."

"As far as I'm concerned it led to my dad's killing himself and indirectly devastating my mother, my brother and me. As a member of the club, you are guilty."

"I had a feeling it was all related to the marina investment mess when I heard that Glenda and James had been murdered. I just didn't think it would happen to me, or if it did, I'd be sharp enough to protect myself. Guess I miscalculated."

"Yup, guess you did."

When Jake had reached the desolate road deep in the country, he pulled a gun on Dr. Haire and told her to follow his directions. Edith was given a vial of a powerful relaxant and told to inject it into her thigh. Jake had made it clear as he did each time that there really was no choice but to inject the drug or be shot dead. Edith, unlike the others, took the syringe and before plunging it into her thigh, pointed it out of sight and pushed the plunger excreting the drug down her thigh and then she injected only a small portion of the drug. She knew it was a potent relaxer so within seconds she pretended to be under the influence of the drug and went limp.

Jake picked her up, noticed the wetness on her body but figured some of the drug had seeped out or something. She was clearly as out of it as all of his other victims. He lifted her and placed her into the bed of his pickup. He methodically snapped the vinyl covering and then to his surprise, as he was about to snap the last snap, he could see a vehicle coming down the isolated country road, a road not even on the map. The vehicle was about two hundreds yards away when he spotted it.

Jake could feel the adrenalin leap into his veins. He had been spotted. The gig was up. The perfect crime was no longer perfect. He couldn't put the tube from the exhaust into the bed of his pickup to kill his victim quickly. He got in the truck and drove in the direction of the vehicle. It looked like a cop, but maybe it wasn't.

The driver of the on-coming vehicle was the owner of the property and he was mad that someone had violated his no trespassing signs. The two cars sped toward one another on the one lane dirt road alongside acres and acres of corn. As the vehicles approached one another, reminiscent of the death defying game of chicken to see who would veer first, the landowner took a pistol from under his seat. He lowered his window and while smack dab in the middle of the road, slowed to a stop. He was positioned to confront the trespasser.

Jake had no intention of stopping, but he slowed almost to a stop. The landowner opened his door to get out and Jake immediately gunned it, veering to his right and slamming into the opened door. The landowner had a few seconds to move to the center of his car to avoid being hit by Jake's truck. Jake was thankful the vehicle was not a police vehicle, but the perfect plan was now foiled.

Jake was on his own now. For the first time, he was without a perfect set of directions. He knew that he had to gas his victim and continue with the plan to tie the dead Edith Haire to a piling in the Oscoda marina.

Jake didn't know the area so once off the private property, he sped, in broad daylight, down a county road past farm fields and an occasional farmhouse. Edith had been tumbling around in the bed of the pickup, almost fully conscious. She could tell that the truck was moving along a paved road and at a fairly good speed, but she also knew that if she didn't escape, she would be the next victim in a long list of bodies discovered in deadly waters.

Edith used her strength to undo some of the snaps from the vinyl covering. She knew her captor had a gun. Finally, she knew a plan to kill her had been disrupted, so he was probably very upset and not thinking logically.

Edith decided she didn't have a choice. It was either die crashing onto the side of the road and hurdling down an embankment or be dead in the water. She took her chance and jumped from the vehicle. She slammed onto the berm, rolled several times and eventually came to rest down in a gully. She was not dead, at least not at the moment.

⌇

Sara Prescott was putting two and two together and coming up with four. She knew the names of the murdered doctors. She knew her sons were prone to violence and she feared that it might be Jake, more than John, who was the marina maniac. But, she was in denial. She couldn't bear the thought of her sons killing people. She regretted the day she talked to the boys about the details surrounding Brad's suicide. She could tell by their reactions that they, and especially, Jake, might seek revenge. Maybe it would have been better to tell the boys of their father's plans to kill them, but she felt they should go through life admiring the man who was their father, so she kept the secret to herself, but the last thing she expected was that her son would seek to have all eight of them killed.

Sara couldn't bring herself to call the police to suggest that Jake and John may in some way be involved. A mother had trouble admitting her sons could leash such terror around a state, so she'd just burrow into the belief that her boys were not involved.

She decided to call John and ask him about it, however.

"Hello."

"John, this is Mom. You doing OK, son?"

"Yeah, doing OK, I guess. What's up?"

"John, let me come right out and ask. Is Jake the marina murderer?"

"Ma, we need justice here. We've all suffered enough for so long."

"He is the killer. Is that what you're saying?"

"Yes, he is doing this for Dad, and for you, for the other families, for all of us. You always taught us that there would be consequences for our actions. These people faced no consequences for killing Dad and ruining your life and leaving us without a father. Yes, Jake is the marina murderer and I am doing what I can to help him. He's my brother, Mom. I have to help him."

John could hear his mother sobbing on the other end of the line.

"You OK, Mom?"

"Oh, John, honey. I'm so sorry, so sorry."

"Mom, let us handle it, OK. If anybody contacts you we don't exist. Understand?"

Sara got control of her emotions and continued her telephone conversation. "John, take care of yourself and help Jake get some help for his problems. Will you do that for me? He wouldn't listen to me, maybe he'll listen to you."

"Sure, Mom."

"Goodbye, son." The phone went dead.

She regretted not forcing Jake to be seen by a psychiatrist who could have helped straighten out his obsession with mutilating and his tendencies toward violence. She regretted lying to the boys about why their father killed himself. Once again, the truth would have undoubtedly set a lot of people free.

Sara knew the devastation Jake felt in not getting accepted at any medical school. She felt it too. She and Brad had planned to send the boys to Europe, to special camps, anything to prepare them for the admission process to medical school. Once Brad died she didn't have the resources to prepare Jake or John, for that matter, to adequately compete with thousands of others for being accepted. So, his not getting in was her fault, or so she thought. If she had been a better mother, he would have made it, but he failed and his failure was a reflection of her failure as a mother.

Sara Prescott had a decision to make, face the humiliation of seeing her sons captured and tried for murder, going through trials and watching their lives be wasted in prisons, or escaping it all. Her dilemma could be solved in the same way that Brad had escaped, suicide.

She called her best friend Barbara Murphy, but she wasn't home. She was the friendly voice she needed at this moment. She took it as a sign perhaps because she fashioned a rope into a noose and just as Brad had done, went into the garage and secured it to the rafter where the family car had been. She stood on a ladder and stepped off for the fateful snap. At the same time as she stepped off the ladder, the township water meter reader was walking by the back of the home and glanced into the garage. He saw Sara's body still moving and hanging from the rafter.

The meter reader immediately called 911 and lifted Sara up to relieve the pressure of the noose. Her neck didn't snap as she hadn't placed the noose into a position where the snap would bring certain death. Sara was unconscious, however. The paramedics arrived with the police on their heels. As had happened seventeen years earlier, death, or the attempt at death, had caused the neighborhood to light up like a carnival.

꙳

Carol and Lou usually took their walks in the evening, but on this day, they decided to spend a portion of the afternoon on the beach, walking, and relaxing. As they walked toward the water's edge, they couldn't see a man, several yards down the beach looking at them through powerful binoculars. Once the man saw them start down the beach he put away his binoculars and headed toward them. It was quite rare that Lou and Carol saw someone they didn't recognize on the beach.

They noted the man coming toward them. He didn't look like the common beach walker. He was fully dressed including shoes and socks which on this summer afternoon at the beach was inappropriate. He looked as if he had a mission, not stopping to look at anything on the beach, but focused, and moving toward them.

As he approached Lou and Carol, he said, "Mr. Searing?"

"Yes."

"I need to talk with you. I know who the marina murderer is and I need to tell you so I can be at peace and potential victims can live."

"I'm listening," Lou said looking at Carol with a 'this can't be real' look.

"I will not identify myself. The killer's name is on a piece of paper in this envelope," the stranger said, taking the white business envelope from his summer sport coat pocket. As he held the envelope in his hand, ready to hand it to Lou, the stranger's cell phone rang.

"Excuse me."

"Sure." The three stood on the shore as the stranger took his call.

"Hello."

"Tom, you must get home immediately. Sara Prescott has been taken to emergency. I'm afraid someone tried to kill her."

"Oh, God, no. Who?"

"I don't know, Tom. I don't know specifics."

"Suicide, might it be suicide?" Father Murphy asked.

"Nobody is talking, Tom. The ambulance was on the way to the hospital when I got home. A police officer only said they have some evidence and it could have been a homicide. She looks at you as a son, Tom. If it is at all possible, please come here immediately. She is at the Chelsea Memorial Hospital. I'm going there now. I pray she will be alive when you arrive."

"I'm south of Grand Haven now. It will take me some time to get there, but I'll get there as soon as possible."

"Thanks, Tom."

"Goodbye."

Father Tom looked at Lou. "I've got to leave immediately. I'll contact you again."

"Wait, the envelope! You were going to tell me the name of the marina murderer."

"Not now. I'm sorry."

Tom turned and broke into a run heading north along the shore. Lou and Carol could see him head up toward a set of condos where he had undoubtedly parked. Lou took his cell phone from his pocket and called a friend who lived in the area. He was hoping his friend could see him coming out of the parking lot and could get a license number and identify the car, but the phone rang four times and a voiced message came on. Lou shook his head and put his phone back in his pocket.

"That was strange," Lou said to Carol.

"Looks like you came close to solving this thing. Did you recognize him?"

"No. He's someone who wants to see the killing stopped, but something in that phone call must have either shocked him into forgetting why he came to me which is not likely, or caused him to change his mind. I'll take him at his word that he will contact me again. I can only hope he's right."

Lou and Carol, headed home tossing an occasional piece of driftwood for Samm to retrieve.

~

Meanwhile back at the Health Clinic in Oscoda, Elaine asked a nurse if she had seen Edith.

"No, was she to be up here now?"

"Yes, she was going to bring me some things and maybe a couple of books. I think she was going to the Page Turner Book Store."

"Hmmm, no, haven't seen her. She'll probably be here in a few minutes." Edith would never be late, or at least not this late without calling and explaining her absence. Elaine lay in her hospital bed and cried. The grief was too much. She and Edith had talked about the marina murders but didn't want fear to control their behavior and their vacation. Elaine knew Edith would be found dead under a marina somewhere. Everyone else had. She'd lost her best friend and that was hell, pure and simple.

By late afternoon, Dr. Haire had not returned to her yacht. The police chief called Brett Turner at home as someone recognized her as being in his book store. The chief asked him what he knew of the missing Dr. Haire.

Brett informed them of the emergency call and that Dr. Haire left with security from the health center. When a call was made to check out the story, it was then apparent that Dr. Haire was a victim of a carefully contrived plot to kidnap her.

It was shortly before 6:00 p.m. when all marinas and police departments got word that Dr. Edith Haire was missing and was undoubtedly the next victim of the marina murderer. All marinas were on alert and all law enforcement agencies were alerted that a body could very well be under a dock in a Michigan marina before the sunrise.

The Oscoda sheriff's department committed to be in boats throughout the night in the marina area with lights always on the water. No murderer was going to tie a dead Edith Haire to a piling in their marina.

⌒

Lester Shanks was a dairy farmer who lived several miles due west of Oscoda. Lester was doing chores and working up an appetite for a good, hearty dinner which his wife Lizbeth made with loving hands. His dog Snappy shared the working hours with him.

Snappy had her jobs to do and she did them to perfection. Lester never had a dog like Snappy and he figured when Snappy died, he could never find another dog to replace her. Les always said God threw away the mold when He created Snappy.

It was about 6:30 p.m. when, with a burst of energy, Snappy took off like a bolt of lightning. She ran down the dirt road as fast as she could go.

Lester was beside himself. She would never let rabbits, other dogs, cats, or any four-legged animal get under her skin. She hadn't chased a car in years. *What's got into Snappy,* Lester thought out loud.

Then, just like Rin Tin Tin, Snappy came running back to Lester, barking and agitated and trying to communicate something important. At first Lester tried to discipline her for taking off and not staying close to the barn and tending to the cows. She kept on barking and starting to run toward the road.

"Oh, all right. You're bothering the neighbors with all that yapping. You got a skunk down the road?"

Lester walked toward the road with Snappy barking, wanting him to hurry.

"I'm moving as fast as I can. Quit your yappin'! I'm coming."

Snappy ran ahead, and Lester followed at a fast-paced walk. Finally after walking for a couple of minutes, Lester could see that Snappy had stopped and was looking at something in the ditch. Lester doubted his dog would get excited about a deer hit and killed by an automobile.

Eventually Lester reached Snappy. He said, "OK, what's got your attention, old girl?"

Lester looked down toward the ditch and there before him was a body, and the body was still, very still. He walked down into the roadside ditch and saw the body was face down. At first, he was sure whoever it was, was dead. He wondered if he should go back to the house and call the police. Maybe he shouldn't tamper with the body. Maybe this was an attempted murder and the police would be upset with him for touching or moving the body. Maybe evidence would be disturbed.

However, compassion overruled his common sense. He reached down, turned the body over and saw that it was a woman. He said, "You okay, lady?"

He felt her wrist and there was a pulse, albeit a weak one. Now Lester was torn, should he take time to get back to the house and get the police and an ambulance or stay and try to help her at the scene?

He decided, perhaps against better judgment, to stay. Snappy walked around and smelled Edith's head and then licked her face.

"You okay, lady?" Lester asked. No response.

Lester looked at her. Her body was severely bruised and he was certain she had a few, if not several, broken bones. She had no shoes.

Lester took his shirt off and got it wet with water from the ditch. Luckily, the lady had not come to rest in the water because even though it was only a few inches deep she could have drowned. He wiped her face and hands.

Lester needed to get some help. He told Snappy, "You stay here, Snappy. I've got to go home and call an ambulance." Snappy barked, as if to say she understood.

Lester walked as quickly as his body could manage back toward his home realizing that his chores were getting further and further behind. He reached his home, opened the door and said to Liz, "There's a lady in the ditch down the road a piece. Snappy went crazy and got me to follow her down there. Gotta call the ambulance."

"I'll call, Les. You go back. Do you need to take anything?"

"Yeah, a blanket, I guess, maybe some water."

"Well, you get that and I'll call the sheriff and stay here to guide him when he arrives."

Liz got on the phone and called. Lester grabbed a blanket, filled one of his coffee thermoses up and left to return to Edith.

Shortly after Liz called, the faint sound of a siren could be heard. It got louder with each minute. Lizbeth waved to the driver as he rounded the corner and came toward their farm. Liz pointed straight ahead and the ambulance continued down the road until the driver could see Lester standing off to the side.

As soon as the paramedics arrived they went right to work, tending to Edith, checking vital signs and giving her the first aid she needed. She was placed on a stretcher and put into the ambulance. By now, the police arrived and surveyed the scene where Dr. Haire was found. They carefully transported Edith into the ambulance, talked to Lester, and headed into town having learned nothing from the Shanks.

Jake eventually found a place that would give him privacy so he could complete his mission to kill Edith Haire. When he unsnapped the cover from the bed of the Silverado, there was no body to be found. He had no idea where he had lost his human cargo, but realized he couldn't backtrack because he could run right into the police. He decided to head home.

Jake knew that if Edith Haire lived or even if she didn't, every cop in the state would be looking for a white pickup, that is, if Edith were alive and able to tell the authorities that he was driving a white Silverado. He chose to drive on as many back out-of-the-way roads as he could till he could reach the safe shelter of his rented home.

It took much longer than usual for Jake to get to Harrison, but eventually he arrived without being questioned by an officer. He parked outside and then had an inspiration to call his best friend and ask if he could park the pickup in his garage. It was a mechanic's garage on the edge of town. It was a weekend and the garage would be closed. If the cops tracked him to his home, the Silverado would not be visible.

His friend met him downtown at the garage. "You've been gone quite awhile, Jake."

"Yeah, well, got no job so I can travel. Summertime you know and the weather is good. I did find some work as a dishwasher up in Mackinaw City. It allowed me to sleep in cheap places and it got me several weeks away from this town. Anything happening around here?"

"Nah, this town is about as exciting as watching clothes go around in a dryer, which some folks do for kicks, as you know."

"Yeah. Still working on the weights?"

"Not without you in town to give us someone to measure up to."

"I've been slacking off too. Gotta get back to lifting."

"Tomorrow? You game?"

"Yeah."

"Meet you at the gym."

"Right, be there. Thanks for letting me use your garage."

"Not a problem."

"Here's a couple bucks for a beer just to show my appreciation."

"Thanks, Jake. I'll give you a ride home, hop in."

CHAPTER SIXTEEN

Saturday, July 18
Grand Haven, Oscoda
and Harrison, Michigan

It was 5:15 a.m. when Lou awakened from a good night's sleep. Carol was not awake yet and Lou didn't wake her. He put on some clothes and opened the door so Samm and he could get some fresh cool air and walk along the beach.

Lou sat down on the sand, closed his eyes and sank deep into thought. He thought of their children and the grandchildren and of Carol and how fortunate he was to be surrounded by love and by wonderful people. Lou guessed he had taken much of this for granted over the years. Days just blend into weeks, which blend into months and then years and pretty soon, the years go by and you don't seem to stop and be thankful, thankful for blessings, and opportunities and to realize how bountiful is the harvest of ideas, friends and other joys of living.

Lou sat there, head bowed, and gave thanks, perhaps for the first time in a long time only this time he really meant it. The thanks he was offering were not simply words or insincere mumbling, but true thankfulness, for he realized he had been given marvelous gifts, and he vowed to never take a day for granted for the rest of his life.

Lou soaked up the silence as he sat on the beach. He entertained no thoughts for a minute or two, just peace and quiet. He opened his eyes and saw Samm sitting next to him, almost meditating in her own way.

Lou stood up, raised his arms as if to greet the day and hold the sun. Lou walked into the house and there was Carol standing in the kitchen. He gave her a hug and the two of them sat down to a good breakfast.

⨞

Maggie was on her way to the Searing home in Grand Haven. She had learned that Edith Haire was missing and wanted to work out of their home till the case was concluded, which she felt would be soon.

The next few hours, the phone never stopped ringing. Scott called to see if bringing the children over for a day at the beach was still in the plans. Lou said, "There's never been a better time, come on over!"

At about 9:20 the phone rang and it was a woman who refused to identity herself. It was Molly who unbeknownst to Philip Heyboer, decided to do what she could to try and save the lives of her friend and the remaining members of the investment club.

"I learned of you from the chief of police in Manistee. I've got information for you and I'm calling you right away. I'm not keeping anything from law enforcement, but you deserve to know. Your murderer is probably Jake Prescott."

"How did you come upon the information?"

"I choose not to reveal this at this time, but I have shared what I am about to tell you with the Chief of Police in Manistee. Potential victims are three in number. They are: Dr. Edith Haire, Dr. Philip Heyboer, and Dr. Cris Gallow. I do not know where Doctors Haire and Gallow are or how to reach them. Dr. Heyboer lives in Michigan City, Indiana, and knows of the potential threat to his life.

"OK, thanks for the tip. We'll get right on it. Can I have your number in case I need more information?"

"Yes, it is area code 920, then 345-5555. Nobody must know I called. The chief knows this as well and has given me his word that this call will remain confidential."

⨞

Lou called Mickey to let him know about the stranger who gave him the suspect's name and the tip that he had just gotten. While on the phone Mickey said, "Lou, Dr. Haire has been found."

"Dead under a marina dock?" Lou asked, fearing the worst.

"No, alive actually, in a ditch ten miles west of Oscoda, out in the country."

"Conscious?"

"I haven't had a full report on her medical condition, but she's alive and has a 50-50 chance of regaining consciousness. She's got a real bad head wound and some broken bones."

"That's wonderful news that she's alive."

"In a matter of minutes every law enforcement officer in this state will be looking for Jake Prescott and we'll ask for a search warrant once we have a place to search. We're getting real close to finding this guy."

"Let me know if you need our help, Mickey. We plan to be here most of the day, I would imagine. Our grandkids are coming over for a day on the beach. Call for any reason."

⊰⊱

Lou said to Maggie, "Just got a call from a woman who wouldn't identify herself. She's got a tip on our murderer. Does the family name Prescott have any meaning to you?"

"Not really. Wait, I recall seeing that name recently. Can't place it though. Maybe in a newspaper? The funeral home list of names!" Maggie exclaimed. "I'm fairly certain I saw a 'Prescott' on the list of people who were at the Verduin funeral."

"People usually put addresses in those books don't they?" Lou asked.

"Usually. I'll get right on it. The family takes that book from the funeral home. I'll call Mrs. Verduin and see if I can get a name verification and an address."

"Of course, Prescott is not that strange a name, it could be a different Prescott."

"Yes, but we can check this one out, anyway."

"Agree."

Maggie called and obtained the name and address, 419 Grand Ave. in Chelsea. While she had Mrs. Verduin on the phone, Maggie asked if she knew a Sara Prescott. She said she had never heard of her, but she said her husband had many clients and friends whom she did not know.

Maggie called information, got a number and called. A man answered who did not identify himself.

"Hello."

"Hello, Sara Prescott, please?"

"Ah, she's not here. I suggest you call the Chelsea Hospital. I don't know if Mrs. Prescott will be in any condition to talk with you."

"What's she doing in the hospital?" Maggie asked.

"I'm not at liberty to discuss this. If you want to talk to her, contact the hospital."

"Thank you." Maggie hung up and called the hospital. She was put through to Sara's room where once again a man answered.

"Hello."

"Hello. May I speak with Sara Prescott?"

"I don't think it would be a good idea at the moment, she's sedated and pretty groggy. Who is calling?" John asked.

"An old friend. Who am I talking to?"

"This is John, her son."

"John. I'm sorry about your mom."

"I think she'll be okay."

"I hope so. Is all of the family there?" Maggie asked.

"No, my brother Jake couldn't make it."

"But you'll be there for your mom?"

"I just arrived from up north and I'll be returning there soon, but Mom's good friend Mrs. Murphy will be here. I think I heard that her son, Tom is on his way as well."

"I'm glad she'll have good company. Listen, John, when Sara is awake, please tell her a good friend called and wishes her well. Oh, John, do you know if your mom was at the Verduin funeral?"

"Yes. Uncle Phil was a good family friend."

"I couldn't make it and was curious how it went."

"What is your name?" John asked. "I didn't get it."

"Jane. Just tell her Jane called."

"OK, I will."

"Oh, John. Where does Jake live now?"

"He's in Harrison."

"Thanks. I'll let you get back to your mom."

Lou called Chief McFadden to tell him what Maggie had learned. Mickey and Jerry had been doing their own work. "Once we heard the name 'Jake Prescott,' we put the name in our database," Mickey said. "If he's been arrested, his name would appear. We learned that he'd been arrested for drunk driving two years ago. He lives in Harrison, Michigan."

"Good. Let's get him."

"I'll contact the police chief in Harrison and we'll pay the man a visit. I'll get back to you if I learn anything."

꒰꒱

By now, there was a warrant for Jake's arrest. When the Harrison police drove up to Jake's two story home there was no light on and the car was missing. They knocked and when nobody answered, they just figured nobody was home so drove on back to the station. They tried to call but Jake didn't answer. The police immediately began procedures to obtain a search warrant.

꒰꒱

In the Oscoda Health Center, Edith remained unconscious but her vital signs were good. The doctors thought for Elaine's mental health and for Edith's as well, that they share the same room.

"I still can't believe it's you and that you're alive," Elaine responded emotionally. "Am I having a dream or is this for real?"

"It's for real, Elaine," the nurse replied. "We want you to keep talking to Edith. We think she may be able to hear you and your voice is critical to helping her come out of this coma."

"I think I'm going to cry. I cried a lot of tears yesterday thinking you were dead, Edith, and now you're alive. I'm glad you're going to live, Edith. Very thankful about that. We'll get better and be back to sailing in no time." Elaine just kept up a constant chatter hoping beyond hope that Edith could hear her.

Earlier in the day, there was a strange activity that went unreported. The supervisor of the clinic challenged the presence of a stranger. He had no credential to be present in the clinic and was told to leave immediately. He did.

"Scott and family are here! I saw the van pull in," Carol said, walking toward the door to welcome three-fifths of the joys of her life. Lou looked out and saw his grandsons getting out of the mini-van and running toward Carol, whom they called "Nana." Lou said to Maggie, "She loves those grandchildren with all of her heart. And, Carol loves Scott and Amanda as if they were her own."

"I thought they were her own?"

"No, their mother and I divorced in the early 1970s. Carol had left the convent when we met, after serving thirteen years as a sister in the Ursuline Order."

"I knew that, but for some reason all these years, I thought she was Scott and Amanda's mother."

"No, but she's told others that when we got married, the most wonderful gift I ever gave her was the gift of my children. In fact, I can't imagine a mother loving her children any more than Carol loves Scott and Amanda."

"Looks like everyone is blessed. To have Carol in any family is pure joy and for Carol to have Scott, Patti, and boys, as well as Amanda, Joe, Hannah and Thomas in your family is also a blessing."

"Yes, definitely."

"Hi, Grandpa," said five-year-old Ben with a smile as he came into the Searing home. Nick, age three, followed and headed right to the toy chest in the family room. Jack was a bit uneasy in his walk as he was just waking up having gone to sleep during the drive over from Grand Rapids.

"You ready to spend a day on the beach and in the water?" Lou asked.

"I brought my inner tube," Ben said holding the black, air-filled, rubber circle of fun close to his body with his right arm and hand.

"Well, good, you'll need it to stay afloat on that big body of water out there."

"Yeah, you know what, Grandpa?"

"What?"

"Mommy said I can throw sticks for Samm to chase."

"Well, Samm will like that. You'll have a friend for life, Ben."

"Yeah, and you know what?"

"No, what?"

"She said we can have S'mores after dinner, too."

"She did, did she? Well, that's almost a given after dinner on the beach. But, you need to be a good boy today and to be careful around the water. OK?"

"OK. And, you know what, Grandpa?"

"What, Ben? We've got to get out to the beach and have some fun."

"Samm wants to play with me."

"I'm sure she does, Ben. She loves having you and your family here. You've got much more energy than Nana and me. She sees you and she knows it's playtime!"

Lou gave all a hug when they entered. Hugs were important to him. Scott and family greeted Maggie warmly. They didn't know her well, but they knew Lou worked closely with her investigating murders. They admired her and related well to her on those occasions when all of them were together.

"Hi, Maggie, how are your son, John and his family doing?" Patti asked. She always asked about John because they shared the same birthday, May 26, and as a matter of fact, they were born in the same town and same hospital. She never knew him. But, once she learned of their shared day of arrival on earth, she always expressed concern for him and his family.

"Oh, he's doing just fine," Maggie said. "I'm afraid he's beginning to take up golf quite seriously, like Tom. I hope, for the sake of his wife Margaret and their daughter Kathy that he doesn't become addicted like Tom. It's a good pastime, but it can grab you and not let go."

"Is John still living in California?"

"Yes, but Margaret is suggesting that they move to Michigan."

"Wouldn't that be great?"

"Yes, having him and his family close by would be a gift, believe me. I'm envious every time Lou mentions that you folks will be sharing time, like today."

"Uh huh, it's nice and I'd like the boys to grow up knowing their grandparents on both sides of the family. I know Lou and Carol miss seeing Amanda and her family since as you know they live in St. Louis, but they seem to have quality time when getting together is possible."

The boys were in their swimsuits. The afternoon was a hot one. Scott had applied sunscreen to Ben, Nick and himself and they were out the door ready for sun and fun on the shore of Lake Michigan. Lou would follow soon, but first he called Chief McFadden in Manistee.

"Got anything new on the marina murders?" Lou asked.

"The Clare County sheriff has gotten an arrest warrant for Jake Prescott and a search warrant for the home and his vehicle."

"Any problem having those issued?"

"Not at all."

"Do you need me?" Lou asked.

"Yeah, I'd like you and Maggie to come up to Harrison to be on hand when we arrest him and look around in his living space."

"When will you be leaving?"

"Actually, I'm heading out now. You and Maggie don't need to get there when the arrest is made, if we can find him, but soon after would be good."

"OK, we've got the family here right now. Maggie is here and we can head up."

"I'd appreciate it, Lou," Chief McFadden said.

"This is important. If you want us there, we'll be there."

"Thanks. Let's make McDonalds our rendezvous spot and we'll have radio and phone contacts as well."

"See you in Harrison, Mickey."

Lou told Maggie of the discussion. She had not brought her overnight bag in from her van, so she was ready to go. Lou also explained his plans to Carol, who understood his wanting to help out Mickey McFadden.

Lou walked out the door and headed to Scott who was making a detailed sand castle on the shore with Nick. Lou could see the artistic talent in Nick. He had a way of stacking that wet sand at only age three and Lou immediately thought he might have a gene presupposed for a talent in art. Who knows?

"Scott, Maggie and I have got to get to Harrison. We're about to wrap up the marina murders case. Sorry, but I've got to go."

"No problem. Thanks for letting us share your backyard pool here," Scott said, referencing Lake Michigan.

"Anytime."

Lou shouted goodbye to Ben, Nick, and Jack.

"Where are you going, Grandpa?" Nick asked.

"Grandpa's got some work to do, Nick."

"You're not going to eat any S'mores?"

"Probably not. Hey, my name's on one. I'll give it to you, Nick. How does that sound?"

"Good. Thanks."

"I'll see you soon, Nick." And, with that Lou quickly packed his toiletries and a change of clothes. He went out to join Maggie who had already activated the hydraulic device that allowed her to be lifted from the driveway up into her accessible van. All Lou needed to do was join her in the front seat and they'd be off to Harrison.

Lou kissed Carol goodbye. "I'll call with what's happening."

"You be careful now, you hear?" Carol said lovingly as she did each time Lou headed for possible danger.

"I will." Ever since the shooting near Rudyard in a case Lou and Maggie solved several years ago, Carol didn't want him heading off to harm's way. Lou couldn't blame her, but told her there was no reason to fear, he learned his lesson that day.

Maggie backed out of the driveway and they were on their way to bring this case to its conclusion.

ॐ

While Lou and Maggie were on their way north and getting close to Harrison, the Clare County sheriff's deputies were once again knocking on Jake Prescott's door. Again, there was no response. With a search warrant in hand, they broke the door down and entered, along with a representative from the State Police Forensic Laboratory. This would assure the search of the home would be text book.

Officers had revolvers drawn and bullet proof vests on. Jake was hiding in an upstairs bedroom closet. He knew that his arsenal of weapons and his incredible strength would be an asset. Being outnumbered and surrounded by a lot of cops was a negative. However, if he could have a gun to the head of one of the cops, his chances of negotiation were good.

Jake hid behind clothes and was able to stand on a shoe storage box and with clothes on hangers in front of him, he was totally hidden. It would only be if a cop shoved clothes to the side that he'd be discovered and if that happened, he was ready to fire a round into the body of the unsuspecting cop.

A lot of noise erupted as the police broke into Jake's home. He heard several people enter as well as shouts of someone calling for anyone to come out. Silence. The police figured that nobody was home so they let down their guard.

Jake could hear footsteps coming up the hardwood stairs. Within thirty seconds the closet door opened. The officer saw nothing but hanging clothes so closed the door. Jake remained in the closet, but he cracked the door to hear a little better and to be able to see when anyone would enter the room. He was certain that someone would be coming back, because he had a file cabinet in his bedroom that contained a lot of papers.

Jake believed that the next time someone came in, the intruder would not have a weapon drawn because they had concluded that

Jake was not in the home. He waited patiently. He could hear activity downstairs and he wondered what might be found.

The police and forensic crime lab people took photos, dusted for fingerprints, went through a small desk but couldn't find anything that could be used to tie Jake Prescott to the murders of five doctors in Michigan marinas.

The lead detective said, "Did anybody search in the bedroom?"

"I went in looking for him, but no one was there," Deputy Leach replied.

"I mean to look for any evidence?"

"No. I did notice a file cabinet."

"OK, Sam, you go in and see if you can find anything. We'll go outside and see if we can see anything."

Deputy Sam Leach walked up the flight of stairs and walked into Jake's bedroom. Jake was right, the weapon was in his holster and not drawn. The deputy opened the cabinet and had his back to Jake. At the perfect moment, Jake burst from the closet and wrapped his arm around Sam Leach's neck and held him in a hammer lock.

"Not a word and I mean it. One word and your neck will snap. Understand? You're my ticket outta here and if we get out, you live, if I don't get what I want and need, you're history. Understand?"

Sam Leach nodded and hardly could breathe. Jake had a tight hold around the deputy's neck. Jake used a torn sheet to tie Sam's ankles and hands behind his back and then he stuffed some of the sheet in his mouth and wrapped a torn off strip around his face so he couldn't speak or see what was about to happen.

Jake stayed upstairs and didn't make a sound and wouldn't until the others came looking for him.

It soon became obvious that Deputy Leach had not appeared and it shouldn't have taken him so long to search the bedroom.

"Sam, you about finished?" Detective Sergeant John Duggan shouted upstairs. There was no response.

The other members of the search team looked at each other. "You guys stay here and cover me, I'm going up."

Sergeant Duggan walked upstairs saying, "Sam, you about finished?"

As he was about to reach the top of the stairs, Jake appeared and shouted, "Drop it, drop it, now! This cop's dead with any smart moves. Drop the gun, now! Sit on the steps, sit down! Move!!"

Detective Duggan let his gun fall down the stairs as he sat down. "Get ahold of yourself, fella. We'll work this out."

"You're on my property without my permission. There's a price to pay for that."

"We've got a search warrant. It's all legal. What do you need, son?" Duggan asked, since Jake was about two generations his junior.

"For starters I want everyone out of my home except this guy who's staying here and you will stay where you are. You got a radio?"

"Sure. We can talk with it. I'll tell the others to leave. Is that what you want?"

"Yes, and no bringing in cops, SWAT teams or an army of guys. I'm serious. A few bodies under a dock are nothing compared to what I can do with the arsenal I have up here. So, just clear out your men and I want nobody else coming around here. Don't challenge me on this, you hear? If my demands are not met, people will die and I'll start with this guy, and then you. Understand?"

"Yeah, you've made yourself pretty clear," Detective Duggan answered. He then shouted, "Guys, listen up. I want you outta here. No replacements, nobody coming around here. This guy's armed and dangerous. I'm serious, no cop cars in this area, nothing till you hear from me. If anybody comes around, we're dead. Now, get out of here and get away from the house and out of town with no replacements. Repeat, no heroes. Leave now."

"Good job, you give directions well," Jake said, while pointing the gun at John Duggan's head.

Jake had directed Detective Duggan to come into the bedroom where the officer was tied up. The only difference in the two officers was that Sam Leach was bound and gagged. Jake wanted Duggan to be able to talk so as to get him what was needed to survive.

"You the marina murderer?" Detective Duggan asked.

"Yeah," Jake admitted.

"You're in this kinda deep, son. It doesn't look good for you."

"Shut up and listen. If you want to live, you're going to have to do what I say."

"What do you want done? You sure don't want to go outside this home do you? Here, you're in control, out there, you ain't got a prayer, son. I mean you ain't got a prayer. Talk about Butch Cassidy and the Sundance Kid, you won't even get a shot fired before you're blown away."

"Shut up! I didn't ask for any advice. Did I ask you for advice?"

"No, just thought I'd give...."

"Then shut up!" After a few seconds of silence, Jake realized that the cop was right. He had two hostages and some time. How he used the time and how he used his head would define his future. He tried calling his mother. No answer. He called John and told him to get to Harrison as soon as possible. John was already in the Mt. Pleasant area on his way to Jake's home. Jake told him what was happening and to wait outside of town till he called him.

ॐ

At the sheriff's office, the situation was clear that Jake Prescott was holed up in his home with two police officers. The marina killer was now cornered, located, and caught. Even if Jake could get out of his home, every road to Harrison would be shut down, helicopters stood ready to track his every move, dogs and SWAT team members were ready to capture him if he attempted to escape.

So, as far as the police were concerned, they had their man, dead or alive, the only issue now was getting Leach and Duggan safely out of the home. That was the challenge.

With each passing minute, Maggie and Lou were a mile closer to Harrison and a rendezvous at McDonald's. The time went slowly for those captured and those planning how best to save lives and still get their man.

At about 7:10, Mickey pulled into McDonalds. He went inside and ordered a shake and some fries and sat down to wait for Maggie and Lou. He planned to call the Clare County Sheriff as soon as the three were together and ready to get to work.

About five minutes later, Maggie's van pulled into the parking lot. Mickey, Lou, and Maggie had no idea that a vacant lot away was the home of Jake Prescott with two officers being held captive inside.

"Well, looks like your buddies don't care if you live or die, old man. Cops and detectives are in town, right next door at Mickey D's. You two want to draw straws to see which of you go first or do I just flip a coin?" Jake asked.

"Your call, kid. You're the one with the gun. But, I'll tell you this, once we're gone, you're gone. You kill us and they'll hit this place with the atom bomb and believe me, they will. Two cops dead and five people in the marinas are dead and you think they'll have any mercy? Not a prayer. So, go ahead and end it for us, but it's your ticket to hell."

Once again Jake realized that the old cop was right. These two were his chance to live. He could sound tough, but, the cop was right.

Jake had to make a statement to the cops and the detectives. He had recognized Maggie and Lou from his brother's description. He didn't know who the third person was but figured he was the law.

He took his gun and smashed the window firing quickly at Lou, Maggie, and Chief McFadden. Maggie slumped over in her chair. Lou jumped in front of her to take hits from anymore fire. Mickey quickly sheltered himself behind an opened car door. The shooting was over and Lou didn't feel any pain or stinging sensation as he had in Rudyard, the only other time a bullet had ripped through him.

But, Maggie had been hit. On instinct, Lou pushed her out of view of the house next door. It looked like the wounds were in her legs. She glanced at her thigh. "I've been hit, Lou."

"Where? In the legs?"

"Yeah, pants have holes and blood is coming out. I can't feel anything, but that's because of my paralysis."

Mickey had already called for an ambulance and let 911 know of the shooting at McDonald's in Harrison.

Lou cut and ripped her slacks where there was blood and they both looked at wounds that were the size of pencil erasers. Lou tore off his short sleeve shirt and wrapped it tight around her leg and also around her calf where a second bullet had entered.

"That was just about the stupidest thing you could have done, kid," Detective Duggan said, shaking his head.

"Got to follow up on my word."

"Well you did that, but the game's over, the place will be covered with cops. You could have used your head and lived a little longer, and I sort of figured you were kind of smart. Behind all that muscle was a brain, but now, you're crazy and acting irrationally."

"Shut up!!"

The siren from the ambulance was quick and paramedics were on the scene doing their jobs. They tended to Maggie and then rushed her off to the MidMichigan Medical Center in Clare. She demanded that Lou stay on-site and do whatever he could to solve this case. Typical Maggie, solving the case was her highest priority. Following the ambulance was John Prescott. Jake had called him to tell him not to lose sight of Maggie.

Lou was assured she'd be okay. Thankful as the bullets entered her paralyzed legs and not any vital organs. Lou knew that hospital personnel would call Tom and brief him on Maggie's condition.

The sheriff and other law enforcement personnel had cordoned off a two block area around Jake's house. The sheriff made his presence known and demanded that Jake give himself up.

Jake turned to Detective Duggan. "All I want is for you to do something for me and I'll give up."

"What's that kid?"

"Contact my mother, Sara Prescott. Tell her she was a great mother. She did all she could to raise me and my brother. Tell her I'm sorry, but I simply had to seek revenge for her, for John, for the other families, so that there would be some justice, just some justice because in this country there should be justice. You should not be allowed to destroy people and then live a life on yachts and drive expensive cars and fail to allow qualified young minds into medical school."

"I'll tell her, I promise. You give it up now, kid. You haven't got a prayer if you don't."

"Yeah, I know. I will. You tell 'em I'm coming out. I'm finished."

"Best decision you've made, son."

John Duggan took his radio and spoke into it. "Sheriff, kid here wants to give up. He'll come out, no weapon. You can trust me. I'm not being forced to say this, Sheriff. Don't anyone fire on him. He's not armed. He's willing to go with you."

Jake, head bowed, walked toward the sheriff who took him by the arm and escorted him to his vehicle where he was frisked and cuffed and put into the cruiser for the short drive to the County Sheriff's Office. It was peaceful and nothing like what all had expected—a deadly shootout with much bloodshed and violence.

With Jake being taken away, a team of detectives and forensic experts returned to the apartment to seek evidence of the marina murders. Lou asked if he could go inside. Permission was granted.

Lou put on latex gloves and looked all about. Like a homeless soul looking for an empty can for a dime in a trash bin, Lou pushed a few papers around in the wastebasket. He didn't find anything, but the techs were finding all that would be needed to convict Jake Prescott of murder. The DNA of hairs in the Escanaba clothes basket and hairs in the apartment shower stall would surely do it. Fingerprints around the apartment and fingerprints on the magazine in Escanaba would also be plenty of evidence. Finally, the kid's own admission of guilt would nail his coffin shut in the state penitentiary.

Lou walked out into the warm air on a Saturday evening. Now that the case was closed, he needed to get to Clare to be with Maggie and to contact those who loved her.

ᴣ⁊

On the way to the hospital, Lou called Carol to report that while he was okay, Maggie had taken some fire and was in the hospital. Lou told her that the wounds were not life threatening and that he would call with any additional information. Carol was relieved that Lou was fine but frightened to hear that Maggie was in the hospital.

When Lou got to the hospital in Clare, Maggie was resting

comfortably in her room. She was patched and soon to be released from the hospital.

"Any damage to bones or anything?"

"Nope, just muscle I guess," Maggie said, quite relieved. "I don't feel anything obviously. Just got some holes in me. They gave me something for infection. I don't think I have to stay overnight."

"Well, if the doctor thinks you need to stay here, that's what will happen. I want you getting excellent care and so would Tom. We wouldn't get home till after midnight anyway."

"Looks like we were in the wrong place at the wrong time."

"Yeah, he was holding a couple of officers hostage in his home which was next door to McDonalds where we agreed to meet Chief McFadden."

"I didn't think he'd know us."

"We weren't innocent victims. I'm certain of that," Lou said.

"I guess the score is one to one now, Lou. You took a hit in Rudyard and I took one in Harrison."

"I'm not keeping score, but guess it comes with the territory."

"Thanks for shielding me out there, Lou."

"Not a problem."

"You could have been killed."

"Yeah, but I wasn't. You'd have done the same thing for me."

"Yeah I would've."

"Does Tom know about this?"

"I talked to him and told him. He said he would come right up, but I told him it was only a few bullet wounds and I was fine. I'd be home soon and he could be a doting nurse at that time."

"I called Carol and told her."

"I know. I called her too. You got to her first. I thought I'd tell her instead of you. Women can discuss these things a bit better. She loves you and just isn't a big fan of your putting yourself at risk. But, she also knows that you enjoy this work and so she'll grin and bear it, I suppose."

Just then a doctor appeared. "How are we doing, Maggie?"

"Fine. This is Lou Searing, my partner in crime, so to speak."

"Pleased to meet you." The two men shook hands.

"Thank you. Nice to meet you," Lou said. "Thanks for helping my friend here."

"You're welcome. She's one tough woman."

"Any permanent damage?" Lou asked.

"No, she's lucky in that regard. My concern was that as medical technology reaches a point where people with her type of spinal injury can walk, that this damage today will not interfere with that."

"And?"

"And, I think she'll be OK. The bullets tore through muscle and a little cartilage. That should heal on its own in time. There'll be some scar tissue and a scar where the bullets entered and in one case exited the body. I've prescribed some medication to fight infection."

"Is she to stay overnight here?"

"I don't think so. We don't need to keep her under observation. She's free to go if she wishes."

"What do you think, Maggie? Are you up to it?"

"I think so, Lou. I'd like to go back to Grand Haven even though we'd get there very late. I don't want to stay in some motel."

"Sure, we'll get you in your van and I'll drive it back to Grand Haven."

ॐ

Jake Prescott was taken to the county jail, booked and processed. He'd be arraigned in the morning and charged with five counts of murder, and attempted murder of Edith Haire and Maggie McMillan. The judge would surely deny bail. As Jake did not have money to hire a lawyer the judge appointed a lawyer to defend him.

After the court appearance the next morning, Jake asked to see his friend, Father Murphy. Two hours later, Father Thomas Murphy came into Jake's cell. "May God's peace be with you," Father Murphy said, giving Jake a warm embrace. Jake nodded and thanked his friend for coming.

"You wanted to see me," Father Murphy said.

"Yeah, I do. I want to go to confession. I've killed five people and I don't want my soul condemned to hell. I am truly sorry."

"I am sorry too, Jake," Father Tom said with head bowed. "I wish I could have convinced you not to kill these people or that I could have intervened to protect you and others.

Jake, seated with elbows on his knees and his head in his hands, listened with a tear or two falling to the floor.

"There must be restitution, Jake. It might be giving up your freedom for the rest of your life. A lot of families are as devastated as you were when your father died." Jake nodded. "I suggest you pray daily for their forgiveness." Jake nodded.

"God forgives you of your sins, Jake. He loves you."

"Thank you, Father."

"God bless you, my friend. May God grant you peace." Father Murphy rose, embraced Jake and walked from his cell. As Father Murphy left the county jail he realized that the carnage was over. He had remained true to his vow not to reveal anything said in confession, but he would have five people on his mind for years to come. He would always feel responsible for their untimely and horrific deaths.

As a boy, Thomas Murphy had tried to protect Jake and did so often, but once he became a priest, he couldn't protect his friend, nor could he protect those who were marked for death. Father Murphy could only offer absolution of Jake's mortal sins that would hopefully save his friend from the depths of hell.

CHAPTER SEVENTEEN

Sunday, July 19
Grand Haven, Michigan
Chicago, Illinois

Carol and Lou got up early and with Maggie still sleeping, went to church. On the way they summarized the last two weeks. "Terrible two weeks, Lou," Carol said shaking her head in disbelief.

"Yeah, five deaths in marinas and two significant injuries to Maggie and Dr. Haire. That's a lot of damage to people," Lou said.

"It sure is, but thankfully it's over." Maggie and Lou had talked about the two weeks on their way home the night before. They really couldn't see how they could have prevented any of the deaths. By the time they picked up on some clues it was too late to prevent a killing. So, they did the best they could and with the help of an unknown woman, they finally caught up to a very sick young man.

Lou and Carol walked into church and sat where they usually do. The Mass was celebrated by Father Thompson. When Father said, "Now we will pray for our own intentions," Lou had a long list, but he only gave worshippers about five seconds. Lou kept his head bowed and went through his list anyway: Carol Searing, Maggie McMillan, Mickey McFadden, Jerry Maguffin, Jeremy Billings, Trisha ... The list didn't seem to end but Lou tried to keep his concentration on the next phase of the Mass.

People were worshipping in Michigan City, Indiana, as well. Many heard the piercing sirens of several emergency vehicles. The sounds almost drowned out the singing of hymns as the police and ambulances flew past a number of churches in the downtown area. The vehicles were heading for the marina and the yacht of Dr. Philip Heyboer. They had gotten a call from Molly saying that Dr. Heyboer was in need of medical attention.

Dr. Heyboer was not floating under a dock beside his yacht *Filling A Prescription.* He was inside his yacht, short of breath, heart going 90 mph, and sweating like he had finished a marathon, and as far as his body was concerned, he had. Apparently he had heard that Edith Haire had been kidnapped and Dr. Heyboer knew the next victim would be himself or Dr. Gallow. Just the thought of the potential trauma caused his heart to take off and for all the signs of a heart attack to prevail.

Dr. Heyboer was taken to the hospital, treated, and released. Molly had called the police and asked for twenty-four hour protection. It was granted.

⟿

When Carol and Lou got home from church, they heard Maggie calling for Carol. Carol went into her bedroom to see what was wrong. A few minutes later Carol came out, "She's in a lot of pain, Lou. She doesn't look well."

"Is she taking her medication for infection?"

"I asked her. She said she was up most of the night in pain and yes, she took the medicine."

"Hmmm, this shouldn't be happening, Carol. The doc in Clare prescribed some medication for possible infection. Please go back in and see if you can find out what's the problem."

Carol returned to the bedroom and talked with Maggie.

"I feel nauseous, like I'm going to faint," Maggie told Carol quietly. "I just shake like I'm in a freezer. I think I have a fever too. Please call Tom, will you? I'm scared, Carol. Really scared."

"I'm calling Tom, but we've got to get you some help."

Carol came out of the guest bedroom. "This isn't good, Lou. We've got to call Tom and get her to the hospital."

"Let's just call our doctor and see if he can come out here now."

Lou called Doctor Wagner and luckily found him answering emergencies on a Sunday morning. "Can you come to the house? Maggie McMillan, my co-investigator, is quite sick and needs your help."

"I'll be right over, Lou."

"Thanks, Doc."

Within five minutes Doc's car came into the driveway and he approached with the traditional black bag in hand.

"Thanks for coming over, Doc."

"Sure. Where's Maggie?"

"First floor bedroom, turn left at the end of the hall."

Carol went in with him. "Can I be here, Maggie?" Maggie nodded consent.

"What's the problem, Maggie? Can you talk about it?" Doc Wagner asked.

"I was shot yesterday evening. I was treated at the hospital in Clare. They patched me up and sent me home with some pills to fight infection."

"What did they give you?"

"The bottle's on the table, here by the bed, I've taken most of them."

Doc Wagner looked at the label and nodded as if agreeing with the prescription. "Let me get your temperature, blood pressure and let me look at the wounds.

Doc went about his analysis. Carol left them alone as she and Lou waited for Doc to come out and give them his diagnosis.

About ten minutes later he appeared. "Got me stumped. At first I thought it was an infection from the wound, but I don't see that. Then I thought it might be an allergic reaction to the medication, but her symptoms show no evidence of that. Then I thought her nausea and faintness might be due to blood pressure, but it's high normal and her heart beat is strong."

"Do we take her to the hospital?"

"This is strange, folks. She needs to be at a specialized hospital. I'm afraid I don't know what's wrong, but I know enough to know that she needs more help than I or any doctor in the area can give her."

Lou picked up the phone and called a friend, Tom Howard who was a pilot. He answered.

"Tom? Lou Searing here. Maggie's sick, our Doc's here at the house. He can't define it, says she needs medical help that no one around here can provide. She's got to get to Chicago."

"If you can get her to the Grand Haven Airport, we'll have her in Chicago in less than an hour," Tom Howard replied ready to help out. "Your Doc can come along and be in constant touch with the Chicago hospital so he can carry out any procedures during the flight."

Lou went into the bedroom. Doc and Carol followed. "Tom Howard is going to see that you get to Chicago and be seen by the doctors who can treat you. We called your husband and he's heading there as well. You'll be getting the best care by knowledgeable doctors. He's even taking Doc there so you can have medical attention all the way."

Maggie stared into space. "Do you understand?" Lou asked.

She seemed delirious, but nodded enough to let him know his message sunk in.

Doc stayed and tended to Maggie. He directed that she be given cool washcloths on her forehead while he monitored her temperature and blood pressure.

Before leaving for the airport, Doc called his colleague to report his unexpected trip to Chicago. He also called his wife to explain his quick trip, telling her he would return later in the evening.

At this point, Lou admitted that he feared for Maggie's life. When he looked at her and sensed the confusion in Doctor Wagner's face, Lou really thought she might not make it. Carol called the ambulance to transport Maggie to the airport but didn't want them to leave until Tom was about to take off. This would allow her to board and be in the air within minutes.

The ambulance arrived and Maggie was taken to the airport. She was helped into the plane along with Carol and Doc Wagner. Doctor Wagner used his cell phone to connect him to the Chicago area hospital where Doc directed she be taken for a consult and treatment by one of the top internists in the country, if not in the world.

Doc passed along all of her symptoms and the Chicago doctor noted them. The physician asked questions, and then asked to be provided with periodic updates of her vital signs. He also said that she'd have a room waiting for her. She would be brought in by helicopter from Midway Airport.

Carol was a calming influence on Maggie. The two were like sisters and could easily communicate feelings and needs. She was a perfect companion for the flight.

Lou returned home, put his cell phone in his pocket, and with Samm wanting a stick or two thrown, walked along the beach happy that the case was closed, but very sorry that Maggie was so sick and wondering what the problem could possibly be.

⌇

Lou received a call around noon from Carol. She reported that they made it to Chicago, as if she were driving to Grand Rapids. The ambulance greeted them and took them to a medical helicopter that airlifted them to the hospital. Carol said that a team of doctors met Maggie and have been working on her, trying to decide a course of treatment. Carol's last word was that Maggie was unconscious, vital signs were not looking good, but she was alive.

Maggie and Lou had been on some tough cases and had endured threats and close calls in previous investigations, but this one was most troublesome.

⌇

That evening. Lou was watching the Tigers on TV as he was trying to take his mind off Maggie's condition. Right out of the blue, with Bobby Higginson at the plate, an idea hit him, this case isn't over. There is another involved and Maggie's illness is a result of some interaction with this second person. The thought was surreal as if some messenger whispered it into his ear.

Lou got up, turned off the TV and went to the phone. He called Mickey McFadden to tell him his thought.

"Your idea comes at the perfect time. Lou. I just got a call from Rose Crandall at the Chalet Apartments. You remember Rose?"

"Oh sure, Maggie had a good talk with her."

"Yes. Well, she claims that as the talk around the breakfast table centered on a suspect being arrested, one of the residents said she knew of the family. She said the man who was arrested, Jake, has a twin brother, John. Rose is thinking that we should find John Prescott and see what he knows."

"Well, I knew of the twin brother, but I guess I didn't think he was involved. If he is, there's my second person, Mickey. Did she give any clue as to where I might find him?"

"All she said was that this lady at breakfast thought he worked in some state run laboratory and was a medical student at some university, probably Michigan State."

"OK, I'll check into it. Thanks."

◗

Carol called. There had been no change in Maggie's condition. She was still unconscious. The doctors had been doing blood analysis and taking tissue from various parts of her body for study.

Lou took Samm for another walk on the beach and realized that his joy of having this case closed twenty-four hours ago had been replaced with continued frustration that the case was not solved or at least not completely solved.

Lou went inside, watched "The Practice" on TV and wished his cases could all be solved in an hour. He went to bed and fell asleep with a prayer for Maggie's return to good health.

CHAPTER EIGHTEEN

Monday, July 20
Grand Haven and Bay City, Michigan

Lou awoke alone in bed and it took a second or two to realize that Carol was in Chicago, that it was Monday, and that he had work to do. Lou did feel like a jog on the beach, so got up and did that with Samm running alongside. When Lou jogs along the shore of Lake Michigan he often recalls the movie "Chariots of Fire" with the athletes running along the seaside. Lou's jog was much slower than it used to be. He used to run races almost every weekend back in the 1980s. He did a few triathlons and a marathon, only one to say he did one, but with no desire to rack up an impressive number of marathons. He came, he saw, he conquered, but almost died, so with the "marathon" on his resumé, Lou decided to stick to shorter races.

The day promised to be a beautiful one. It would be hot, but with low humidity. Sunbathers lived for this kind of day. Lou enjoyed his run and went inside for a cup of coffee and a light breakfast. Lou would expect a call from Carol any minute and then he had calls to make himself.

Lou had a good feeling about the day. He felt that Maggie would come around and that the case would break, if, in fact, he was right, that there was more to this case than Jake Prescott.

༃

After breakfast, a shower, and getting dressed for the day, Lou sat down with the phone. His brother Bob retired from the Michigan state police as a highly respected detective. He had introduced Lou to some of his colleagues and there was one officer, Mike Cirrito, about whom Bob once told Lou, "If you ever need help and you think the state police can help you, call Mike Cirrito. He's the best, simply the best." Lou called Mike.

"Mike, this is Lou Searing; you know my brother, Bob Searing."

"Oh, yes, Bob and I go way back. How is he doing?"

"You know, I rarely see him. I think he's doing OK."

"Good. He's a fine man."

"Yes, he is."

"What can I do for you, Lou?"

"Well, Bob told me once that if I ever needed any help to give you a call."

"Yeah, sounds like Bob. He's always finding work for me to do, but for Bob and certainly his younger brother, I'd do it with a smile on my face."

"Thanks, I appreciate it."

"What do you need?"

"I'm looking for a guy I'd say around 25, but I can't be certain of that. His name is John Prescott. I understand he works in a state lab, probably Department of Community Health. He was hired probably within the last year or two. He might be a medical school student at MSU. What can you do for me?"

"Sounds fairly simple. You want an address, phone number? What info do you want on him?" Mike asked.

"Yeah, the basics like that, but if you can find someone like that, I'm going to want to know if he's been at work the last two weeks, what kind of vehicle he drives, a photo of him, if he's been in any trouble with the law for starters."

"OK, I'll be back with you in 15 minutes."

"Fifteen minutes? You Superman or something?"

"There's no phone booth around here for me to change into my outfit," Mike said with a chuckle. " This should take one phone call, maybe two. Don't go far from the phone, Lou."

"Thanks, Mike. I'll wait to hear from you."

"Be with you soon, Lou."

Lou read the newspaper and before he was past the local section, the phone rang. It would either be Carol or Mike. It was Mike.

"Lou?"

"That was fast."

"You gave me an easy assignment. The assignments from the Commander are the tough ones."

"What do you have for me?"

"John Prescott is 24 years old, six-feet-tall, very muscular, works out in the gym a lot. Drives a red Ford Ranger XLT, he's a Lab Worker Six, which means an entry level job studying tissue cultures from people who've contracted meningitis or rare forms of viral or bacterial infections. He came to the state job about 2 years ago and you were right, he's a student at MSU med school, he's kind of a quiet guy, no friends, does his job and spends his time in bars and weight rooms.

"Apparently he has a white coat syndrome, always wearing a white lab coat that brings teasing comments from co-workers because he also sometimes has a stethoscope around his neck, he gets teased because there is no need for such an instrument. Some colleagues call him "Doc J." behind his back. He's been at work on and off using vacation days sporadically in the past month. He's got no criminal record, 4 points on his driver's license for speeding. That's all I could find in three minutes of work. Is that it, Lou, or can I help you with anything else?"

"Can I get a photo of him?"

"Your fax should be ringing and a photo should be in your home in a few seconds."

"Is there any family information in front of you?"

"Only a name to contact in an emergency."

"What's that name?"

"Jake Prescott in Harrison, Michigan, 517 555-9203."

"As they say in the American Legion halls and the Catholic school cafeterias, 'BINGO,' Mike. You're probably going to get a letter of commendation to add to your personnel file. Great job. Thanks."

"Not a problem, please tell Bob my fishin' pole's been callin' his name!"

"I will, and thanks again, Mike."

᛭

Lou hung up and went upstairs to his office. He looked in the fax tray and there was a page with the photo of the lab worker. He was an identical twin brother of Jake Prescott. The resemblance was so close you couldn't distinguish between the two in a line up.

This put Lou into a whole new game. It was obvious that the marina maniac was not the work of one man, but of twin brothers. Lou also figured out that John could have been in the Clare hospital Saturday night, wearing a white coat, and carrying a stethoscope, portraying a doctor and could have in someway infected Maggie with a sample of infectious bacteria.

Lou immediately went to the phone and called the number Carol gave him in Chicago. He was fortunate to find Carol in the Intensive Care waiting area.

"How's Maggie?"

"Not good, Lou. They can't isolate the problem and she's starting to go down hill, I'm afraid."

"Is Doc there?"

"Our Doc, or Maggie's specialist?"

"Either one."

"Yeah, Doctor Wagner is with me. I'll put him on."

"Doc, I've gotten some information that Maggie could have been infected with some bacteria from a state lab in Lansing that studies infectious diseases."

"We're waiting for lab results now as we suspected that too. What could it have been? Do you know?"

"Don't know, but a suspect has surfaced in the marina murders and the suspect may have access to viruses and bacteria." Lou went on to explain what he knew.

"I'll let the doctors here know that. We'll call the state lab and see what cultures John Prescott was working on. That should give us the strain and then all we need is the antidote. Thanks."

Doc handed the phone to Carol as he quickly went to a phone.

"You doing OK, Lou?"

"Yeah, looks like this case isn't over as we had thought."

"'I just hope Maggie survives this, Lou. I've never seen anyone so sick, but she is hanging tough. Her body's fighting it, I'll give her that."

"OK, I've got to go. Stay in touch. Love you."

"Love you too, Lou. Be careful."

"I will."

⁂

Lou called the Clare County Sheriff and asked to speak to the detective handling the case of Jake Prescott. A man came on the line.

"Hello, this is Lou Searing, an investigator of the marina murders."

"Yes, Lou, this is Detective Ackerman. How can I help you?"

"In the evidence room or bag or whatever is a book found in Jake Prescott's apartment Saturday evening. It has names of doctors who were murdered and the word 'Revenge' in red. When I looked at that I didn't note the next name on the list. I need that name."

"Hold on, I'll get it for you."

Lou waited for about a minute which seemed to be an eternity. The detective came back on. "Dr. Cris Gallow, Otologist."

"Thanks, is there a boat name as well?"

"Yeah, *Hearing a-Wake.*"

"Thanks."

Lou hung up and called Mickey McFadden. He told him all that he had learned to date. "I thought the case was closed after the arrest of Jake Prescott. Because of the book we found in Jake's home we can predict that the next victim will be a Doctor Cris Gallow, an otologist with a boat named *Hearing a-Wake.*"

"I've got it noted," Mickey said.

"We need another marina alert as we need to find this doctor and her boat if it's on the Great Lakes."

"OK, I'll get it out within minutes. Thanks, Lou."

***

Cris Gallow lived and practiced in Bay City. A tradition in her office was to choose one day in the summer and take the staff on a cruise into Saginaw Bay. They would have a day on the bay and return to the marina for a cookout and games. It was Cris's way of thanking her staff for all their hard work during the year. The staff looked forward to this outing because it was fun, a total break in the routine and it also allowed them to see Cris in a relaxed and out-of-character role. This year's event was to be tomorrow.

Cris Gallow was in her marina, using the last day of her vacation to be on her boat cleaning up and bringing drinks on so that when the staff prepared to arrive in the morning, all would be set.

The news of the killings had reached Dr. Gallow and she felt she would be able to handle any approach by the killer. Shooting her at a distance would be certain death, but any kind of face to face confrontation would be for her, or so she thought, a piece of cake.

John Prescott was parked on Evergreen Drive, sitting in his Ford Ranger with binoculars trained on *Hearing a-Wake*. The marina was on Water Street, across the Saginaw River. He watched Cris wherever she went.

John knew that everyone's guard would be down. The word had gone throughout the state that his brother Jake had been caught and the marinas were now free of any problems once again. There were no posters, no warnings, and nobody was on guard mistrusting every stranger who walked around.

John read his brother's detailed instructions one more time: *Dr. Gallow will be taking her staff for a day in Saginaw Bay on July 21. There will be some preparations for this party the day before. This is the approach you will use with her. The Telephone Relay System for the Deaf will be used to contact Dr. Gallow. You have been taught how this system works so you will implement it effectively. You will call the relay center at one-thirty and ask to be put through to Dr. Gallow. She will come on the line and this is what you will say 'My name is Steven Wilson. You treated me several years ago when I had a mastoidectomy in my left ear. I have gone almost completely deaf and I don't know why and I'm terrified. May I please see you this afternoon?'*

She will say yes and invite you to come to the marina or to meet her at her office. Her reputation is to never deny a patient access to her, especially one in great need, even emotional need. You thank her profusely and indicate you will be right down (marina or office). You know what to do from this point on as we've talked about the perfect setting for the monoxide poisoning.

⟲

Mickey got a call from the marina's harbormaster in Bay City telling him that Dr. Gallow did have a yacht in his marina and was in fact there and appeared to be taking supplies onto her boat. All appeared to be normal.

Mickey called Lou at home and when he heard what he had to say, he replied, "I'm going to Bay City, Mickey. Fax the photo of John Prescott to the police and harbormaster and put everyone on alert and pull over any Ford Ranger in sight."

Before the word of caution could get to the Liberty Harbor in Bay City, John pulled his Ford Ranger up alongside Cris's Chevy Blazer.

"Excuse me, Dr. Gallow, I'm Steven Wilson, I just called a moment ago. Thank you for seeing me."

"You're welcome. Let's go to my boat where I have some instruments." Dr. Gallow motioned to come and began to walk toward her yacht. John immediately put a gun into her back and said, "Not one word or you die. Turn around and get into my truck."

As if Cris Gallow had realized five years ago when she took karate that this minute would appear, she instantly moved with perfection. The skills that had earned her a black belt were immediately and effectively portrayed as John Prescott truly didn't know what hit him. He was on the ground, dazed and looking up at Cris Gallow, who was talking on a cell phone with a pistol pointing at his head.

The police arrived, arrested John Prescott and took him off to the Bay City jail. Dr. Gallow went along to assist with reports.

When Lou arrived, it was all over. He had missed the drama, but did have a chance to talk with Dr. Gallow.

With John Prescott's lawyer present Lou and the police were able to get him to admit to infecting Maggie in Clare. He cooperated by telling them that the infecting agent was a rare bacteria from Argentina that the state lab was studying. Lou immediately called Doctor Wagner in Chicago only to learn that the lab people in Lansing had already given them the information they needed from John's lab assignment and reports.

Lou decided to spend the night in Bay City. He was too tired to drive for four hours back to Grand Haven and besides, thunderstorms were predicted.

Chapter Nineteen

Tuesday, July 21
Bay City and Grand Haven, Michigan
Chicago, Illinois

The first thing Lou did upon waking was to call Carol in Chicago. He needed to hear some good news. Lou was able to reach Carol and he learned that the doctors had isolated the bacteria, provided the antidote, but at this moment there was little change in Maggie's condition. She was still alive and would be closely monitored.

Lou ate hot cakes and sausage with orange juice in a McDonald's and then drove on home arriving close to noon. Lou called Chief McFadden at the Manistee police department as he wanted to be sure that Mickey and Detective Maguffin had all the information and that it was accurate.

"I'm glad it's over, Lou," Chief McFadden said. "Thanks for all of your help. Sure hope Maggie is going to be OK."

"Me too. Thanks for asking me to get involved. I'm sorry we couldn't stop these killings early on, but at least all of us were able to explain it."

"Rest a bit, Lou. You and Maggie have given this case almost all of your energy."

Lou hadn't heard from Carol in several hours, but again, no news was good news. Needless to say, Samm was happy to see Lou. She probably thought she'd been abandoned.

Samm wanted to go for a walk and do some stick chasing and Lou needed to feel the sand and water beneath his feet so the two of them walked along the sandy beach and let the waves lap upon their paws and feet. It felt good and it began to cleanse and help Lou to get his head back to a sense that all was really okay in the world.

Later in the afternoon, Lou was about to lie on his bed for a short nap when the phone rang. It was Carol calling to report that they were about to board Tom Howard's plane for a return trip to Grand Haven. "We should be there about five your time."

"That's great. Is Maggie coming along?" Lou asked, wishfully thinking.

"No, they're keeping her in the hospital, but she's conscious now and she's going to be okay. The doctors tell us there may be some lingering effects but they were able to stem the infection and now it's up to her body to heal itself. That infecting agent was so rare that the pathologists in Chicago had no means to identify it. John Prescott had been studying the bacteria and may even have created his own strain. Apparently, if the patient can keep on living, chances are very good for a full recovery."

"Thank God for that. That's the best news I've had in the past two weeks.

"By the way, Dr. Gallow was a karate expert and she decked John Prescott in a second. John provided a full confession to his role in helping his brother. It's over. I'll tell you all about it when you get here."

"Maggie can talk to you on the phone, so you may want to call her. I'm sure she'll be glad to hear that the case is over. Give her a call, Lou, it would brighten her day. Tom is in the room with her."

"OK, will do. So, you are coming back with Doctor Wagner?"

"Yes, Tom Howard says we should be touching down in Grand Haven in about an hour max."

"You have a safe flight and please thank everyone for their help."

"I have and I will continue to do so. See you soon."

"Yes, hurry on home to a long and tight hug, my dear."

"Believe me, I'm ready to get home, Lou, but I'm glad I could be with Maggie and Tom."

Lou hung up from talking with Carol, took a deep breath and called Maggie.

"Hi, Maggie, I hear you're going to be just fine."

"That's what they tell me, Lou."

"Well, you'll be glad to know that the killing is over. We've got the Prescott brothers, Jake and John. Next will be trials and incarceration. You did a good job, Maggie."

"I'm still a bit groggy, Lou. When I get out of here and get home, you'll have to fill me in on all the details."

"I will. Take care of yourself and we'll talk soon."

"Good job, Lou. A feather in your cap."

"Thanks. I think I'll just rev up my Harley and take a fast ride and hopefully shake all of this out of my mind. It's been a stressful few weeks."

"Be careful, I've had enough hospitalization for the two of us for a long time."

"Yes, you have. Regards to Tom. He probably isn't getting to play much golf in downtown Chicago?"

"No, but he's itching to get me home and to join you for 18 holes sometime before the snow flies."

"Tell him, I'm game. Later, Maggie. Goodbye."

꒰꒱

Lou went out to the airport to welcome Carol and Doc Wagner. Tom's small plane seemed to fall out of the sky. It taxied up and out stepped Doc and Carol. Lou gave Carol a long and tight hug. It was so good to see her once again. Lou thanked Dr. Wagner and Tom Howard for their help in saving Maggie's life.

On the way home from the airport Carol said, "I dabbled a bit in your work, Lou."

"How's that?"

"When I was at the hospital, I decided to follow Maggie's thought that there was a logical connection between the doctors who had been murdered. So, while I had little to do but worry about Maggie, I spent quite a bit of time on the Internet at the hospital library and was able to verify a pattern."

"Great. What did you learn?" Lou asked, surprised that Carol had gotten involved. Maybe some of Lou's passion for murder investigation was getting under her skin. Actually, Carol had quite a role in the golf course murder a few years ago at Marsh Ridge near Gaylord, but she usually leaves all of this crime-fighting business to Lou and Maggie.

"Through the Internet, I found the name of the newspaper in the community where each victim lived," Carol began. "Then, I was able to find an obituary for each victim. Knowing the date of the murders helped me pick the edition of the paper I wanted to read and in a matter of a half hour, I was looking at five obituaries.

"I set them on a table in the library and with a marker tried to find something in common with all five. Two things caught my attention. The first was a tribute to James Rothchild in which his contribution to the University of Michigan Medical School was noted.

"The other death notices all mentioned an affiliation with the University of Michigan Medical School. I concluded that the victims all knew each other, all either were students or were on staff in some capacity. So, I drew the obvious conclusion that something happened in that group of students or doctors that led to their being murdered.

"I then called the spouse of three of the doctors and tried to discover a pattern. All three said the eight formed an investment club while medical students or members of the teaching faculty. They met with a lot of success and like gamblers addicted to dice and cards, they got all wrapped up in it, investing more money than was reasonable until some of them sought professional help for the passion of seeing money grow from money.

"One person, Dr. Milhalik in Milwaukee, took me into his confidence and told me of the terrible mistake of eighteen years ago when Dr. Prescott joined the group and lost all of his money. He did recall Sherry telling him that Brad Prescott took his life, and how this brought the eight to their senses. The investment club broke up shortly after the suicide.

"One more thing," Carol said. "I think I've an explanation for the noose and wrists being slit."

"What's your theory?"

"My theory is that the victims were all moved to the marina piling with a noose around their neck symbolic of how Dr. Prescott killed himself and I think the wrist was cut to give the impression that the victims were committing suicide."

"Hmmm, could be. We didn't come up with any pattern of suicide."

"I know, but if you try to think like the murderers, it seems to me that they would try anything to throw off the law when it comes to motive. All it took was a slash of the wrist and maybe it would work."

Lou put what Carol had said with what Jake Prescott had said in Clare and it all finally made sense. Lou called Chief McFadden and explained what he and Carol had concluded in the last half hour. They declared the case solved. Carol and Lou with Samm at their heals walked out onto the warm sand. They walked hand in hand along the water's edge while Samm begged for a thrown piece of driftwood.

"I'm proud of you, Lou, and I love you very much."

"We're so blessed to share our lives. I love you too, and I'm proud of you, always giving time to others and being a marvelous wife, mother and Nana."

The afternoon sun shone down on them and the warmth felt good, very good. They were home, finally home. The killings were over and each hungered for peace. They found it in their love for each other. All would be well.

CHAPTER TWENTY

Tuesday, August 4
Grand Haven, Michigan

It was a warm August morning. Lou and Carol's daughter Amanda and her family were visiting from St. Louis. Their annual visit to Grand Haven was always special for the obvious reasons, but especially because their grandchildren, Hannah aged 4 and Thomas aged 2, so enjoyed the "Big M," as their mother affectionately referred to Lake Michigan.

On this particular day, it was raining and beach activity was on hold for an afternoon. "Hannah, how about you and Grandpa making some chocolate chip cookies?" Lou asked.

"Yeah, let's do that!" she exclaimed.

Hannah and Lou shared a love of chocolate and they knew that, while a bit unhealthy, they'd have some of the cookie dough and they'd double the recipe when it came to chocolate chips.

"You get all the ingredients and I'll get the mixing bowl and cookie sheet," Lou said. Hannah knew right where to find the chips, the butter, and the flour. They had a grand time reading the recipe, mixing the ingredients, and scooping up nice round balls of batter to place in neat rows on the cookie sheet. Grandpa and granddaughter enjoyed discreetly sneaking a chip or two into their mouths as they worked, the behavior of every good cook.

They pre-heated the oven and waited for the little red light to go off before popping the dozen balls of batter into the oven.

"You find out what people want to drink, and I'll set the table," Lou said.

Hannah took drink requests and how many cookies Nana, her father Joe, her mom Amanda, and her brother "T", a nickname for Thomas, would want. She wrote them down and gave an indication that a college job of waitressing could be a real possibility in a dozen plus years.

The cookies came out of the oven smelling delicious with melted chocolate oozing from the plump and hot mounds of baked batter. They popped in a dozen more and invited the folks to the dining room table for a mid-rainy day treat.

"These cookies, made from a special recipe, shall forever be named the Hannah and Grandpa Chocolate Chip Cookies or HG Triple Cs," Lou declared, as if giving a toast while looking into Hannah's eyes. She gave Lou a big smile and a chuckle. All enjoyed the warm treat with their coffee, milk or tea.

"Please pass me the HG Triple Cs," said Carol, winking at Lou and enjoying the smile on Hannah's face.

Lou looked out the window toward the Lake and could see the sun shining through the clouds. Lou got Hannah and Tom's attention and said, "Get your swimsuits on, and find your inner tubes, the day will brighten up!" Hannah and Tom scurried to get in their swimsuits and to invite Samm to go to the Lake with their mom, dad, and Nana in tow.

Lou stood watching Hannah, Tom, Amanda, Joe, and Carol walking to the shore with sand pails, inner tubes, and a ball, and he thought, Life can't get any better than this, sharing an afternoon with my family, making a double batch of chocolate chip cookies with Hannah, and having the sun shine on a happy day at the beach. How fortunate I am, how lucky to be so full of joy. Lou took his camera from the kitchen counter and went to capture a moment in time when all seemed right with the world. Lou was at peace.

Epilogue

Jake and John Prescott were tried and convicted of the murders of five people. It was determined that Jake's mental health was good enough to stand trial. Both men were sentenced to life in prison without the possibility of parole. Jake was charged with kidnapping and killing Dr. Knoble, Dr. Rothchild, Dr. Harrison, Mr. Verduin, and Dr. Mihalik; and the kidnapping of Dr. Edith Haire. John was charged with assisting in the murder of Dr. Rothchild and Dr. Mihalik, threatening the life of Dr. Gallow, and of attempted murder of Maggie McMillan.

Testimony at the trial confirmed that John Prescott was present in the hospital in Oscoda and in Clare. It also came out in the trial that Jake Prescott had become obsessed with the eight doctors in the investment club. He made it a point of knowing all about their lives, their day-to-day activities, their mode of operation. He had enlisted a host of people to eavesdrop for him and to feed him information all under the guise of obtaining evidence for an eventual suit. Those who knew and helped Jake had no idea he was using all of the information to plot the deaths of the eight.

The slit wrists were to try and sell a suicide theory. The theory didn't work, but according to Jake, he thought it might, so he made the procedure a part of the murder.

The list of people to be killed lacked one name, Philip Heyboer. Jake talked about killing all eight members of the investment club, but he couldn't kill his Godfather and a good friend of his father. Philip Heyboer, ironically the only person who worried over his pending death, was never an intended victim.

Jake and John spent their years of incarceration working in the medical center of their prison. Their behavior was exceptional and their work was commendable.

Father Thomas Murphy became very active in prison ministry and was being mentioned in some circles as the perfect priest to become the diocese's next Bishop. He corresponded frequently with Jake.

Sara Prescott recovered and for months was under a physician's care.

Edith Haire eventually came out of her coma. With extensive therapy she regained her mobility and was able to return to her practice and to her love of sailing. Elaine regained her health as well and the two enjoyed many more sailing trips on the Great Lakes.

Rose Crandall was given a certificate of commendation by the city of Manistee for her help in solving the crime. The presentation was made in the cafeteria of the Chalet West Apartments. All of the residents gave Rose a standing ovation and as she accepted the award she said with a smile, "You'll never guess what I saw last night." Everyone hung on every word, for soon a story the likes of which they'd never heard would soon fill the air.

Dr. Philip Heyboer and Molly Crowe were joined in holy matrimony and enjoyed a honeymoon in Honolulu, Hawaii. Philip did meet with Sara, Jake, and John in Marquette, Michigan, where the young men were serving time. He explained the truth which was that Brad Prescott was not double-crossed. He made a conscious and risky fiscal decision. When the deal went bad he, being unable to shoulder the blame for his financial mistake, told Sara that he was double-crossed by the investment club. Sara simply passed the misinformation along to her sons. While truth was being shared, Sara told the boys that their father planned to kill them as his escape from the crisis and to get the insurance money which would significantly offset his debt. Jake now understood that he had killed five people for a revenge that was never needed. His revenge was all because of a lie, told to his mother, by his father, a father who had planned a drug interaction that would have led to Jake's death.

Maggie McMillan eventually was back to her healthy self. Through the use of antibiotics in an experimental program and thanks to her fine immune system and healthy way of living, she was determined by her doctor to be healthy once again.

Carol and Lou Searing continued to enjoy living on the shore of Lake Michigan south of Grand Haven. Lou did return to Arcadia for a full day of fishing and glider flying with Chuck Mange. As Carol cradled their cat Luba in her arms, Lou turned on the computer and watched as his fingers flew over the keyboard writing the novel which he titled, *The Marina Murders*. Their other cat Millie and their dog Samm snuggled at Lou's feet. Life was good.

THE END

A Parting Thought

A common response of people when they hear that I self-publish my books is, "I've always wanted to write a book," or, "Someday I will write a book." Inside all of us are stories yearning to be shared. Technology gives all of us the opportunity to tell our story. If you have these thoughts, to write your own book, please act on them. There are numerous recourses in bookstores and on the Internet to assist you. You won't regret it, and many will enjoy what you yearn to share. Best wishes to you.

Coming Soon

Lou and Maggie find themselves on the S.S. Badger, crossing from Ludington to Manitowoc, when murder interrupts a smooth sailing. You won't want to miss, Murder on the S.S. Badger, the 6th book in the Louis Searing and Margaret McMillan Mystery Series.

Buttonwood Press Order Form

To order additional copies of *The Marina Murders,* or the four previous mysteries in this series, visit the website of Buttonwood Press at www.buttonwoodpress.com for information or fill out the order form here. Thank you.

Name_____

Address_____

City/State/Zip_____

Book Title	Quantity	Price
The Marina Murders ($12.95 – Softcover)		
Buried Secrets of Bois Blanc: Murder in the Straits of Mackinac ($12.95 – Softcover)		
A Lesson Plan for Murder ($12.95 – Softcover)		
The Principal Cause of Death ($12.95 – Softcover)		
Administration Can Be Murder ($12.95 – Softcover)		
TOTAL		

Rich Baldwin will personally autograph a copy of any of his books for you. It's also a great gift for that mystery lover you know!

Autograph Request To:

_____

_____

_____

Mail Order Form with a Check payable to:

Buttonwood Press
PO Box 716
Haslett, MI 48840

Fax: 517-339-5908
Email: RLBald@aol.com
Website: www.buttonwoodpress.com

Questions? Call the Buttonwood Press office at (517) 339-9871. Thank you!